the
outsider

MAISEY YATES

the outsider

CANARY STREET PRESS

CANARY STREET PRESS™

Recycling programs for this product may not exist in your area.

ISBN-13: 978-1-335-08182-7

The Outsider

For questions and comments about the quality of this book, please contact us at CustomerService@Harlequin.com.

TM is a trademark of Harlequin Enterprises ULC.

Canary Street Press
22 Adelaide St. West, 41st Floor
Toronto, Ontario M5H 4E3, Canada
CanaryStPress.com

Printed in U.S.A.

To Michelle, Jill and RaeAnne
for the most excellent plotting session that resulted in
this book. And to Flo, for loving Bix as much as I do.

CHAPTER ONE

Bix Carpenter knew how to do two things well. Survive and make moonshine. In her experience, one was often linked to the other. And especially now that she was officially out of the family business, it was good that she had the knowledge to carry on herself.

Well. The family business itself had been dissolved when her father had been sent to prison. Her half-siblings—younger and older—were either strangers to her or didn't want anything to do with her. Which was fair, because she didn't want anything to do with them either.

But she still had her contacts in the liquor world, and she knew what she was doing.

It could be worse. It could be meth.

She told herself that a lot.

Though, she had to be honest and admit that one of the biggest reasons it had never been meth was that there had been a massive explosion in one of the trailers in the park back when she was fifteen or so, and any designs her father'd had on cooking the more volatile substance had gone out the window then and there.

If you were doing illegal things to survive, there wasn't much sense doing an illegal thing that could kill you.

She could almost justify making alcohol. Her father had passed on so many opinions on the Oregon Liquor License Commission and the racket they were running that she could nearly make a case for the actions being *benevolent*.

But mostly, she didn't care.

The truth was, life had beaten any desire to be benevolent right out of her.

She'd had a criminal record since she turned eighteen and could no longer rest on the possibility of her juvenile record being expunged. She had never really cared. No one in her family lived on the right side of the law. The law, in her estimation, was mostly designed to set up roadblocks to keep people like her down. At least that was her experience.

Her experience was the only one she cared about.

Empathy for others was hardly going to put a roof over her head.

But thankfully, this new place had. The spring in the area had come highly recommended to her by some other moonshiners who her dad had known back in the day, and they'd made alcohol here years back that they'd claimed was the best around.

She'd only just barely made it here. Her van's starter was shot, and she needed to earn money to get her going again. She was all right if she could get a jump—sometimes. But she wasn't going to head down to Humboldt with things going that badly, and being in a position where she was going to be dependent on the kindness of strangers.

For two reasons: She didn't do dependence, and she didn't believe strangers were kind.

So she'd taken the van over here, pulled it into an alcove along the highway and as deep into the woods as she could, concealed behind some trees.

Then she'd decided to set up her still.

The spring was further into the woods, and while she could sleep in her van it wasn't convenient and it was nearer to the road than she liked.

She'd been slowly scoping the property out for the last five days. And it seemed to her that it was unusual for anybody to come to this end. She wasn't entirely sure where things began and where they ended, but as far as she could sus out this was a massive ranching spread, with more outbuildings than she could count.

And it definitely had more outbuildings than anybody went into with regularity.

This thicker, more wooded part of the mountainside hadn't had a single soul wander through the whole five days she'd been up here. She'd moved into the cabin, which gave her a little break from the van and got her farther off the road, with her knapsack and her supplies, and hadn't been bothered at all.

Maybe she could settle here for a while. That would be nice.

She'd been running for so long.

Thankfully, she didn't have any warrants *presently*. Though, the one thing about prison was at least you had a place to sleep. And food.

Not that any of her stays had been extensive.

She was well acquainted with misdemeanors, but nothing that had gotten her more than a few weeks and probation. Which, in her family, was underachieving. If anything.

She was trying to decide if she was grateful that she'd been forced to quit smoking simply because she couldn't afford the habit. Right now, she wished she had a cigarette. But that was the kind of thing that tempted her to shoplift, which was the kind of thing that often landed her in the sort of silver bracelets a girl didn't like to wear.

She chuckled to herself and settled back in the clean corner of the cabin she currently called home.

It was quiet. She kind of liked that. She wasn't used to quiet. When they lived in the mountains in their cabin, there were still a lot of loud familial fights. When they'd lived in the trailer park, they'd been able to hear the whole neighborhood fighting. She'd been on her own for a couple of years now, but she'd never lived anywhere quiet.

She looked at her fishing pole, and wondered if she should head down to the river. Technically, she supposed she was a poacher. But she ate everything that she caught, and her dad, she believed, was right about a few things.

One of them was the fact that the state monetizing things like fishing, trapping and hunting by making you get permits made it impossible for people to be self-sufficient.

And if there was one thing Bix prized it was her independence and self-sufficiency.

That was two things. But whatever.

She had some ramen and other easy, cheap foods in her pack, but fish would be nice.

Decisively, she got up and snagged her pole, heading down a path in the woods that she knew led to the river. She bent down and started digging in the dirt, finding an earthworm and baiting her hook as she walked down to the river's edge.

She wasn't often thankful for her dad. But he had taught her how to get along. So right then, she sent up a nice thought for him—and whatever cell he was in currently—and cast her hook into the water. She had a couple of fishhooks in her backpack, but she had to be very careful in rivers like this. If she got her hook hung up on the rocks and lost it, then it was going to make her life a lot harder. And she really didn't need her life to be any harder than it already was.

She felt her line jerk, then go tight, and she yanked upward, making sure that if there was a fish on, she'd gotten it secured. And then she started to reel it in. The movement on the line told her that she absolutely had something.

She said a little prayer of thanks to whoever was watching out for her. Then she realized it was herself.

"Thanks, me," she said, as she reeled the line in, and brought in a wiggly rainbow trout.

She was looking at the fish when she heard a sound. She looked up, and there across the river, emerging from the trees, was a man.

He was tall. And broad. Well muscled, with a tight black T-shirt and cowboy hat. There was an air of authority about him that made everything inside of her go quiet. It was familiar.

He wasn't specifically. It was the vibe he gave off.

A cop.

That was what he reminded her of. She could feel that big pig energy radiating from across the river. She was frozen, with a wiggling fish on the end of the line that she was holding up, and she knew that he saw her, and yet he hadn't said anything. She wasn't going to lose her fish. She grabbed it, defiantly, and dispatched it. Then she gathered her things and took off at a run, up the path, and headed back into the woods. He wouldn't be able to see where she went.

Her heart was pounding. Terror and adrenaline pumped through her in equal measure.

This spot was perfect. She was not going to let the sighting of one man ruin it. She would give it twenty-four hours. If he came back, came sniffing around, she would leave. But she had a roof over her head for the first time in a while, and she didn't want to lose it. She looked at the fish and knew a moment of despair. Because she was not going to be able to risk lighting a fire tonight. She didn't want to waste it either.

She was never going to kill an animal and then not make use of it. Even if it was an ugly fish.

She blinked hard, denying all of the emotion that rose up inside of her. She wasn't going to cry.

It was cold outside. Or at least, pretty cold. And she knew she had a couple of options. She dug in her backpack for a plastic bag, and took it out. She decided to wrap the fish carefully, and bury it in the cold dirt.

Deep enough that hopefully it wouldn't attract any bears, and that it would also be insulated. She trusted the idea well enough, or at least, trusted it as much as she did anything. Because hey. If there was one thing Bix Carpenter knew, it was how to survive.

"I THINK WE might have a squatter."

"And what evidence do you have, Sheriff?"

Daughtry King leaned back in his chair, and took a long drink of his beer. He could argue with his brother about him calling him Sheriff. He was a state trooper, not a sheriff. He didn't even work for the sheriff's department. But then, his brother obviously knew that, and was just being difficult.

A hallmark of Justice King if ever there was one. Oftentimes he could appreciate that—today not so much. He was tired. And if he said anything about being tired then his brother would remind him that taking two jobs was his idea.

True.

But, he considered it part and parcel of trying to do something to redeem the King name.

So when he'd decided to go into law enforcement, he hadn't even bothered to have the discussion about the fact that he was trying to carry a new legacy for the family on his shoulders. Especially at the time, Arizona hadn't cared at all. Denver and Justice still didn't. Landry understood. But then, his younger brother had always seemed to care just a bit more about the things their father had done to them. And what they might have to do to fix it.

Especially now that his brother was a father—well, his brother had been a father for thirteen years; it was just that the kid had lived with him, and the rest of them hadn't known—but now that he was actually the custodial parent of his daughter, and had another kid on the way, if anything Landry cared even more.

Mostly though, being understood wasn't high on Daughtry's list of things he needed.

"I saw them. Across the river. Fishing."

"Sounds like we have a poacher."

"Well. That too."

"You don't think it was one of the ranch hands?"

"It was a kid, I think. I mean, had to have been. Skinny. Not very tall. Hard to tell, though. Giant baggy sweatshirt and dirty pants. It didn't look like one of the ranch hands."

"And you're going to say that this is lawman intuition?" Justice asked.

His brother was such a smart-ass.

"Yes," he said. "Because I've seen things. You just get used to evaluating people."

The truth was, there wasn't a whole lot of crime in the area. It was patrolled primarily by state police, and there was a small outpost, and a few officers. But it was all the same crime you found anywhere else, and most especially in areas where there was poverty. Shoplifting, drugs, domestic violence. When life got hard, people got desperate. And he'd seen a lot of that. The person across the river had a desperate look about them. The way that they had clung to the fish . . .

The thing was, he was kind of tired of arresting the same people. That was what happened in an area like this. Every so often there were people who passed through, new kinds of trouble, but that was temporary. A lot of it was the same person driving without a license. Their sixth DUI that year. The same violent husband who you saw, but could never hold, because his wife would change her story the next day and refuse to press charges.

The same kids drinking. The same drug users. And back out on the street the next day. And around and around it went.

If he had gotten into law enforcement to solve anyone's problems but his own he would've been very discouraged by now. But luckily, he had just enough of his dad's narcissism that his primary goal had been to make the community associate his family name with something different. Now at least Officer King was associated with the family name. So, there was that.

Justice's best friend, Rue, came into the room. "What's all this?" Rue asked, hands planted on her hips. Daughtry noticed a ring flashing on Rue's left hand and made a mental note to ask Justice about that.

"Daughtry thinks that there is a squatter and fish poacher out on the ranch."

"Oh," said Rue, frowning. "That's scary."

"It's not scary," said Daughtry. "It's a half-pint trout poacher. There's nothing scary about that. But I promise I'll go out first thing tomorrow morning and have a look."

"Ah," Rue said. "The big scary man that carries a gun for a living doesn't think it's scary, so what does a woman know about safety?"

"It isn't scary," said Daughtry. "Because I think it's like a fourteen-year-old kid. I only saw them from a distance but they were small."

"Well, what are you going to do?"

"I'm going to do what any decent human being should do. I'm going to see if they need help."

BIX STIRRED WHEN she heard the sound of footsteps near the cabin. She froze. This was what she had been afraid of. The man was back.

She hadn't left any sign outside that would indicate there was a person in the cabin, but he was only a hundred yards or so away.

That would definitely clue the person into the fact that someone was nearby. Or at least, had been.

He already knows that. Because he saw you. So just don't panic about it.

Panicking didn't help anything.

She just hoped he didn't find the van and have it towed. That would be a disaster.

Him finding the still wouldn't be ideal either.

Moving as silently as possible, Bix crept up to the window, and peered just above the ledge. She could see movement outside, but the glass was so dirty it was impossible to make anything out clearly. The good news was that meant it was difficult for anyone out there to tell what was happening inside.

But just in case, she opened up the crawl space hatch, and slipped down inside, closing it behind her. She had stashed all her stuff down in there earlier except for her blanket. The door to the cabin opened, and she heard heavy footsteps above her. She quit breathing.

Maybe this was better. Yeah. Maybe it was better. Because he would check all around here, and he wouldn't see her. So, he would let it go.

You just want to stay for a while. You're always so desperate for a home without wheels.

She shoved that thought to the side. It didn't do her any good.

She waited. The minutes ticked by. They seemed like hours. Wasn't he satisfied yet that there was no-body in here?

Finally, the footsteps went back toward the door, and it closed behind him.

And then she waited for what felt like an eternity. Because she knew she was in a dark space where there were probably rodents and spiders, and she hated all of it, thank you.

Bix was self-sufficient, and able to do what needed doing. But she wasn't entirely without phobias of weird creepy animals. It was just that usually she had to deal. Finally, she took the chance and exited the space.

She waited several hours before she really started moving. She decided to make a fire. She prepared her fish, and she cooked it. And it was delicious.

Her packaged food could wait. It was a good day when she had something fresh like this.

She had some traps, and she was tempted to try to find places to set some up. She never set traps anywhere someone could get hurt, and she needed to get the lay of the land before she did anything like that.

More than anything, she wished that she still had her gun. That had been shortsighted. Getting rid of that. She had sold it for a few hundred dollars, which had felt like a boon at the time. Because ammunition was a damned sight too expensive anyway, and it had seemed like maybe it was just better to off-load it and get what she could. But it limited her food options in a way that really sucked.

Oh well. Fish was healthy. And the river seemed to have a supply. It was just too bad she had to stand out in the open to fish.

It wasn't until late afternoon that she decided to go and check on the still. It wasn't exactly high-tech. But she had to get creative, especially since she had to try to transport the still with her when she moved. And frankly, the bigger pieces were just impossible. So, a cheap pot and a five-gallon bucket were the big parts, and cheap enough to replace, and anything specialty was small enough to pack up in her bag.

It wasn't the most subtle-looking thing, out there in the middle of the woods. Her current bucket was bright orange.

She went over and bent down beside it, and what scared her the most was that she didn't hear anything. Not a footstep. Not a breath. Just the voice.

"Well. I thought I just had a squatter. Seems I actually have a whole criminal."

She straightened and turned. And there he was. The man. In a uniform. Well, hell. He wasn't *just* a man.

Turned out her intuition had been bang on the money.

Turned out, he was a cop.

CHAPTER TWO

HE LOOKED DOWN at the scrubby creature kneeling on the ground in front of him. The same creature he'd seen across the river just last night. He had assumed that he was looking at a teenage boy. Bony shoulders, baggy clothes and a dirty face.

But hell. It was a girl. Her blond hair was tucked up in a beanie, a few stray strands sticking out around her face. There was a smudge of dirt on her cheekbone. And her cheeks were much too hollow. Her lips were chapped, and there was a scrape on the bottom of her chin.

She was pathetic.

He stood there staring and began to revise even more of his initial thought. He'd pegged her at maybe fourteen right at first. But no. She wasn't fourteen. She was older.

Maybe.

There was a glint to her eyes, an intelligence that made him think she couldn't possibly be that young.

"Who are you?" she asked.

"Name's Daughtry King. Officer Daughtry King."

"Is there a problem?"

"The illegal still behind you is a problem."

He watched her eyes dart back and forth. He knew that she was doing the math equation. He just didn't know what the figures were.

"It's not mine. I mean, I don't even know what it is. I was just looking at the funny buckets. I was wandering through the area, taking a hike."

"Strange, because you were here last night."

"Camping," she said.

"This is private property."

"I didn't know," she said. "I'm really sorry. I . . . I'm not in trouble, am I? I've never been in trouble before."

Her eyes went glassy. Her lower lip trembled.

He didn't buy it.

There was something wholly disingenuous about the saccharine tone she said that in.

"Stand up," he said.

She looked around wildly, and for a second, he felt bad.

She seemed terrified.

But it only took a moment for him to realize that it was a facade. She wasn't terrified. This was an act, and he was getting irritated.

He reached down and grabbed her upper arm, hauling her to her feet.

She screeched and jerked backward. "You get your hands off me! I'm not doing anything wrong."

That feral outburst, he realized, was closer to the truth of it. Of her. She wasn't scared. She was mad.

"Tell me your name, and what the hell you're doing here," he said.

"I *told you*. I was taking a walk in the woods. *Camping*. Taking a walk while I was camping."

"You can't even keep your story straight, ma'am."

"Ma'am?" She wrinkled her nose. "The hell is that?"

"Manners," he returned. "Are you not familiar? Well, clearly you aren't, as I've introduced myself to you, but you haven't introduced yourself to me."

"I'm a woman," she said, making her voice small again. "A *little* one. You might be a police officer, or you might be impersonating one, but either way, a woman has to be careful. And not just trust men because they say they are trustworthy."

"That is true," he said. "But the difficulty is, ma'am, you're on my land. So not only am I an officer of the law, I'm the landowner. I have every right to know what you're doing here, and what your name is. I need to see some identification."

"Identification?" she scoffed. "It's a hell of a thing that a person needs a piece of paper to prove they exist. Another way for the state to earn money by *doing nothing*."

"Then tell me who you are."

"My name is Bix," she said. "And I'm just passing through. I'm not here to make any trouble."

"But you were here to make a still?"

"I don't even know what a still is," she said, defaulting to that blandly innocent tone again. "I just thought it was a bucket. With some hoses. I stopped to have a look at it."

"It looked like you were inspecting it, and pretty competently too."

"Look at me," she said, gesturing toward herself. "Do I look like I would know what to do with one of these things?"

"You absolutely do," he said, his voice flat.

She looked exactly like what she was. A woman down on her luck, desperate enough to do anything. She was too skinny, she was dirty, and hell, in spite of himself he felt his chest tighten with compassion.

It was so easy to get jaded. And not just in his line of work, by *living*. The truth was, there wasn't a hell of a lot of crime in Pyrite Falls. But the crime there was was repetitious and soul grinding. He was familiar with it. The fact that he could still feel a bit of compassion mattered to him. Meant something to him.

It at least made him feel like he wasn't a husk. Which was nice.

Figuring out what to do with her was less nice. The truth was, every stray that wandered through town wasn't his responsibility. But a stray that wandered onto his property felt . . . a little more like she might be.

"Is *Bix* short for anything?"

"No," she said.

He wasn't sure he believed her. He wasn't even sure if she went by Bix or if it was something she'd plucked out of the air.

"Right. Well. Do you have somewhere to go, Bix? Someone waiting for you?"

"I . . . Yeah. I've got a husband. Waiting for me to come home. If I don't come home, he's going to get mad. And worried."

He was certain she was lying about that.

"Do you have a house?" he pressed.

"I've got . . . a house."

"Do you have a house other than a cabin on my property?"

"*House* might be overselling it, but I have a place. I have a van. I just . . . I've got to buy a part to fix it, that's all. And then I'm leaving. Not just your ranch, but the state. So, you don't have to worry about me. I'm not a problem. I won't hang around. I just . . ."

Lord have mercy. This creature was going to end up being his problem.

"Cut the bullshit, please," he said.

She blinked. "Are cops allowed to say *bullshit*?"

"Sweetheart, cops do nothing but shovel bullshit all day. We can damned sure call it like it is. This is your still."

She bristled. "I have the right to remain silent."

"You do. But I'm not arresting you."

It was his property, after all. And it wasn't like she had time to have actual alcohol in the still, so whatever her intent was, she hadn't gotten far with it. Anyway, doing something to this girl would be like . . . kicking a puppy. A pathetic, homeless puppy.

She blinked. "You're not arresting me?"

"No. I'm not. Just . . . tell me honestly, Bix, what the hell was happening here?"

"I'm being honest. I'm not staying. I just need to earn a little money so that I can get out of town. My starter's blown and I can't get the damn van to start. You can give me a jump if you want, and I'll be on my way."

"To where?"

"I'm headed down to California."

"To do what?"

"I don't owe you that information," she said, giving him the lofty look of a queen, when the only royal thing about her was that she was a royal pain in the ass.

"Here's the thing. You may not owe me information, but the way that I see it, you don't have any control here. I can arrest you if I want to. You're trespassing, you're squatting and you're engaging in illegal activity on my land."

"Squatters have rights," she said, jamming her finger toward him. "You can't arrest me for staying here. And you can't just kick me off."

"The hell I can, babe."

And that was Daughtry King. Not the cop.

She narrowed her eyes. "What do you want from me?"

"I just want to know who you are, what you're doing here and how I can help."

He hadn't expected that third thing to come out of his mouth. It was clear she didn't either.

"Well, that's not true. That's never true. You don't just want to offer help. No man ever has. You want to know who I am, why I'm here and get a blowjob."

He nearly laughed. "No offense, but that didn't occur to me."

She did look slightly offended. Oh well. She looked like a street urchin. She was bony and pathetic and covered in dirt. The idea that . . .

Hell. Who was he kidding? She wasn't wrong. A lot of men would've taken in her desperate state and seen fit to make those kinds of demands. Hell.

If he sent her on her way in a van with no starter, looking like a bundle of sticks wrapped in a baggy sweatshirt, he was sending her out to be potentially harmed or taken advantage of in some way.

He couldn't consign the little stray to the world. He just couldn't.

"Come with me."

"I don't want to be arrested," she said.

"Do police usually ask if you want to be arrested?"

She squinted. "Wouldn't know. Like I said. I'm pure as the driven snow."

Then he did laugh. "Right. Okay. That's how you want to play it, go ahead and play it that way. Let me put my cards on the table. You need a part for your car, so that you can head down south. You need to earn some money. You can work for me. At the ranch. You got any skills?"

She blinked. "I . . . Yeah. I got lots of skills. I can hunt and fish and trap. I can fix cars."

"Can you clean stalls?"

She blinked. "Sounds easy."

"How about construction?"

She nodded. "Yeah. I've done my fair share."

"Then we'll have no trouble finding stuff for you to do."

She narrowed her eyes. "Why?"

Because you became my problem, and I can never leave a stray behind.

"What do you mean *why*?" he asked.

"Why are you helping me?"

Because my dad wouldn't have.

"Because we've got plenty of shelter, plenty of food and plenty of work. What you're doing out here, that's work. Even if it's illegal work. Even if you won't admit to it. If you're willing to come do legit work for me, then you can do that for a couple of weeks and be on your way."

Yeah. He could offer her money. But he didn't want to do that. He wanted to offer her something she could earn herself. Mostly he . . . he felt cautious about the whole thing. She was a woman alone in the world. She'd clearly been treated badly before. He didn't feel all that great about turning her loose. Not that he had any control over that. But if she decided to stay . . . Maybe it would be good for her. Have a couple weeks of meals and not sleep so rough.

"People don't just help each other," she said. "They look out for themselves."

"Yeah," he said. "Some do. But I'm a police officer because I want to change things. It isn't just because I want to arrest people. What I want is to live in a world where more people help than hurt. All right?"

"I don't know about that."

"I'm just coming off shift," he said. "Why don't you come on back to the ranch house with me and we can have dinner."

She frowned. "This sounds like a recipe for rape and murder, and I'm not actually interested in that."

"Is it so hard to believe that I just want to help you?"

"Yes."

Fair enough.

"We won't be alone back at the ranch house. My whole family is there."

"Your . . . your family?"

"Yeah. Come have dinner. You've been staying on the property, I could've come and raped and murdered you at any point. I can do it now. I don't have to take you back to the house."

She appraised him. Her eyes fell to the gun on his hip. "True," she said.

"Come on back. Get a plate of food, have a shower. If you still want to leave, leave. But you're not hanging out here on the edges of the ranch."

"You'll give me a jump?"

"Yeah. If that's what you want."

She screwed up her face, appraising him with hard, squinting eyes. Then she seemed to relax slightly. "All right, Sheriff. I'll go with you."

"I'm not a sheriff," he said.

"It's all the same to me. Oink, oink."

"Cute. Haven't heard that one."

She barely came up to the middle of his chest and she was mouthing off. She clearly wasn't that scared of him, no matter what she said.

"You don't have a husband, do you?"

"Is it so hard to believe that I might?"

"You don't look a day over eighteen."

"I'm *twenty-six*," she said.

She was lying. He didn't know why he was so certain of that, but he was.

"Okay," he said.

"You don't believe me."

She looked wounded.

"Since I've met you, you've cycled through about four personalities. So, no. I don't believe you. I think you're desperate to keep me from finding out your real situation, and I also think you don't want me to know your name."

She huffed. "It doesn't benefit me."

"If you want a paycheck, I might have to know. I'm going to run you through payroll."

She looked scandalized. "You want to put me in the system?"

"It's easiest for taxes—"

"Taxes?" She looked scandalized.

"Taxes are actually how my job is funded," he pointed out.

"Yeah," she said, dryly. "Exactly. You're the System, dude. I don't want to be in the system."

"I imagine you're in the system to some capacity."

"Well. Yes." She looked around, her expression shifty.

"Do you have some stuff you want to grab?"

She looked momentarily defeated. "Yeah. I just . . . If I can get my backpack. And to let you know, there's a big hunting knife in it. If you try to touch me, I will gut you."

That he believed. It was the first thing that had come out of her mouth that he thought was a pretty solid truth.

"Noted."

She led the way back to the cabin. She hopped down the way like a rabbit on a trail, and it was difficult to keep up with her. She pushed open the door to the cabin, the one he had searched yesterday.

"You were here," he said. "Yesterday when I came in to search."

"Yeah," she said. "I was hiding."

"Where were you hiding?"

"If you don't know the hiding spots on your own fucking property, it's not up to me to tell you."

She had attitude. She grabbed a knapsack and a fishing pole from the corner and hefted it up over her shoulder. "Right. Let's go then. Let's do this dinner-and-shower thing. Do I have to listen to you preach the gospel before I can have a hot meal?"

"Ask my brother Denver to share the good news with you. See what he says."

She looked vaguely intrigued by that. "Mister, I have heard every form of good news you can possibly imagine."

"How's your soul?"

"Don't know. Had to sell it for parts a long time ago."

That hit him square in the chest and resonated a little further than it ought to have.

He cleared his throat.

"Well. Let's head on back to the homestead, Bix."

CHAPTER THREE

BIX DIDN'T KNOW if she was doing the right thing or not. Normally, she had a pretty fair sense of what to do, based on gut reactions. She *always* trusted her gut. Hell, a woman in her position had to. But this guy was a giant red flag. Wrapped in a uniform. He was everything she didn't like. He was a big strong man who was *also a cop*.

She wanted nothing to do with him, and yet he was offering her something she wanted very badly.

She wanted to be warm. She wanted to be clean. She wanted to be full. And the idea of work. A real job that paid an hourly wage, that maybe would get her a little bit further than trying to get the moonshine made and sold before she headed south . . .

Well, the problem was he'd found the still. So, her plan to get some product made and sold to finance her trip was fucked anyway. She wasn't sure about taking the work, but she knew she might as well have the dinner.

She knew a moment of feeling quite miserable as she followed him through the forest. They came out the edge, and there was his cop car.

"Get in," he said.

She went toward the back seat.

"Up here," he said, gesturing to the passenger door.

She frowned. "Wow. Never ridden in the front of one of these before."

She opened up the door and slid inside, and only then did she realize that she'd betrayed more of herself than she meant to.

"Ridden in the back, though?" he asked when he got in beside her.

"I plead the Fifth."

"So yes," he said.

"No, I'm just exercising my constitutional rights."

"A word to the wise, Bix. Anything you say can be used against you, but what you don't say will form opinions."

"Aren't you just a six-foot-four-inch magic eight ball."

"Shake me and find out."

She snorted. She knew that she smelled like sweat, and the earth, the trees. She knew a moment of embarrassment sitting next to him. All clean and well pressed in this uniform. He was muscular, broad shouldered. His jaw was square, like an old-fashioned Hollywood movie star. His nose was straight, and his lips looked like they might even be appealing if he ever smiled.

He was flat out *handsome*. She didn't normally waste time pondering the handsomeness of men.

Threat or *not a threat*, that was all she needed to know about men. And whether they were handsome-shaped or not didn't inform that assessment.

Neither did him being a cop.

She'd rather take her chances with a convict, generally speaking.

Depending on what they were convicted of.

Cops were just government-funded mafia in her estimation and she'd do well to remember that.

She rested her elbow on the door's armrest, and the rest of her chin on her fist. She winced. She had forgotten that she had a scab there. She couldn't even remember now how she'd done it. But it just added to that feeling of inadequacy. He owned a ranch. He was someone who had things. She wondered what his family was like. They must be wonderful. They must have pushed him to have dreams. To have goals.

Goals other than being a shady criminal.

She shoved that to the side. There was no earthly point in feeling sorry for herself. It wasn't useful. Not in the least.

It only took a couple of minutes for them to turn off the paved road and onto a dirt driveway.

"This is Four Corners Ranch," he said. "It's been owned by four ranching families since the late eighteen hundreds. My family is one of them."

Elitist. Inherited wealth. He would have no idea what it was like to have inherited nothing but poverty and a sketchy relationship to morality.

"Interesting," she said.

She was not interested.

They rolled up to the farmhouse some five minutes later. It was idyllic. Lovely. Two stories with a wide front porch. There were trucks parked out front, and she had the feeling that there was a whole mess of people inside.

She couldn't remember the last time she'd hung out in a group. Well, a group where they weren't making moonshine.

"You all right?"

She wasn't sure how she felt about him being intuitive to her mood. Maybe intuition hadn't been required. Maybe her discomfort was obvious and she'd just so profoundly forgotten how to be around another human.

She'd thought any feelings she had about people judging her had vanished a long time ago. But the idea of going in there . . . to see his family, who were probably all as clean and beautiful as he was, looking like a raccoon that had just been dumped out of a garbage bin was a hit she didn't think her pride could take.

He'd already looked and seen something was wrong. So, she might as well just swallow said pride now and ask for what she wanted.

"Is there . . . ? Can I have the shower before we see anyone else?"

His face relaxed, and the pity she saw there was wounding. She didn't like to be pitied. But right now, she was a bit pitiful, it had to be said. So maybe she just had to own it. Take what she could get.

Raccoons from garbage cans couldn't afford to be choosers. Or something.

"Let's drive over to my place. I thought that you would maybe want a little more security . . . you know, to not be alone with me."

"To your point," she said. "You had a gun on you this whole time."

"True."

He pulled slowly away from the farmhouse and drove her farther down the dirt drive. "I got my own place just down here. Denver lives in the farmhouse, but the rest of us live on the property."

"Denver is?"

"My oldest brother."

"Oh. How many siblings do you have?" She wasn't really used to making small talk.

"Three brothers and one sister."

"That's a lot of siblings."

"It is. How many siblings do you have?"

She snorted. "No fucking idea. I've got bros in different area codes." She stared at him as if she expected him to react to that. "Anyway, I've got one half brother that I lived with and know pretty well. But I can't actually be sure how much seed my dad has sowed out there."

"Well. In total fairness, I suppose I could have some half siblings out there."

She looked at him, frowning. "Really?"

"I don't really know what my parents are up to either."

She sat with that, uncomfortably. Because he did not seem like the type to have wayward parents.

He seemed like the type to have it all together.

Especially given the way that he talked about the family all being together for dinner.

Her family had eaten together sometimes. Usually chili out of a can on a TV tray.

He'd successfully surprised her with the revelation that his family might not be normal.

"Do you smoke?" Since he was going to be a whole surprise and everything. She might as well see if she could get a little nicotine out of the deal.

"No," he said.

"Rats."

They pulled up to the front of a neat-looking cabin. This looked like the kind of place he should live. It was woodsy and clean. Respectable, but somehow rugged.

She was putting way too much thought into him.

"Why?" he asked.

"I don't smoke either. Anymore. Because I can't afford it. I would like a cigarette, though."

"It's bad for you," he said.

She looked up at him, made sure to angle her face just right so he could see the scab under her chin. "Is there something about me that says I'm all about living a superhealthy lifestyle?"

He gave her a dispassionate look, those intense blue eyes flickering over her. It made her feel vaguely uncomfortable.

"I don't suppose."

"Do I look like I've ever touched kale?"

"Can't say as you do."

"I don't even know what kale is," she said. "I'm a whole-ass mess."

"Well now, you're not that bad."

She got out of the car. "Here for a good time, not a long time."

"You don't look like you're here for a good time either, Bix. You look like you've been around for a hard time."

"Rude," she said.

But there was something about that that slid under her skin and made her feel fragile.

It *had* been a hard time.

Something about acknowledging that made her throat go all tight.

Wow. Suck it up, Bix.

There were plenty of people who had it way worse. There was a whole catalog of shit she hadn't been through. And some she had been. But whatever. That was life. She wasn't born with a silver spoon in her mouth. Hell, she wasn't even born with a plastic spoon in her mouth. She didn't take anything for granted; she couldn't afford to. And she didn't sit around feeling sorry for herself, because she didn't have that kind of time.

She sniffed and walked toward the front of the house. He moved up behind her, and unlocked the door.

She tried to keep from flinching. He was so close that she could feel the warmth emanating from his body.

He just smelled so good. He managed to smell like the pine trees, the dirt and the air, but it didn't seem like lingering poverty clinging to his skin.

It smelled fresh. Clean.

He threw his keys on the coffee table next to what looked like a very nice couch. It was a small place, but it was perfectly well ordered, just like the outside. And everything inside was in great condition. It was warm in there. She felt a stinging pressure at the back of her eyes, and she ignored it.

"Hang tight," he said.

He disappeared down the hallway and returned with a black sweatshirt and a pair of black sweatpants. "These are going to be a little big."

She blinked up at him. If they were his, they were going to be more than a little big. But maybe they were his wife's?

For some reason, she felt instantly bothered by the fact he might have a wife.

"These belong to some woman you fucked?"

She didn't know why it came out like that. She didn't know why she was being mean. He might actually be doing something kind for her. But she couldn't wrap her head around it. And so, she couldn't accept it. And she sure as hell couldn't be nice.

"No," he said. "They're mine. From police academy. But the drawstring on those pants cinches pretty tight."

He led her down the hall and pointed toward the bathroom. "Here you go."

He closed the door, and she locked it. She turned on the water, and just stood there for a full minute, not quite sure what had happened. Not quite sure how this was how the day had gone. She took her sweatshirt off and her beanie came with it. Then she took off her T-shirt, and her bra. She looked at herself in the mirror for a long time. She wished she hadn't.

The woman standing in front of her was so thin that Bix hardly recognized her.

She could see her ribs; her stomach sank in pitifully. She looked at her breasts critically. They weren't very big. And that was even more true with the weight that she'd lost.

Her face was thin and drawn. Pale. She took the rubber band out of her hair. Her hair was greasy, stringy. Dull.

She swallowed hard and turned on the shower, ran her hand under the water and found herself delighted by the warmth. She couldn't worry about how she looked when she had a hot shower to look forward to.

She slid her jeans off her hips and didn't bother to look at herself again. She got into the shower, and she really did just about cry. The water felt so good. So soothing. She had been cold down to her bones, and she just felt . . . dirty.

She swallowed at the lump in her throat. Her chest felt bruised. She knew it wasn't because she had just looked at her skinny chest in the mirror.

She lathered up the soap and ran it over her skin, then took her time washing her hair. She didn't want the shower to end, but she was hungry. And there was dinner on the other side of this. She got out of the shower and tugged on the sweatpants. They had an elastic band down at the ankles, thankfully, or she would've been trailing fabric down beneath the bottoms of her feet. As it was, it just bunched up there comically. She grabbed hold of the drawstring and pulled as tight as she possibly could, cinching it up around her waist.

She could barely get them tight enough. She knotted the string ruthlessly. She lifted up the sweater, and she had to laugh. Because it literally said Police Academy on it. Of all the things. Her dad would have an absolute cow.

But her dad wasn't here. This cop *was* here.

Of all the things.

She put the sweatshirt over her head and gloried in the feeling of the soft fabric against her bare skin. Gloried in the feeling of being clean.

She gathered up her dirty clothes and stepped out of the bathroom.

"Do you have a washing machine?" she asked.

"Yeah. Do you have more clothes in your backpack?"

"Yes," she said.

She was acutely aware of the fact that she was barefoot, with wet hair. There was something weird and intimate about it. She didn't especially like it. She wasn't used to *intimate*.

"You can wash all your clothes if you want."

"I . . . I would. Thanks. You don't happen to have an extra pair of socks, do you?"

"I definitely do."

Her shoes would still work, but clean socks would be amazing.

He explained where the laundry room was, and she followed his instructions to get there, dumping all of her clothes in the washing machine and starting the load. By the time she went back to the living area he was there with a pair of black socks. She sat down on the couch and pulled them over her feet, taking pleasure in the simple activity. She put her shoes on and wiggled her toes.

"You ready to go have dinner?"

"Sure," she said.

It was like she'd washed some of the anger and suspicion off her skin. And she couldn't say if that was a good thing or not. In general, it wasn't. She knew.

But this felt so good, and she felt mollified.

Safe.

"We can take my truck back over to the house. No reason to take the cop car."

She climbed into the passenger seat beside him. "Are you married?" she asked.

He looked at her as he started the engine. "No. Does it look like a woman lives in that house?"

"I guess not," she said.

She wouldn't really know. That was the kind of thing people knew maybe when they had functional families in their background. Somebody who could picture what a normal family home looked like. That certainly wasn't her.

"Does your family know . . . that you're bringing a . . . ?" She could hardly call herself a guest.

Nor could she bring herself to say *garbage raccoon* out loud.

"Yeah. I texted them and let them know I was bringing over a new employee."

"I didn't say that I was going to take the job."

"Why wouldn't you?"

Everything in her rebelled against that. Everything in her wanted to have a fight.

How dare he? How dare he act like he knew what was good for her. What was best.

But the problem was, he had a point. She was all about survival. She was all about doing the practical thing.

"How much would you pay me an hour?"

He named a figure that made her eyebrows shoot up. It was like a dollar more than minimum wage.

"Really?"

"If you do good work, yes. I don't see why not. Seems like you're pretty handy, and I could use the help."

"I . . ."

"So, what's the holdup?"

"I want to know what the catch is."

"There's no catch. This is a big ranch, we employ a lot of people. We have work, you need work."

"Do you have any idea how hard it is for me to get a job?"

"You have a criminal record, don't you?"

"I . . ."

"Bix," he said. "I'm going to do a background check on you when you give me your name so that I can put you on payroll. You might as well just tell me."

Well, fine. She knew when she was beaten. Pretending otherwise was an embarrassment she couldn't bear.

"Yes," she said. "Okay? I have a criminal record. And you . . . Can you imagine going into a job interview looking like I do most days? Nobody's going to hire me. I look . . . I look like what I am. A street rat with too many misdemeanors under her belt to be a good bet."

She didn't know why she felt embarrassed or angry to say that to him. She wasn't ashamed of herself. Not in general. She'd been given a bad hand. She played those cards pretty admirably, she thought.

"Well, I don't hire that way."

"Why?" she asked, feeling the need to push him away. "You're just . . . you're just so nice?"

"No. I'm not nice. Don't go assuming the best about me."

"Wow. I thought cops were supposed to know how to read a room. You think that I'm assuming the best of you? I'm trying to figure out what the hell is happening. I don't actually think you're nice. Because I don't think anyone is nice. Not in a way that isn't entirely self-serving. And don't be offended by that, that's what I think about everybody."

He snorted. "Noted. What is it you think I'm trying to get out of this?"

"On a good day I assume human trafficking. When I'm feeling a little bit more suspicious, I'm inclined toward ritual sacrifice."

"Well shit, and I thought my cover was going to be blown when you saw the pentagram and the altar in the backyard."

"I'm just warning you, whatever deity you try to send me to is probably going to send me back."

She wrinkled her nose. And said nothing about the fact that she would at least be a virgin sacrifice. He didn't need to know that. Nobody did. It wasn't like she thought it made her good or anything. *Nothing* made her good.

It was only that it was something that belonged to her. Something that the wretched dregs of the world hadn't managed to steal. No shitty guy in a tiny apartment, or a dilapidated trailer, had talked her into letting him in her pants for five minutes in exchange for weed or shelter or whatever. She had decided a long time ago she'd rather sleep rough if need be. Again, not because of any kind of moral high ground. It was stubbornness.

The need to have some say over her own life. Her own body.

She'd had a couple guys try to get handsy, and one of them had ended up with a pocketknife through the fleshy part of his hand. Little bitch had cried. And couldn't do a thing about it. Because if he'd tried to go whining to the police it wouldn't have gone well for him either.

She wasn't lying to Daughtry, though. She really didn't believe anyone did a damn thing out of the goodness of their heart. It was all to serve some greater good for themselves. Or to feed demons inside of them. She wondered which it was for him.

Demons. That was what her gut told her.

She didn't know why.

"Am I your grand atonement for something?" she asked.

He turned to look at her, one eyebrow raised. "If you were?"

"Lousy pick, dude. But it doesn't matter to me. I just like things to make sense."

"Come on now, you can't be under the impression that the world is actually inclined to make sense."

She huffed. "Well no. Not really. I know better than that. But I would like to know what manner of sacrifice I actually am. And on what altar? Because that's the bottom line, Sheriff. There's always something."

"My dad was a piece of shit," he said. "And the truth is, if you had rolled up on the ranch back when he was in charge? I don't know what he would've done. But it wouldn't have been helping you. Sometimes living in opposition to what you were raised to be is the best you can do."

Those words settled down beneath her skin. Twisted around inside of her. She didn't like them. Not especially. They made her uncomfortable. Because she hadn't done that. Not even a little. She had lived exactly along the lines of what you would expect somebody with her background to live.

She had followed in her dad's footsteps.

But right and wrong were pretty elastic concepts as long as you weren't hurting anybody. That was what she'd always been raised to believe.

You had to look out for yourself because nobody else was going to.

They just weren't.

She couldn't have any kind of sympathy for another person if she didn't have her own survival sorted out.

"Well. That makes me feel better," she said.

"Why?"

"Because I don't trust in random acts of kindness. They just aren't real. Not to me. Not in my life."

He made a noncommittal grunting sound, and just then they pulled up to the front of that farmhouse.

At least now she felt human, even if she did look like a small child dressed in clothes that were too big for her.

"My oldest brother is Denver, then there's Justice. Landry will be there with his wife, Fia. They have a daughter named Lila. My sister, Arizona, is there with her husband, Micah, and their son, Daniel. Rue is my brother Justice's best friend. And that's the crew."

"I'm not going to be able to remember that," she said.

"Yeah. But I figured you might want to know exactly what you're getting. And . . . just so you know, they're not quite as civilized as I am."

She snorted. "I'm not as civilized as you are, Sheriff. I should fit right in."

CHAPTER FOUR

As THEY WALKED through the front door, he thought about what Bix had said. And he realized that it was probably true.

"Hey, everybody," he said when they came in. They were all expecting him to come in with someone, so they were crowded around looking expectantly. "This is Bix. She's passing through the area and needed work. So, I figured she could stay here on the ranch for a while and do just that."

"Hi," she said, her voice a little bit smaller than it had been before.

He had felt some real pity for her when they had first pulled up to the house and she'd asked to go take a shower first.

The poor little thing was dirty, and he could see that she was embarrassed about it. She was wearing his ill-fitting police academy garb. She was clean now, though. Her blond hair hung down her back, and her skin was bright and clear. He noticed for the first time that her eyes were round, and a particularly interesting shade of robin's-egg blue. She had freckles sprinkled across her nose, and her top lip was a bit fuller than the bottom one. Which lent her a sort of pouty expression. He still couldn't quite guess her age. He knew she wasn't being honest about the one she'd given him. He just still didn't know why.

He had a feeling it had to do with not wanting somebody in the system to know her. Which was hilarious, because once he actually got her name, he wasn't just going to know her age; he was going to know the details of her rap sheet.

Maybe he was being indiscriminate bringing her into his family home. He had searched her backpack while she showered. She did have a knife in there, just like she'd said. But he hadn't found a gun. He didn't think that she was actually dangerous to him or his family. No. She was just down on her luck.

"Howdy, Bix," said Denver, taking a step forward, fully assuming his patriarchal role. "Nice to meet you."

"Yes," said Arizona. "It's always nice to have another woman around. This place is a sausage fest."

That was when Rue came out of the kitchen. "What's that about sausage fests?" Rue asked.

"I was just saying, there are too many men around here for my comfort."

"There's more and more women all the time," said Rue.

"Yeah," said Denver. "It's even now."

"Maybe the issue is that I just don't like *you*."

Marriage had tempered Arizona some. Only some. She was still a sharp little scoundrel.

"So yeah, this is everybody," he said. "Let's eat."

The kitchen table was becoming increasingly full. He was proud of that. Because they had grown up keeping to themselves. They had grown up without any kind of real connection to their mother, and the connection they had to their father was toxic at best. But then things had changed. And slowly, over time, they'd started to build something between each other.

Rue had befriended Justice when her parents had worked on the ranch and had stuck close ever since. They had connections. They had people. Landry and Fia had worked out all their issues. They had their daughter. Arizona and Micah had gotten back together. Yeah. They had built something good. Something warm in place of what had been. And now Bix felt like she was a part of that. Or emblematic of something they were able to do that was . . . good.

So, there was that.

She sat down at the table, and he sat beside her, feeling somewhat protective.

She looked over at him, and her expression was unreadable. Dinner was already set out, and when she looked back at the food, he could read her expression.

"Eat as much as you want," he said. "We have plenty."

It was all the invitation he needed to make. She heaped food on her plate. Potato salad, rolls, steak. Baked beans, and a chicken leg. She tucked into it with relish, and then helped herself to more. Denver looked across the table at him and nodded once. He could see that his older brother had taken measure of the situation and approved.

It wasn't often Denver approved of him.

As far as Denver was concerned, their duty was to the ranch. To each other. Daughtry felt much more beholden to the community. To right the wrongs that their father had done.

The wrongs that he had participated in.

Denver didn't have the same level of atoning to do that Daughtry did.

But when it came to strays who worked on the ranch, Denver took that shit seriously.

And he knew that Denver would be right with him when it came to making sure that Bix got out of here with more than what she came with.

Denver and Justice talked about ranch business, and Landry gave an update on the barn construction.

"Pretty soon we ought to be able to break ground on cottages too," he said. "I think it would be good if there were a few places for guests to stay when we were hosting a destination wedding."

"Yeah," said Daughtry, "sounds good to me."

"You all ranch cattle?" Bix asked, surprising him by speaking.

"Yep," Denver said. "We have fifty head. But additionally, we've been expanding the place. Beef is profitable. To an extent. But when you're farming and ranching you always have to be nimble. It's a hard life. But we have the land, and so we're definitely obligated to work it and make it do as well as it can. Landry had the idea to renovate one of the barns into a venue for meetings and weddings and the like. So then I was thinking after that we'd build places for people to stay . . ."

"Are you going to be providing food?"

"We have a lot of food," Fia, his sister-in-law, chimed in. "We bake pies and can make basically anything and are set up to do it over at Sullivan's Point."

"So, you all work together," she said.

"More or less," Justice said. "We try anyway."

"Everything runs a lot smoother these days," said Denver. "Back when our parents were in charge of the place the families had become rivals more than partners. It was Sawyer Garrett over at Garrett's Watch who came up with the idea to reinstall the collective that we used to have. We share finances, we help each other through the hard times."

"Well, aren't you just the Waltons," she said. But she smiled, so it didn't sound quite as edgy or mean as it might have.

"Not quite," said Denver. "But we do the best we can with what we've got. We try to help each other."

"Even though everybody thinks we're assholes," said Arizona.

"That isn't quite it," said Rue. "You intimidate people because they don't understand you."

"Misunderstood," said Arizona. "Like the majestic wolf."

"Or the honey badger in your case," Justice said to his sister.

Bix was looking back and forth between everybody, apparently amused and clearly trying to follow exactly what was going on. It was a lot of family dynamic to dump a stranger into, but she seemed entertained if anything.

"Well, I'm happy to get the dishes," Bix said, standing up from the table and rolling up her sleeves. "You all did all the work. And provided the food."

"You're not going to do the dishes by yourself," said Rue.

"No, you aren't," Justice agreed, standing.

"You take up too much space, Justice," Rue said. "There isn't that much room at the sink."

"Are you telling me this is woman's work?" he asked, lifting a brow.

"No, I'm telling you maybe Bix and I want to hang out."

"Well . . . thank you," Bix said.

They went back into the living room, and Denver took his seat at his favorite armchair, with cattle horns sticking out the side. It had been their dad's favorite chair. He sometimes thought Denver sat in it just to enjoy the fact that he had taken it from their old man. Not because he thought he was like their dad, but because he was relishing all that he had taken from him.

Daughtry had a feeling he was about to get the third degree so he opted to take a minute to ask Justice about Rue. "What's with the rock on Rue's finger?" he asked.

Daughtry couldn't for the life of him read the expression on his brother's face. "Oh, she's engaged."

They all swiveled their heads to look back into the kitchen, then stared at Justice. "And you didn't mention that?" Denver asked.

Justice shrugged. "She's been dating Asher for like eight years. It's not shocking."

"When's the wedding?"

"March." He stared at them. "They've actually been engaged for a while. She just got a ring recently. He's been deployed and all that. But when he was in town a few weeks ago he gave her the ring. And now he's gone again, which is why she's been over here so much."

"You . . . good with that?" Landry asked. "With her getting married?"

Justice made a dismissive noise. "Yes. She's happy. She's the nicest, most organized, most together person I know. She makes me look like the biggest degenerate on the planet, and I love her for it. I'm glad she found someone who's like her."

Daughtry had never fully understood the relationship between Justice and Rue, but if pressed he would have said it had some . . . sexual tension there. But maybe not. Maybe he'd been wrong all this time.

"So. Give us the story," said Denver.

It took Daughtry a minute to realize Denver was no longer talking to Justice.

"Not much to tell. Her van broke down on the outskirts of the ranch. She needs money to fix it. She's kind of down-and-out."

"That's very nice of you, Daughtry," said Justice.

"He's a martyr," said Denver. "He's not nice."

"That's mean," said Landry, feigning shock.

"I'm mean," Denver said blandly.

"The way I see it," Daughtry said, ignoring his brothers, "we can find her some odd jobs to do, get her set up and send her on her way. But she's going to need a place to stay."

"Where exactly?"

"I'm not going to farm her out to you. We'll have to get one of the other houses on the property habitable. Until then . . . Well, tonight at least I thought I'd sleep on the couch and have her sleep in my bed."

Denver and Landry exchanged a look.

"Really?" Daughtry said. "Do you honestly think—"

"No," said Landry. "That's the thing. I do not think. Not of you. You would *never*. I'm just wondering if she's going to think . . ."

"I already made it clear to her that I'm not expecting payment for this," he said, his lip curling. "Because you know there's plenty of guys that would only help her so that they could take advantage of her."

And the question swirling around inside of him was why he was helping her.

Because he was a good person? Maybe it was really just because it was the opposite of what his dad would've done. That was what he told himself in the beginning. It was what he'd told her.

His brothers were looking at him with cool speculation. It was his sister who came to his immediate defense. "You're just a good one, Daughtry. You have the ability to help and so you do. There's nothing deeper than that to it. You don't need to."

"You're doing what any of them would do," said Fia. "Whether they think so or not. You're all good men. You would never leave a woman vulnerable."

That he did believe. His brothers were all good men. They weren't like their father. They didn't try to bleed everybody around them for whatever they could get.

Daughtry had made sure that his entire life was a condemnation of the way that his father had behaved. The way that he had behaved.

That was the problem. His brothers could rest in the fact that they weren't their father.

Daughtry couldn't.

He made sure that his life was all about black-and-white. All about laws and rules in order, because he had seen who he was without it. He didn't like that person. He was determined to never be that person again.

It was easy for him to decide what to do when he put it in context with his job. What was the point of being a police officer if he didn't help? It was the kind of thing that made his day a bit easier to navigate.

And he was all about that. Moral simplicity was his jam.

He looked at the time. "I'm going to go collect her. Take her back and get her to sleep."

"How old is she?" Denver asked.

"She says she's twenty-six."

Denver shook his head. "Well, that's a lie."

"I know. I just don't know how much of one it is. But I'll find out once I get her full name out of her. I'm going to put her on payroll legally and officially. But she's had a long day. She doesn't need to be in there doing dishes."

"Maybe she wants to," Denver said. "Don't treat her like a half-drowned kitten when she's a whole woman capable of standing on her own feet."

It was a strangely pointed thing for his brother to say.

"I don't want her feeling like she has to pay us back."

He moseyed back into the kitchen and leaned in the doorway. Bix was scrubbing dishes as quickly as possible, with Rue putting them away.

"Sorry," said Daughtry. "I'm going to take your scrubber."

"We aren't done yet," said Bix. "And I can't make her finish alone."

"I'll help," said Justice.

"You've had a long day," Daughtry said.

The expression she gave him was one of utter confusion. "What?"

"You've had a long day. You're probably tired."

"Well. Yes. But . . . I don't understand why that . . . I don't get why . . ."

"What?" he asked.

"I don't understand why that matters. Or why you're concerned about it."

"Seems like a normal thing to be concerned about."

"Okay."

She moved away from the sink like a little robot and dried her hands on her sweatpants.

"Bye," she said to Justice and Rue.

"Bye, Bix," said Rue. "Hopefully we'll see you for dinner tomorrow."

"Maybe," she said.

He led her out of the kitchen to another chorus of goodbyes, and when they were outside, walking to the truck, she stopped. "That was . . . It was very nice. I'm not sure that I should stay."

"Why not?"

"Because. I can't get used to this. It's not ever going to be my life. It's never going to be normal. It's never going to be . . . I can't get used to eating that much food."

"Counterargument," he said, feeling sympathy for her swelling in his chest. "You're building up your strength."

"Nobody has ever . . . You being afraid that I'm tired . . . No one has ever cared about that before. It's never mattered. And it's not something that I'm going to be able to keep."

He wished that weren't true. And yet, he couldn't argue with what she was saying. It probably was true. But it sure as hell sucked.

"Well, someone should have," he said.

"Not going to argue with you, Sheriff. But nobody ever has. And I have a life to live. So, I can't sit around getting soft."

"Sit around for a little bit and get strong then. Food, rest, all that's helpful."

"Maybe."

"If you want to leave the minute that you have enough money to get a new starter, you will be out within a week. You can't tell me that you were going to be out of here that fast making moonshine."

She squinted. "I wasn't making moonshine."

"Really?"

"I'm not admitting anything," she said.

"You're a difficult little critter. Get in the truck."

She obeyed him, which surprised him, and then they were off to the house.

"I'm actually staying with you tonight?"

"I don't have any better options open at the moment. I also don't have a guest bed."

The silence that filled the truck was heavy. "I'm sleeping on the couch," he said. "To be clear."

"Oh."

"I'm not waiting to drop another shoe on you."

She was tense, he realized. She had been from the moment he'd met her. Her shoulders held tight, her whole body tight. Poor thing.

"That's unusual."

"Yeah. I get that. I'm sorry about it."

"No need to be sorry to me," she said.

"Fine. Not sorry. Don't care if you're tired. But from a practical standpoint, it would be best if you got your rest so that you can work. I'm going to drive you out to the ranch house tomorrow morning, and Denver will give you your assignment. I have to go to work."

"Do the rest of them work on the ranch?"

"Yeah. I do too. Just when I'm not working my shifts for the department."

"Right."

He killed the engine and they got out of the truck, walking toward the house. "Come here," he said.

He led her down the hall and pushed his bedroom door open. "You can sleep in here."

"I . . . Well, thanks."

"No drama."

He went into the room and opened up his closet, taking out a folded-up blanket and snagging one of the pillows off the bed.

"You . . . You're going to sleep on the couch?"

"Yeah. It'll be fine."

Not really. His feet were going to be crunched up at the end. But that didn't matter.

"What?"

"Yeah," he said. "Fine. Don't worry about it, Bix."

"I'm not," she said. "If you're uncomfortable, that's just because you're a sap. I don't give a shit."

"Good. That's what I like to hear."

"Great," she said.

Then he walked out of the room and closed the door behind him, leaving his foundling in there.

He paused at the vacant bedroom two doors down from his own. He could always just get a bed and put it in there. She wouldn't be here that long. It was probably more efficient than trying to get another one of the buildings ready.

He would think on that.

Until then, he had a very uncomfortable night to spend on the couch. And if it was penance a little bit . . . that was just fine too.

BIX DIDN'T KNOW what to make of the situation she found herself in. Everybody at the King house had been nice. Very nice. And the food had been amazing. And then he had noticed that she was tired and . . .

She rubbed her chest where it felt sore.

She didn't like feeling emotional. Not like this. It was annoying. She didn't feel like it was fair. There was no call to go getting sappy or attached or anything like that.

He was just a guy. He was a guy that was helping her out.

What did it matter? What did he matter? He didn't. They didn't.

This was almost a con. When she thought about it. Because she was going to go right back to selling moonshine. She wasn't getting on the straight and narrow or anything like that. He wasn't actually making a difference in her life.

Whatever the hell he thought he was doing.

She went to the bathroom and took a minute to look around that space. He had a tub in there. She was going to use it. Tonight, or maybe early tomorrow morning. But she realized she needed to get her clothes moved out of the washing machine and into the dryer.

She walked out of the bedroom and made her way down to where the laundry room was. She dug through the washing machine and grabbed her clothes. Put them in the dryer and examined the settings. She didn't know what the hell they meant. She took her best guess and hit the button. She figured she couldn't go too wrong with More Dry.

She wanted her clothes to be *more dry*, after all.

When she got them started, she walked out of the laundry room, and then stopped. There he was, at the end of the hallway, backlit. Shirtless. He just sort of stood there. And her mouth went dry. Because he was . . .

He was *built*.

She had known that. She had been able to tell that, seeing him in his uniform. That he had broad shoulders and a muscular chest. That his waist was narrow. He was tall. Exceptionally tall.

But that hint of his physique in the uniform hadn't fully prepared her for this.

For the sight of his well-defined pectoral muscles dusted with dark hair, the firmly ridged abs on his stomach.

She did not get foolish about men. Because she couldn't afford it.

Her personal economy was always such that sexy men were just way too expensive.

But right now, she was immobilized by it. By him.

"Sorry," she said, suddenly realizing that she was standing there ogling him.

She turned around and went back to her bedroom.

She closed the door firmly behind her and locked it.

Lord Almighty. She had not needed that. She didn't need her head filled up with images of his chest. His stomach.

He should warn people about that.

That he was a snack and a half.

Good thing she was immune to men. Really. Because she was.

Also, a good thing she'd stuffed herself at dinner because she needed no snacks.

"Can't afford it," she repeated to herself over and over again as she went into the bathroom and started to run some water in the bathtub. She'd just had a shower a few hours ago, but access to warm water was a luxury. And being this close to a bath meant she simply couldn't resist.

And taking further advantage of her hospitality seemed like it might make her feel better.

So, she started running the water, and took her clothes off, but then tried to ignore the way that the fabric brushed against her body. While that image of him half-naked still lingered in her mind. What the hell was wrong with her?

She grimaced and stood outside the tub, tapping her foot. Waiting. She got in and sighed when the water closed in over her shoulders. It was an amazing tub. A deep one. Probably special order because he was so tall.

And big and broad.

She felt an arrow of desire lance her. *Unexpectedly. Weirdly.* It was such a foreign experience for her.

Always theoretical.

She squeezed her legs together and did her best to ignore it. She had to keep herself safe. Nobody else cared as much about her own safety as she did. He might be helping her, but it would only be to a point. What she'd said to him earlier was true. She couldn't afford to go getting sentimental. She couldn't afford to get comfortable.

She soaked in the tub until she turned into a prune, then got out and dried herself off. She put the sweats back on and looked at the bed.

He slept in this bed normally. It was also big. She felt slightly like Goldilocks in that moment. But the bed was definitely Papa Bear's. And it was big. Not just right. It was disconcerting. And his.

She pulled back the blankets and slipped between the sheets. She was immediately enveloped by that scent she'd noticed earlier. It made her heart jump. It was weird. She didn't like it.

She shifted, and rolled over onto her stomach, but that didn't help, because that just put her face in his pillow. Which also smelled like him.

She huffed and moved closer to his nightstand. There was nothing on it. Nothing but an alarm clock. There was no art in the room. The bedspread was plain. If she had a house, she would actually put nice things in it. She opened up the nightstand drawer, feeling nosy.

It was empty.

Except for a box of condoms.

That hit her strangely in the chest.

She took the box out and saw that it was open. She pulled a strip of condoms out and ran her finger along the packets. "Who do you use these with, Sheriff?"

It was incredibly invasive and nosy, and she knew it. But . . . it was interesting. These windows into him as a human. As a man. Not just this strange kind of savior-like figure.

She shoved the condoms back into the drawer and decided she didn't need to know about it.

And she sure as hell didn't need to think about it.

It was . . . it was crazy. And it was dumb. So there. She didn't care about his condoms. She just wanted some sleep. And this was the first bed that she had actually been in in a while. Other than the cramped little mattress in her van. So, this was nice for a while. It was a stopover. She refused to think of it as anything else. She was too smart to believe that this would last. That was a good thing. It was a damned good thing.

CHAPTER FIVE

WHEN SHE WOKE up in the morning, she had no sense of what time it was. And that was weird. More than a little weird. She was also warm. And comfortable. She didn't have a single ache on her body, and she wasn't contorted into a strange shape. Quite the contrary, she was sprawled out in the center of a king-size bed.

She jerked awake, tangled in all the bedclothes. And then she remembered.

Daughtry.

The King family. They had brought her in. They'd fed her. He'd let her sleep in his bed.

He had an amazing chest.

He had a drawer full of condoms.

Some of that information wasn't useful, so she set about deleting it from her brain. She had overslept. For sure. There was no way he was still around.

She slipped out from beneath the covers and realized that she was going to have to get her clothes out of the dryer. Cautiously, she opened up the bedroom door, and crept out into the hall.

She smelled bacon. She moved slowly down the hall, making her way toward the kitchen. And there he was. Standing with his back to her at the stove. He was wearing a black T-shirt that stretched tight over his muscles, and a pair of dark denim jeans that cupped his ass like a pair of hands. His feet were bare. Something about that made her heart stutter.

"Morning," he said.

He reached out to his left and picked up the mug. He didn't turn to face her as she assumed he took a sip of the coffee.

"You're still here," she said.

"Yeah. I figured I'd give my shift a miss today. Got it covered."

"Why?"

"I thought it was more important to spend some time showing you around. I didn't want to turn you loose with my family just yet."

"But you could."

"It's true. I could. I want to have a realistic talk with you."

"Can I have bacon first?"

Then he did turn, and her heart jumped hard against the front of her breastbone. He was the kind of stunning men never were. Not to her. That sculpted jaw, covered in dark stubble, the strong column of his throat. His broad shoulders. His thick, muscular arms and well-defined forearms.

And he was just . . . a human man. Standing in the kitchen, making breakfast. He wasn't a superhero off saving the world. And when he wasn't in his police uniform, she couldn't feel like he was an adversary. Well. She imagined she could if she tried really hard. She reached down deep and searched for a bit of resentment she might be able to pull up.

But she didn't want to find any, actually.

On the stove there was a plate of bacon, and a heap of scrambled eggs in a pan. There were biscuits. Hash browns. And pancakes. And she was starving.

"I haven't seen this much food since . . . Well, since last night. But before that, it was a long damned time."

"Eat," he said. "Because you're not going to be able to get any work done as long as you're that bony."

She scowled.

"Don't body-shame me," she said, moving forward and grabbing hold of the piece of the bacon and taking a bite off the crisp end. She could've cried. Except she was Bix Carpenter, and she didn't cry.

"I'm not *body-shaming* you. It's obvious that you want to have a bit more meat on your bones than you do. Are you going to tell me you got this thin on purpose?"

"No," she said. "But I don't see the point whining about it. Sometimes in life you have extra food. And sometimes you don't have any. There's no point feeling sorry for yourself over it. I don't care if I'm skinny. I can still do things when I need to do them. I can still work for you. And now, I got a lot of fuel available to me. So, I'll do my best to top up now."

"All right. I've heard a lot of philosophy from you. Why don't you fill your plate and have a seat at the table, and we'll have a discussion about how this is going to work."

He handed her a plate, and she started piling the food high.

"Coffee?"

She wrinkled her nose. "Never developed a taste for it."

"Orange juice?"

"Please." Her tongue went tight, her mouth watering as she anticipated the sour juice. Having choices like this was . . . amazing. But she didn't want him to know just how grateful she was.

She sat down at the table, and he gave her a big glass of juice. Then he sat down across from her.

"All right. Give it to me straight. All your information, so that I can get you put on payroll."

"Bix Carpenter," she said.

"It's really not short for anything?"

"I think it's short for neither of my parents gave a shit."

"Right. And where do you come from?"

"Idaho originally. But we've been all over. Mostly western Idaho and eastern Oregon. But a bit up into Washington. Sometimes down to California."

"What do your parents do?"

"Not a damned clue what my mom does, since I haven't seen her in about twelve years. As for my dad, I think he makes license plates."

"He's in prison?"

She rested her forearms on the table and looked at him full on. "That was the joke, Sheriff."

"And what was it you all did?"

"We made moonshine. That's what we did." She didn't see much point holding it back now. That was the thing. He was going to find out.

"Right. That it?"

"Yes. My brother, my dad, they got into some heavier stuff. There were drugs sometimes. But I never had anything to do with that. We were always together. Sometimes we tried our hand at splitting up for a little bit, because it was easier. But we usually drifted back."

"How old are you?"

She shook her head. "Doesn't matter."

"It does."

She sighed. "I'm twenty-three," she said.

"Why did you tell me you were older?"

She shrugged. "I don't know. I wanted you to be-lieve that maybe I had more of a life. Like maybe I had somebody looking out for me. The truth is, I don't. The truth is my dad, and my brother were the only two people that really had any involvement in my day-to-day life. And now they're in prison. For a while."

"Because of the drug running."

"Yep. I knew it was bad news. I did. I told them that. But they didn't listen to me. My dad doesn't . . . He likes to think around the system. He doesn't believe in limitations. He believes that society is stacked against people like us."

"And what are people like you?" he asked.

She suddenly had the feeling that she was in an interrogation room. Damn that man—he'd softened her up. She almost had to admire it, because he was good.

It was just like being down at the station. It was just that he'd fed her. And there was a beautiful view of the mountains outside, rather than it being one-way glass with more cops staring at her from a hidden vantage point.

"Just . . . We're poor. Okay? Uneducated, white trash. It is what it is. We were homeschooled because my dad didn't want the school system to indoctrinate us." She frowned. She said that, and she knew it was a lie. It was what her dad had always said.

"I mean, he probably homeschooled us because he didn't want teachers asking about what was going on at home." She tried to imagine her and her brother, dirty and skinny as they sometimes were, going into a classroom where a teacher might have blown the whistle on them.

"Also, my dad would've had to enroll us in school, and that would've required him to give them the address and . . ."

"He doesn't like being in the system."

She nodded. "Hell, it's kind of a miracle I'm in the system at all. That my mom got him to let her give birth in the hospital, let me get a birth certificate. I'm probably lucky I have documentation at all. I think as things progressed, as his views changed, he would've avoided that."

"Right. So, no school. And what did you do all day?"

"We worked. Helped with chores and with batching the moonshine. He had a pretty big operation back in those days. He had a place to stay. The property. He didn't end up keeping it. We got raided by the Feds at one point."

"That must've been difficult."

She shrugged. "If there's one thing I learned from my dad that I really do believe, it's that there's no use wallowing in the hard times."

"Right. Well. Now that I know little bit about your background, tell me what you want to do."

"What do you mean?"

"How long do you think you want to work here?"

"You said it would probably take me about a week to earn the money for my starter."

"And then what are you moving on to?"

She shrugged. "Doesn't matter."

"I'm serious. Do you have opportunities elsewhere?"

"I have the opportunities that I always have. I like to make my own way. I don't want to be dependent on anybody."

"But what if you stayed here for a while? Worked here for a while?"

"I'll tell you what, Sheriff," she said, ignoring the strange tug in her chest. "Why don't you at least see how I work before you go offering pity labor."

"Bix, none of this is out of pity. You told me that you had a hard time finding work, and I have work."

"Yeah. Well. Like I said, maybe you should wait and see what you think after you actually see my work, and after you see my rap sheet."

She got up and put more bacon on her plate, ate it until she felt full. And then she wanted to cry. But she wouldn't.

"I have another question for you," he said.

"What's that, Sheriff?"

"I can outfit a place for you. But especially if you're only staying short-term, I wonder if it makes more sense for me to get a bed to put in here."

"You want me to stay *here*?"

"It's up to you."

She squinted. "Let me think about it."

"All right."

She had a feeling that he took way longer to leave the house because of her. After she finished eating, she went and got clothes out of the dryer.

"Do you have stuff in your van that you need to get?"

She thought of her few cherished personal items.

"Yeah. There are some things I might like."

"After we work a bit, do you want me to drive you over there to get some things?"

"Yep. If you don't mind."

"I don't."

It made her want to yell at him. To push at him a little bit. Because why was he doing all this for her? She understood. At least, she understood the reason that he'd given. But it just felt weird. She wasn't used to it. Her dad, her brother, they wouldn't have treated her this nicely. They never had.

She just had to remember what she'd told Daughtry not a few minutes ago. Sometimes in your life you had a lot of something. Sometimes you had a little. Right now, this was happening, and there was food. A warm, safe place to sleep where she didn't feel like she had to jump up bright and early, as soon as she'd gotten the bare minimum of rest, and get back on the defensive.

So, she was going to take it. Not ask too many questions. And not get too attached.

That was her best bet.

CHAPTER SIX

HE HAD A STRANGE, unsettled feeling when he drove Bix out to the barn to get an assignment for the day. Deciding to take the day off, he didn't like the idea of Bix leaving so quickly after she got here. He just felt like whatever he was sending her off to, it wasn't going to be good. And he felt like she was so vulnerable that he didn't like the idea of it at all. He could see that she didn't think so. It was obvious to him she thought she was tough. Well able to withstand any of the bullshit out there in the world.

Obviously, she had done it up until this point.

He didn't feel like she should have to.

He would never have gone out looking for somebody to help, but now she had fallen into his lap like this, and it just seemed . . .

You've latched on to her, but she hasn't necessarily latched on to you.

No. It was clear to him that she was ready to bolt at a moment's notice if any of them put a foot wrong. And he wasn't entirely sure what would constitute putting a foot wrong as far as Bix was concerned. She was an unknowable entity, and maybe that was part of the reason why he was fascinated by her.

People, in his experience, were generally exactly what they seemed.

Oh, some of them had a pretty good mask. But it didn't take much digging to get to the heart of it. His father hadn't presented like a maniacal asshole. At least, not to the children that had been raised underneath his firm hand.

He had been a difficult man. Giving praise and rescinding it. But Daughtry had idolized him. His father was a hard worker. For a lot of years King's Crest was the highest-earning ranch in Four Corners. They were the most successful. He'd said it was because he was dedicated to doing business on the side. He'd laid out the ethics of that business like he'd really thought it through. The Kings, he'd said, were hard workers. Lazy people borrowed money then blamed others when they couldn't pay it back. But if you had a debt, it was the right thing to pay it back. Sometimes he had to be hard to collect those debts, but that was him protecting his family.

Daughtry had bought it all, hook, line and sinker. He'd worked with his dad.

He hadn't realized his dad was a loan shark and a drug runner. And so when Daughtry went with his dad to collect debts, he was cheating people. Along with his dad.

So yeah, he knew that people could fool you. But at this point in his life Daughtry was difficult to fool.

But Bix was a study in contradictions. On the surface, she was almost exactly what he might expect. An angry antiestablishment rebel who came about the belief system pretty honestly. What had the system done for her? Nothing. Even he could see that, and he believed in the system.

He didn't believe it was perfect. It was only as flawed as all the people in it. But he believed that the framework existed to make good things within the system, and that was what he tried to do. Because he prized rules and order above all else. A clear and binary way to act and mete out justice.

But there was more to her. He could see it, in the quick flashes of softness that appeared in her eyes. Little bits of emotion. She did her best to hide it, maybe even from herself. He had become a student of the people around him because he had been bound and determined not to be tricked again.

Not the way that his father had deceived him.

But rather than feeling frustrated or suspicious of Bix for being unreadable, he felt intrigued.

He wasn't used to that.

When they pulled up to the barn, Justice and Denver were standing outside next to a pile of lumber that had clearly been freshly delivered.

"Morning," he said, when he parked the truck and got out.

Bix followed behind him, her movements reminding him of a squirrel. Quick. Agile. Anxious.

She came to stand beside him.

She wasn't wearing the sweats anymore. She had changed to an oversize flannel shirt and a pair of jeans with holes in the knees. She had put her black beanie back on. She was back to looking like a teenage hooligan. Even though he already knew she wasn't.

Even though he already knew that she was capable of looking soft. More her age. More like a woman.

Immaterial. It was just something he'd observed.

"Where's Landry?" he asked.

"He took Lila to go pick up some feed. They said they'd be back late afternoon."

"All right. I took the day off. I have some things to do around my house, but I'll be around later." He shifted. "Bix is willing to do any kind of carpentry work that you have."

Denver turned to Bix. "You know how to build?"

"I don't suck at it," Bix said.

"Know how to use power tools?"

Her eyes went bright. "No. But I would love to learn."

"Oh, we can have some fun," said Denver.

And Daughtry thought of what she had said. About how she would probably get along with his family better than he did.

He was watching it happen right in front of him. He shouldn't let it bother him.

It did.

"See you around, Daughtry," said Bix, waving him off. He wondered why the little scoundrel was so eager to get rid of them.

"I'll be back," he said.

"I know," she said.

"Fairly quickly," he added.

"Great," she said. "In the meantime, I'll be using power tools."

"Don't let her hurt herself," he said, turning away from Denver and Justice and heading back toward his truck.

He got in the cab, and not for the first time, wondered what the hell he had gotten himself into. His first order of business was to find a bed, and he had a feeling his best bet was going to be contacting his sister. He decided against calling, and instead went out to the north field on the ranch, which he knew was where he was most likely to find her on this day of the week.

And there she was. On the back of her horse, her dark hair streaming out from underneath a cowgirl hat. Her husband, Micah, was with her, also on the back of a horse. They looked happy. So happy. And it made his chest ache because Arizona had spent a lot of years being angry and bitter and unhappy.

Their father had been cruel to her. Daughtry hadn't known that at the time. But after she had gotten in a car accident that had left her scarred and with permanent injuries, their father had been outraged at her for being mortal. He hadn't had any patience for her emotions, for her depression. Arizona had put up a thick shield, a wall that was difficult to get around.

Micah coming back into her life had changed everything. Not just because she was in love, but because he had helped her realize that a lot of what their father had said to her, a lot of what had gotten in her head, wasn't true.

He was happy about that for her.

The problem was his father had loved him. Daughtry had been his right-hand man. He had always approved of what Daughtry was doing and that had given him a sick kind of twisted-up metric for measuring good and bad. Right and wrong was something he had never given much thought to. And he did his best to let it govern his life now.

He put the truck in Park and killed the engine. Then he got out and gave his sister a wave. She saw him, and oriented her horse his direction and began to ride toward him. She let the mount fly, clods of dirt flying up behind his hooves. And she made sure to stop dramatically just in front of him. Which threw a little bit of dirt on his jeans. But he didn't mind.

"What brings you by?" she asked, looking mischievous, in a way only younger sisters could.

"I had a question for you. You know Bix, the woman that I just hired to work on the ranch?"

"She looks like a kid to me."

"She's not," he said. "I mean, younger than we are, but an adult."

"Okay. Proceed."

"I need a bed for her. So that she has a place to bunk down while she's working here."

"Okay."

"I was just wondering if you knew if there were extras either at the ranch house or in storage somewhere."

"I have one that we just put out in the storage shed. You're welcome to get it if you want."

"Yeah. I'd appreciate that."

"It's unlocked. Just behind the house. It should be the closest thing to the front. We just got a new bed and put it in there."

"Perfect."

"We have an extra bedroom," she said. "If Bix needs a place to stay . . ."

"No," he said. "I've got room at my place."

"And you actually want her to stay with you?"

He couldn't quite untangle why this felt like the best way forward. He felt responsible. For her. For his family. He felt like she was a mission that he had to see all the way through because he was the one who had started it. It seemed reasonable. Rational even.

He didn't want her at the ranch house. While he trusted Bix more or less, he would be an idiot to trust her all the way. That was just logical.

"She's . . ."

"Your stray?" Arizona asked.

He bristled slightly at that. It was unflattering to both him and Bix. But the problem was it was not far from the truth.

"She's my responsibility," he said, opting to just put a better label on it rather than scold his sister.

"You are a man who loves responsibility," said Arizona. "And a hair shirt."

"You're the only person who can get away with saying things like that to me."

"Wow. What do you do to the other people who say things like that to you? Do you glower at them until they put themselves in handcuffs?"

He gave his sister a deadpan look. "I'm going to go get the bed now."

"Okay. Feel free to take some of my other junk with you."

"I'm not a cleaning service, Arizona."

"You're not good for much, Daughtry."

He shook his head and made his way back to the truck. It was a short drive over to the house his sister shared with Micah and their son. A cute little place, with a picturesque yard. It was amazing the way that his sister's internal changes were reflected in the way she had decided to shape the home that she and Micah shared.

He didn't have time to linger much on that, though. He went to the shed and opened it up, quickly finding the mattress, box spring and basic bed frame.

It was a bigger bed than he had been intending to put in the space, but Bix would probably enjoy it. Not that she had said anything about whether or not she had enjoyed sleeping in his bed last night.

He grunted a laugh as he thought those words. Definitely not in the context women normally slept in his bed. Not that they usually slept in it. It had been a while since there had been a woman anyway.

He was fond of arrangements. He wasn't big on going out, getting drunk and picking women up; that was his brothers' territory. It wasn't that he'd never done it; he just wasn't habitual about it. It was one of those things that fell into a gray area for him. And he didn't like a gray area.

He liked things to be clear. Definitive.

And that was where he preferred a long-standing arrangement over a hookup. There was a woman who delivered vitamins for the cattle to the ranch a while ago. And she had included him as a stop on her route even when they didn't need vitamins.

There had been clear boundaries and clear rules. She had chosen to stop and see him, she had always been totally sober and in her right mind, able to skip the stop if she hadn't wanted sex. His father was just such a manipulative bastard, and he had never, ever wanted to be like that. He didn't want to cajole or seduce. He didn't like anything that fell into that category.

He realized he was a little bit over-the-top about that. That he took it to an extreme. But his actions when he'd been a teenager had been such that he felt extremes were warranted where he was concerned.

He didn't trust himself.

She had moved on to another area, and that was fine. But it had also left him in a bit of a dry spell. He was busy, though, and it wasn't something he thought about overly much.

It was a testament to the fact that it had been a few months that handling and moving a bed put his mind firmly on sex.

He got everything loaded into the back of the pickup and drove it back to his place. He was beginning to feel a little like a Ping-Pong ball, pinging around back and forth. Then he wasn't done yet.

He brought the bed into the empty room in his house and worked toward assembling it. And by the time he was through, it was lunchtime. He could grab something at the house, or he could head over to the barn, where Fia and Denver had no doubt collaborated on some vittles for the workers.

He opted for Denver's food, because he knew it would be better than whatever he could rustle up here.

But when he pulled up to the barn, what he saw made his stomach drop down into his feet.

He looked up through the windshield and saw Bix. She was on the roof, no tether or safety line or anything like that. Scrambling around like a wildcat from one end of the ridgeline to the other.

He put the truck in Park and didn't even bother to turn it off.

He got out and looked at his brothers, who were just standing there with their hands on their hips looking up.

"What the hell is going on?" he asked.

Denver gestured toward the barn. "She's checking to see if the roof leaks."

"Are you *insane*? She could get herself killed." He started to walk toward the barn, but realized there was no ladder. "How the hell did she get up there?"

"She climbed," said Denver, looking impressed.

"Like a rat," said Justice.

"And you just *let* her?"

"You've known her longer than I have," said Denver. "You know, like a half a day longer, but what gave you the impression that she was somebody that asked for permission to do anything?"

He knew his brother had a point. But they could've picked her up and tied her to something to keep her from doing something that dumb.

"She's skin and bones," said Daughtry. "She probably doesn't have the strength to be doing things like that."

"And yet she is," said Denver.

Daughtry hadn't worried that she wouldn't work hard. That was funny. Maybe because he didn't care whether or not he was taken advantage of. That wasn't the point of him offering her work. But it hadn't occurred to him that she would go overboard trying to prove that she was fit to be here. And it should have.

Because she was exactly that person. If he really thought about it. Everything she'd said added up to this. People might make assumptions about her because she had been working on the wrong side of the law, but what she did was work. She obviously believed that a person had to earn their way; she just didn't believe that the way was necessarily what the law said.

And now here she was, going overboard trying to prove herself.

"Bix!" he called out.

She stopped and peered down at him. "Hey, Sheriff. I'm just checking to see where the shingles have gone bad."

"Get down here."

"I'm not done," she shouted back.

And to his chagrin she continued to scamper around up there, until she made her way to the edge, sat down on her rear, bent over and gripped the edge of the roof, and just about gave him a heart attack.

She was dangling, her feet in the air. Until she swung them forward and seemed to find a foothold in the wood. Then she leaned down and gripped another board, until she was secure. She worked her way down like it was a rock face and she was a free solo climber, the amount of strength she contained in her skinny limbs shocking. He couldn't breathe. Not until she was halfway down. Not until she was far enough that if she fell, she wasn't going to get killed or maimed.

And then with about three feet to go, she hopped down. "Did you have something to ask me, Sheriff?"

"I didn't have anything to ask you. I have something to tell you. Don't do things like that. That was stupid."

She crossed her arms, her expression speaking of mutiny. "Justice and Denver didn't have a problem with it. Anyway, there's going to be a whole crew out there working on that roof, because it is in shambles. Sorry to be the bearer of bad news."

"I'm not shocked," Denver said, looking grim.

"This is getting expensive," said Justice.

"Well, I knew it would be expensive," said Denver. "And the truth is, we have the money."

"You're going to pay for it out of your pocket?" Justice asked.

"If I have to."

"All because Landry wanted to make changes around here?" Daughtry asked.

"Because it's the right thing to do," said Denver. "Because we've got to keep evolving if we want to be secure."

"Damn straight," said Bix. "Evolution is the only way to survive. The world isn't going to slow down

for you. So, you've gotta figure out how to keep up."
She looked at him. "And sometimes you have to climb
a few barns."

"Except you don't need to do that," said Daughtry.

"I'm fine. Do you have any idea how many times I
have evaded the law that way?"

He looked at her and frowned. "No."

She smiled. "A lot."

"I think she's great," said Justice. "A regular street
urchin."

"It's true," said Bix. "Oliver Twist doesn't have
anything on me."

He didn't know why, but the literary reference surprised him. Maybe because she'd mentioned that she
had gone to school. That she certainly hadn't made it
sound like their dad had taken a great interest in giving
her a quality education.

Denver checked the time. "Time for lunch delivery."

And as if on cue, Fia pulled up in her car and got
out. Denver walked into the barn and returned a moment later with tables and Fia set out two big silver tins
filled with meat.

Then Fia began to put sides and baskets of bread
out, and then two glorious-looking pies.

Denver smiled at his sister-in-law. "Thanks."

"It's my job," she returned. "And anyway, you
cooked the meat I just heared it back up."

"I don't pay you enough."

She waved a hand. "You don't need to pay me."

Bix looked at Denver. "You do need to pay *me*."

Denver laughed. "Don't worry. I definitely will. You can get extra hazard pay too, since Daughtry is so pressed about your adventure up on the roof."

"I've only known him for a little over twenty-four hours, but I think it's safe to say that Daughtry is always pressed."

That earned her a riotous laugh from his brothers.

"Hilarious," he said, moving over to the table of food and piling on rolls, coleslaw and brisket.

Bix did the same, though she had twice as much food on the plate.

She separated from the group and sat against the barn, her plate resting on her knees, which were pulled up tightly to her chest as she ate quickly, shoveling the food in.

Like she was afraid it was going to disappear.

He imagined that she might be.

He sighed, mostly at himself, and moved across the expanse of dirt to where she was sitting. He took a seat down on the ground beside her, with a couple feet of dirt between them. "I know you're used to having to live hard. But you don't need to prove yourself here. You don't need to put yourself at risk to earn a place."

"I'm not doing that," she said, not pausing her eating. "It was a job that needed doing, so I did it. I like working."

So, he had been right about that.

"Yeah. I get that. You seem like you really get a lot out of this."

"I do," she said. "It's nice to do something that people . . ." She shook her head. "I'm never going to claim to be a hero of any kind," she said. "Ever. But it's a little bit nice to do something that's actually worthwhile. Building something. I mean, making moonshine is making something. I take pride in that. I don't take things away from the world, I add to them. I can't help it if people are irresponsible with their liquor. Everyone needs to be responsible for themselves. And personally, I think the state ought to stay out of everyone's business."

"Yes. I did get that from you."

"The point is," she said. "I might do things that are a little bit shady, but I don't ask for money for nothing. I pull my weight. I earn my keep."

"Yeah. I see that."

"Now. If I think you're a little bit of a sucker who's overpaying me, that's your problem, not mine. I didn't trick you."

"You tried," he pointed out. "When we first met."

"How?" she asked, pausing to lick her finger.

"You pretended that you were afraid of me. You're not afraid of me."

"All right. I didn't say that I was the soul of honesty. I said that I *prefer* honest work. But I'm going to do what I have to in order to get by. Hard-line morality is expensive, Daughtry. And I'm not rich."

He grunted. But didn't really have a response to that.

He looked over at her, and for the moment, she seemed like she was lost in thought. Her pale eyebrows were drawn together, a crease between them. "Have you considered brewing beer?"

"Me personally?" he asked.

"Well, not you personally. The ranch. I think it's a good idea, the things that your brothers have proposed. But there can always be more. I was thinking about what Denver said. Everybody finding something to do. Well, someone could brew beer."

"Do you like alcohol?"

Her expression was unreadable. "No."

"You don't drink."

She shrugged. "I don't."

"But you make alcohol. And now you're suggesting that we brew beer. And you don't even like it?"

"I didn't say I didn't *like* it. I don't drink, but I do taste my stuff before I put it out. I can tell when the product is good. I was trained to figure that out. But I can't afford to go drinking my own moonshine. Hell, there's a metaphor for life in there somewhere. I have to sell what I make. And as for buying alcohol? Waste of money."

"Like cigarettes."

She looked wistful then. "I do miss cigarettes."

"No drinking, but you got into smoking?"

"Yeah. Just the guys hanging around always had some. It was easy to bum off of them. I liked it because it calmed me down a little bit without making me feel like my senses were impaired." She shook her head. "I don't have to justify myself to you."

"I don't suppose you do."

"Let me get you some more food."

She squinted. "Being nice again?"

"No. I also want seconds."

He grabbed her plate, filled it up again, along with adding some more to his. Then he brought it back to her. Her eating slowed on the second round.

"Fia's a great cook," she said.

"Yeah. She is."

"And Denver . . . did the meat?"

"Yeah he's like a grill master. He gets super intense about it. I think if he didn't have the ranch he'd have opened a restaurant. Though that would require him to actually deal with people, which is not his strong suit."

"I mean, I like him fine enough."

"He's . . . I don't know, he's complicated. He takes care of all of us, but hell if I know what's going on in his head half the time. He took in a teenager for a while after our dad's illegal activities landed him in prison. And there's this other family . . . Our dad was responsible for the death of Dan Patrick, and Denver has been sending money to the girls in that family for years. Ever since."

"Your dad *murdered* their dad?"

"He didn't murder him. He put him in a dangerous position, though. And he lost his life. She didn't have anywhere to go. Denver felt responsible, and took her in. Nothing means more to Denver than family."

"He's like Vin Diesel."

"I have no idea what that means."

"Too bad for you," she said.

Silence lapsed between them. "If you want to, I can take you out to the van and get your things."

"I have a job to finish here. Afterward?"

"Okay. I guess I'll grab a hammer too."

After the hours had passed, Bix got in his truck, and they drove out toward her van. She had hidden it as best she could off the highway.

It was . . . not much.

An old, orange piece of junk with curtains in the windows.

Bix scrambled to the side door and unlocked it with the key that was in her pocket. She jerked it open, and it seemed like it required an unusual amount of force.

"I'll just . . . I'll be a second."

She disappeared into the van, and it shook as she moved around inside. He decided that he wasn't going to wait.

He took a step up into the van and looked around.

It was dilapidated. A threadbare mattress on the floor in the back. There was a dresser that looked like it was bolted down to the floor, and on top of it, there were some bins. He looked down inside and was surprised to see . . . books.

He reached inside and took one out.

Rich Dad Poor Dad.

Then he picked up the one under that one.

The Seven Habits of Highly Effective People.

He kept surfing through the stack. *The Four Agreements, The Subtle Art of Not Giving a . . .*

It was full of self-help books.

He just stood there staring at the books, not quite able to make sense of them.

She turned and gave him a furious look. "Why are you digging through my stuff?"

"I'm not trying to be nosy." Except he was.

"Well, you do a great impression of someone who is. Besides you're like . . . a detective. It's your job to be nosy."

"I'm not a detective any more than I'm a sheriff."

"Whatever, Sheriff," she said, waving her hand. "That's all splitting hairs to me."

"Do you want to bring your books back with you?" he asked, ignoring her attitude.

She looked uncomfortable. "I don't care. I could."

"Where did you get them?"

She shrugged. "There are little free libraries everywhere these days. I always stop and look. Don't look free shit in the mouth, I mean, right? So, I just take whatever seems . . . you know, not terribly boring."

Mostly nonfiction, he saw. There was also a worn copy of *Anne of Green Gables*, *Oliver Twist*—that made him chuckle—and a romance novel. *"The Wolf and the Dove,"* he read.

Her cheeks went pink. "I haven't read that."

She was lying. "Like I said, I grab whatever crap," she said. "It's free. And the nights are long. I don't have Wi-Fi."

She didn't. It struck him then, how odd it must be. To be twenty-three, to not have a cell phone. To not be on the Internet. That hadn't been his experience of being twenty-three; it had been ten years ago, after all. But even he had marginal connections to technology.

"Let's bring your books," he said.

He grabbed the whole crate and carried it back to his truck.

She had an armful of clothes when she came out.

"They need to be washed," she said.

"As you already know, I have a washer and dryer."

"Thanks," she said.

She didn't ask why he was doing it. She didn't act overly hostile. It was kind of weird. All things considered.

When they got back to his place, he helped her carry her things inside. He showed her to the bedroom that he'd moved the bed into. "I guess I ought to get you a nightstand and a dresser."

She looked like she didn't know what to say to that. She looked around the room, her eyes totally unreadable.

"I'll just . . . I'll get some things organized, and then I'll do laundry."

"You want to go over to the big house for dinner?"

"Can I . . . ? Could we . . . ? I mean can I . . . ?"

"There's some shit in the freezer if you don't want to go out again. That's fine."

"That would be good," she said, looking relieved.

"All right. I'll leave you to it."

He didn't need her to thank him. He wasn't doing it for gratitude. But it bothered him a little that he didn't feel any lighter. It hadn't gone any further in cleansing his soul than he'd imagined it would.

That's fine. Just keep going. Just stay on the straight and narrow.

What other option was there?

CHAPTER SEVEN

BIX CLOSED THE door to the bedroom. Her bedroom? For now. She was shaking, and she hadn't wanted him to see it. Because it made her feel weak. Made her feel small. And she had been feeling pretty good until she had to go back to the van and look at her life through his eyes. Today with Justice and Denver, she had felt something else. Something new. Like she was free. They were fine. They swore and told crass stories and made her laugh. She made them laugh too, and it had been a good time. She had fun climbing up to the top of the barn. And it had amused her that Daughtry was so put off by it.

She didn't know why he would care. If she fell off the roof she wouldn't be his problem anymore. On some level, it seemed like he would think that was a good thing.

The sheets and blankets on the bed didn't match. But they were clean and soft. There were two pillows, and she didn't really know what to do with that. She didn't need to. It was excessive. It had been one thing to sleep on Daughtry's bed with all those extra pillows. It was reasonable for a man to give himself a whole ton of extra pillows, she felt.

Him giving an extra one to her was just . . . It spoke of a concern for comfort.

And yet again, she didn't quite know what to do with that.

She picked up her box of books and put it on the bed. She didn't share her life with anyone. She didn't share things. It had been humiliating to have him look at the books. She had read *The Wolf and the Dove*.

She had read it at least fifty times.

One of the things she liked about it was how strong the heroine was. Everything was terrible; it was the Middle Ages, after all. The heroine was kidnapped, chained to a bed and held captive by a fierce and handsome warrior.

If there was something about that fantasy that appealed to her . . . it was her business. She wouldn't say that she had any kind of romantic inclinations. Again, she couldn't afford them.

But it was nice to escape into a different world for a little while. To imagine that a dark and dangerous experience could lead to something . . . wonderful.

At least Daughtry hadn't chained her to the bed.

She blinked, doing her best to banish that image. Actually, when she really thought about it, it was difficult not to superimpose bits of that book over her current experience.

Of course, she wasn't a prisoner. And she was the one that had invaded Daughtry's space. Her castle hadn't been invaded by Norman conquerors. She didn't have a castle. She had an old gross van.

It bothered her, too, that she found that so embarrassing. Because she didn't care what he thought about her. He was the kind of person who would always look down on someone like her.

Except, he hadn't done that.

Well, he didn't do it openly. But she had felt the sting of embarrassment when he had looked at all of her books. Like he was combing through her thoughts.

She picked up her copy of *Rich Dad Poor Dad*. She didn't put a lot of stock into this kind of thing. Most of the advice in books like this was for people who already had a certain amount of success. Who already had something to work with.

But it made her feel like she was doing something. She hadn't gone to school. Any education she'd had, she'd worked for. A lot of it was through reading. She was grateful that people passed their books on.

It had the potential to change lives. Or at least, she kind of liked to think that it did. These books hadn't changed her life.

Not yet.

What made her so uncomfortable about Daughtry looking at them was it was clear she wanted them to. That she wanted *something* to.

She was pathetic.

Absolutely pathetic.

There was a stark knock on the door and she jumped. "What?"

The door pushed open. "Bix," he said. "What exactly would you like to eat?"

"What are my options? I mean, sorry. You don't need to do that for me."

"I don't need to do what?"

"Cook me something, or whatever you're preparing to do." She sniffed. "I'm totally fine just staying here by myself. I can rummage through the freezer."

"I'm going to stay with you."

"Why?" she asked.

"Because," he said, his voice sounding rough, frustrated, "I'm bound and determined to take care of you, you silly little varmint."

"I don't understand."

"Well, I don't understand your book collection. Or why you're resisting so hard."

"They're just books."

"They don't look like just books to me. They look like goals. Dreams."

She scoffed. "I don't have dreams."

"Everybody has dreams," he said.

"Bullshit, Sheriff. What's your dream, then?"

He looked thoughtful for a moment. "I guess it's to just keep doing the best that I can. To continue to repair my family's reputation in the town. And to expand the ranch."

"You have a brick," she said.

"What?"

"The ranch. It's your brick. Your foundation. I'm not making excuses, not really. But my dad took my brick and threw it through the window. I'm the proud owner of a generational smash and grab. I don't have anything to start a foundation with." She shook her head. "No one dreams of this. Nobody dreams of that crappy orange van that I had hidden out in the woods. Nobody dreams of having to stay in a bedroom in a stranger's house. I have been so far away from living any kind of dream for so long that I just quit. Maybe if you're a different kind of kid you can dream. A kid holding a brick. Listen, it sounds like your family wasn't great. But you all have this, and you have each other. I don't have that."

"But you don't have these books for nothing."

"Toilet paper is expensive. In this economy you have to be creative."

"I don't believe that," he said.

"I don't understand why you care. Are you just desperate to try to find something in me to justify this ridiculous act of charity that you're engaging in? Daughtry, it's not . . . It's not there. I'm not going to give you what you want. I'm going to work here, and I'm going to move on. And the fact of the matter is, even if I started out doing something different, I would just go back to what I know. Been there. Done that. Got the ill-fitting T-shirt. I've had real jobs. A couple of different times. The juvenile record got expunged. That was supposed to be my chance. I have had a fresh start. But I don't know what to do with them. Because eventually, it gets hard. Eventually, I reached the end of knowing what to do. Eventually, I reached the end of my own strength. And I go right back. To my dad, my brother, to their friends. And that ends at brewing moonshine in the middle of the woods."

He shifted, but he didn't look shocked or angry by her outburst. It was one of the more annoying things about him. He just wasn't reactive.

"If you had a brick, Bix, what would you do with it?"

"Break your nose?"

There was something subtle that shifted in his expression. Something that made her heart go tight. That made her stomach swoop.

"You can't even be serious for a second?"

"I'm serious."

"No. You're a liar. You're a liar who's afraid to give me a straight answer because you're afraid to want something."

She rolled her eyes. "Are you billing me for this hour?"

"If you had a brick," he repeated, "what would you do with it? What would you build?"

"You might as well ask me what I'd do with a handful of stardust, Sheriff. Because I don't have either."

He lowered his head. "I think you want to do something. Otherwise you wouldn't have those books. Even *Anne of Green Gables* and *Oliver Twist* are about making new lives out of nothing."

"Look at you," she said. "You read."

He took a step toward her. It wasn't threatening, but it sucked the air out of her lungs all the same. She didn't think she had ever seen a man as physically perfect as he was in person before. All the lines were straight. Symmetrical. Beautifully drawn. His eyes were the most piercing blue, his hair dark brown and curling just at the back of his neck. He would almost be pretty if it wasn't for his size. Big and rough and broad. A warrior, she'd thought then.

Though there was no point thinking of him that way. There was no warrior coming to save her by holding her captive in a soft bed. It was a compelling fantasy. But one she only indulged in at her weakest moments. And right now, with Daughtry, she couldn't afford to be weak.

"All I know is what I *would've* done," she said, her frustration boiling over. "I would have gone to school. Every day. And maybe I would've made some friends. Friends my age. *Girls*. I would have read every book in the school library. I wasn't even allowed to have a library card, Daughtry. Because it's just another scam to get your information into the system. I would have gotten a summer job, and I would have bought myself nice clothes. I would've had a boyfriend, and he would have taken me to a dance. We would have broken up when we got into college, because I would never have let him hold me back. Because I would choose myself over a teenage relationship, but it's fine because there would have been other guys later. I would have got my degree, and I would have . . . I would've done something. I wouldn't be a skinny nobody living off of your charity."

The last couple of words came out tremulously. And she hated herself for that. She hated that she was having these big, complicated feelings in front of him. That was the thing about living by herself. It was just easier. You never had to explain what was happening inside of you to another person. And consequently she'd never had to explain it to herself all that well. She didn't like this. She didn't like feeling like her skin had been peeled back. Like she had been exposed to him. No. She didn't like that at all.

But of course, she couldn't just be mean to him. Because he was being nice to her. Except, it didn't feel all that nice. It felt like a gift with an elaborate series of trip wires that she could easily get herself hung up on. Because he was making her deal with all this . . . this stuff. Because he was digging.

"You can't have your childhood back," he said. "And believe me, I understand the process of grieving that. My dad was a bastard. He was a narcissist who hurt the people around him, Bix. I get it. My mom left so she didn't have to deal with him."

His mom had left too. It stunned her, and she wasn't quite sure why, to know that this perfect, gorgeous man had also been abandoned by his mother. It made her think that maybe . . . just maybe the issue wasn't her. Because it happened to anybody. Really. If it could happen to him it could happen to anybody.

"I spent a long time regretting a lot of things about my childhood. And then I decided to take control of what I was doing now," he continued.

"I have more baggage than you," she said.

"That is true. It is. I'm not going to lie to you. I'm not going to say it's not . . . not a thing. But there are people in the world who aren't going to hold it against you forever. You just have to find them."

"I like being alone. Because when I'm with people this kind of thing happens."

"Somebody asks you to dig into your inconvenient truths?"

"It's not about inconvenience. There's just . . . Like I said, what's the point?"

"The point is, eventually you have to own that this is your life."

"Do I give you the impression that I'm someone who doesn't own their own choices?"

He shook his head. "No. In fact, you seem very ready to own a whole bunch of bad choices. But when you give your explanations, I have a feeling that I'm hearing your dad come out of your mouth."

He might as well have hit her. She would have hated it less. "I . . . I don't . . . Who doesn't carry forward the lessons they learned when they were a kid? Some of us didn't get to learn lessons outside of our houses. So it's all I have."

"I'm standing right in front of you telling you that you have other options. You can't claim ignorance on this."

"The hell I can't, Sheriff. In order to take your advice you have to prove to me that I can respect you."

"Have I done anything disrespectful?" he asked.

He hadn't. And she realized they were in a small, and closed bedroom, and he hadn't made any sort of untoward moves. She had a feeling he saw her more as a stray puppy than a woman, but then, she also knew that attraction wasn't what made men behave *that way*. It was their desire to control somebody. Well, and to get off. But that wasn't a particularly flattering thing.

So, she wasn't insulted that he wasn't making any moves toward her.

And maybe he was right; it should be more of a commendation to his character than she was allowing it to be. Or maybe that wasn't even what he meant. Maybe he meant that he had this ranch. This house. That he had enough not just for himself, but enough to share. Bix had never been able to practice that level of generosity because she'd never even had enough for herself.

"I want pizza."

"I'll get us a pizza. It'll take me about an hour."

She wondered if she should feel guilty about that. She didn't. Instead, when he retreated from the bedroom and closed the door behind him she felt a sense of relief.

She wasn't going to stay here. It was . . . She had to admit that it was nice of him. To do all of this. He wasn't trying to get anything out of her. She had to concede that too, because if he had wanted her to pay him back, he would have made his move long before now. Unless he was trying to fatten her up.

She snickered. Maybe he was like one of those witches with the candy house. Maybe he wanted to bake her into a pie. Honestly, that would track with the trajectory of her life.

A Norman conqueror who took her captive, not to chain her to a bed . . . but to plump her up like a goose for a Sunday meal.

She looked over at her box of books. Then glared at them. "You haven't helped me at all. You've given me unrealistic expectations."

She sat on the edge of the bed and let out a hard breath as she looked around the room. She would collect her paycheck next week. It would be more than enough for the new starter, and she would continue on her way. She didn't need to listen to him.

She didn't need for him to get in her head. It wasn't possible for her to go back. It was impossible for her to claim even one piece of that silly little dream that she had spouted out to him.

A dream.

A handful of stardust.

A brick. It didn't matter.

She didn't have any of it.

And there was no use crying over spilt moonshine.

CHAPTER EIGHT

SHE GOT PAID at the end of the week, but she didn't leave. She told herself that she would. Every day. It was strange, acclimating to living with someone else. A man. A rather large one who rambled about the space with firm, decisive movements. He made breakfast; he went off to work. She spent the day doing whatever Denver, Justice or Landry assigned her to do. They usually ate at the ranch house, with everybody.

She was still wary of the women, because she didn't quite know how to relate to them. In her world, the only women around were sleeping with the various men who helped her dad make moonshine, and there was a very clear line between them and Bix. Drawn mostly by them. She was one of the workers. They weren't.

There was no such line here at King's Crest. It was equitable, and easy, but still, she was more comfortable with the three men she spent most of the day working with than she was with the women. Though every night part of her ached to figure out how to join their conversation. But she never really had friends, and she didn't know how to go making them.

There were some moments with just Daughtry, but she found she liked him better when they had a buffer between them.

Denver and the other guys never asked her about her dreams. They applauded her when she climbed the barn. They were excessively complimentary about her carpentry skills, and they made sure to praise her profusely over the different suggestions she made for how to fix things on the cheap. They were easier than Daughtry.

They cursed regularly, they liked to tell stories, and that kept conversation light and easy. And best of all, impersonal.

The new roofing shingles came in, and she ended up getting started on that project. And once that week ended, she didn't feel like she could abandon it without seeing it through. And then once it went into part of the following week, it just didn't seem like she ought to leave in the middle of the week.

Every night, she lay down in her bed and looked up at the ceiling. And told herself it ought to be the last night she went to sleep in that bed.

She fantasized about getting up in the morning and asking Daughtry to cut her check for the work from the previous few days, and getting on her way.

She was squirreling away quite a bit of cash at this point. It was way more than she needed for a new starter. It was starting to be a respectable amount for . . .

A lot of things.

The Kings paid well, and her room and board was included. She was beginning to find her feet in a way that she never had the opportunity to do before.

Hell, if she stuck around for just a little bit longer she might be able to put down a deposit on an apartment.

Of course, she didn't have any credit. And there was nobody to cosign for her.

It was always this. The circles. A little bit of hope, a little bit of a setback.

It was why she didn't like to dabble in hope.

Then they broke ground on the four new cottages they were building as guest rentals. She was fascinated by the process. And she ended up staying as the foundations got poured.

And it got harder and harder to remember why she had ever been suspicious of any of them.

Being on the ranch began to feel safe.

She didn't pile her plate quite as high with food.

She wasn't worried about it being taken away tomorrow.

And still, she thought, as she went to bed that night, that in the morning she might decide to leave. But it would be on her terms. It would be her decision.

She had been at King's Crest for about a month when Daughtry came home from his shift with the state police and told her it was town hall meeting night.

"What?"

"Yeah, you missed the last one by just a hair. Once a month we get together and have a big family meeting."

"Don't you guys do that every night?"

"No. I don't just mean the Kings. I mean everybody else. Us, the Garretts, the McClouds and the Sullivans."

"You mean, everybody?"

"Yep. You haven't even seen the whole rest of the facility."

It was true. She had pretty much been sticking to her well-worn route ever since she had gotten here. She hadn't even ever gone into town. It was complicated. She felt safe here. There were people she was beginning to trust. It was nearly painful to admit that to herself, but it was true. It was just different here.

The idea of stepping into the broader ranch world did something strange to her. Because she was so . . . She was still going to leave.

But maybe it would be worth seeing everything first. Seeing all the things.

She and Daughtry hadn't spoken like they had that night over three weeks ago again. They talked. But they kept it light. He didn't ask her about dreams.

In fact, weirdly, even though they lived together, she saw him the least. He worked long hours away from where she worked. When she did see him, it was usually at group dinners, and then they had the occasional breakfast in the morning. But often he was out before she was, and sometimes Landry just swung by to pick her up on his way out to the barn. He drove over from Sullivan's Point. He and his wife only came to about half of the dinners, because they had a child, and sometimes they just did dinner by themselves, but also she knew that his wife's family was very close.

It was weird. To be in this position. Where she wanted to be closer to people, but also wanted to resist it.

"Yeah. I'll go."

"It's great. There's tons of food. Dancing. A bonfire."

It made something shift in her chest. "It's like a party?"

"Yeah."

She had never really been to a party. Not a nice one. Sometimes there were get-togethers after her dad was done making a big batch, or they'd had a big sell-through. A celebration among all the men that had helped. But she didn't feel safe during those kinds of things. Usually, she hid away.

She did her best to school her face into a neutral expression. "Okay. That sounds all right."

"I was thinking." He looked like he wanted to say something, but he didn't quite know how, and that was strange. Because Daughtry always seemed to know exactly what he wanted to say. Even if she didn't want to hear it.

"What?"

"I'm not trying to insult you. I want you to understand that. But . . . I was also wondering if you wanted to maybe see to getting some more clothes."

She blinked. She'd had the same clothes since she was in high school. It never really occurred to her to replace them. She had a belt, and sometimes it was the only thing that kept her jeans up. Truth be told, her jeans were feeling a little tight. She had filled out some since she had come to live at the ranch. Amazing, since she was still working herself to the bone every day. But there was always plenty of food.

"Why would I be insulted?"

"Because I'm not saying there's anything wrong with what you have. But you've been here a month, and I just noticed that . . ."

"That I don't have much."

"Yes."

"Well, your brother has been paying me quite a lot of money, so actually I could go buy my own clothes if I wanted to."

"Understood. But, you have to drive somewhere to get them."

"Oh. Right."

"I have to go over to town—to Mapleton. It's about forty-five minutes away. I just need to get something from the outdoor store there. Do you want to stop and look at some things?"

She wrinkled her nose. "I don't know. I . . . I guess."

"You can get something for the meeting."

"Wait a minute. Is that why I was supposed to be insulted? Or was I supposed to try to not be. Because really you're embarrassed to bring me to the meeting if I look like a raccoon?"

"You don't look like a raccoon," he said.

"Well. How am I supposed to interpret this?"

"It's something I've been thinking about. And I have to go to town today. That is why it's coming up now."

She wanted to be sulky, but she was far too intrigued by the offer. She didn't have a bank account, so all her pay was processed through payroll, and then presented to her in cash. She grabbed a thick stack of it and tucked it into her wallet, and allowed Daughtry to drive her to town.

They had about four hours until the town hall meeting by the time they got to Mapleton. The town was nice. It was strange, being away from the ranch.

"I'm tempted to believe that what you're actually doing is just dropping me off and abandoning me. Like a sad kitten." Until she had said it, she didn't realize how much she was actually afraid that was what might be happening.

Okay. So maybe she didn't feel wholly secure. It was something to do with Daughtry, which was weird, because he was the reason she was here at all. He was the reason that she had gotten the job in the first place. He let her stay at his house.

"I'm definitely not doing that."

"You're not?"

"I would have to drop you off hundreds of miles away, first of all. You'd come right back."

"I have pride," she said.

"You're also a stubborn cuss. So I just don't think that you would ever let me have the last word on this. Nope."

She did laugh, because it was true. If he kicked her off the ranch, that would be her main problem. That he had made the decision. She was going to leave tomorrow anyway.

He went to the outdoor store, and she walked by a few of the little boutiques on the main street while he did. She looked at the prices on the clothes and nearly died of shock.

When he came out with a bag, and crossed the street toward her, he frowned. "You didn't get anything?"

"Not in there," she said, jamming her thumb toward one of the boutiques. "The prices are ridiculous."

"There's a Fred Meyer up the way."

"That might be more my speed."

That was how they ended up there. She gazed longingly at a couple of the nightstands, because it would be a nice thing to have to put her books on. But she didn't say anything. She found a section with some nice summer dresses, and some pairs of cute leggings, and she decided to try them on. She didn't own any dresses. And she would've said that she didn't want to show her legs, not in any circumstances, because they were usually knobby and not unlike a scarecrow's.

But she was pleasantly surprised when she took in her reflection. She had filled out quite a bit, and she looked . . . feminine. She was clean, and while there was no real shape to her haircut, her blond hair was glossy now. Her blue eyes brighter.

The scab on her chin was healed.

Her skin looked clear and . . . She was smiling. She couldn't even remember making the decision to smile.

She came out of the dressing room, and decided she was going to buy all of the things that she had. It was nearly one hundred dollars' worth of things, quite a few items and a lot of it was on clearance. She swallowed hard. One hundred dollars was just so much money.

But she had earned it.

She didn't see Daughtry, so she went to the check stand and paid for her clothes. When she still couldn't find him, she crept out of the store and looked for his truck. And there she saw him. Loading some big things into the bed of the truck.

"Where were you?"

"I decided I had some purchases of my own to make," he said.

She hopped up on the back tire and looked in the bed. The nightstand was in there. Her heart thumped painfully against her chest. There was also a bed-in-a-bag set, and a desk and a chair.

"What's all this?"

"It's for your room. I thought it was a little bit threadbare."

"I'm not staying," she said.

But now she thought maybe tomorrow wouldn't be a great time to leave because he had just bought all this stuff, and that was pretty nice.

It hurt, though. And she couldn't quite figure out why. He was a sucker. A sap. He was doing too much for her. And she hadn't asked him to.

She got into the truck, and was annoyed at where her shoulder strap crossed her breasts. Because her chest felt so damned sore.

"Did you find some things?"

"Yes," she said.

"You're happy with—"

"Let's listen to music," she said.

And she let country songs fill the cab of the truck instead of words, because it was easier. Because she really wasn't used to spending much time with anybody. She had done quite a bit of spending time with people these past weeks. Tonight there was only going to be more of it. That was her excuse. It wasn't really to do with just how much Daughtry had affected her with his purchase.

She regretted, a little bit, not buying makeup as she got ready for the town hall meeting, but she put on a pair of white sneakers that she had bought, and a floral dress. And she looked . . . cute. She didn't quite know what to do with that thought.

She had never really given much thought to being a woman. Except that it was an inconvenience. Because it made her a target in a very specific way. It made her physically weaker than she would like to be; it made things difficult.

Right then . . . she thought of what she had told him, all those weeks ago. She would go to a dance. Maybe there would be dancing at the party.

She swallowed hard, her throat getting tight.

You would think she should be used to all this by now. To being here. The things being . . . unusual. Different.

Whatever.

She stepped out of the bedroom, and when she saw Daughtry standing in the living room, she stopped dead in her tracks.

He was wearing the same thing he always did when he wasn't in uniform, except he had a black cowboy hat on his head and there was something about him that just seemed . . . more.

He looked at her, his blue eyes flicking over her. "That's nice."

"Thank you," she said.

"You want to bring a jacket?"

She sniffed. "I'm not going to get cold."

He took a black jacket off the peg by the door. "Suit yourself."

The truth was, she didn't have a jacket. She hadn't thought about that. All she had was her ratty old coat and a couple of hoodies. And she wasn't going to put those over her cute dress. She would just have to stick close to the bonfire that he had told her existed at this thing that they were going to.

Just stick close to him.

She ignored the little voice inside of her that said that. She didn't need to stay close to Daughtry King. Because even though she was parked here for a little while and enjoying some of their hospitality, she took care of herself. Nightstands and matching sheets weren't going to change that.

CHAPTER NINE

HE COULD HARDLY recognize the woman riding shotgun in his truck right now, versus the woman he had first found in the woods a month ago. This version of Bix was softer. At least in appearance. Her face had rounded after weeks of eating well, and she seemed less edgy. Most of the time. Every so often something would get her hackles up and she would go right back to the feral creature he'd first encountered, but it was less and less often.

Living with her was easy enough. She was like a roommate.

Or a cat.

Yes. Having Bix live with him was a lot like getting a cat. She came out of her room when she wanted food, and otherwise didn't have a lot to do with him.

But right now, wearing that floral dress, sitting next to him in the truck, he felt something shift inside of him.

Like he was seeing a new dimension in her. Even knowing that she was twenty-three, it was hard for him to see her as anything other than a scrappy kid. She was wise in the ways of the world, mostly. But then there would be moments and things that made her seem like a teenager.

But one thing he couldn't forget was the way that she had told him all the things she might've done if she'd had a normal family. The way her eyes had gone bright when she'd talked about going to dances. Going to college. She could deny that she had dreams, but he knew that she did.

And it made him feel . . . an intense desire to fix it for her.

He'd found a place. He'd found a way to begin to atone for his own sins, for the way that he was raised, and the way that he had participated in the life his father had constructed out of lies and a lack of basic human empathy. She was only twenty-three. She could still start again.

He also knew if he said that she would bite his hand off.

"It's up the road a spell, but this is where Landry and Fia live."

"I figured that," she said.

"It's pretty."

"It doesn't surprise me that the place Fia lives is pretty."

"Have you gotten to know her very well?"

Bix shifted beside him. "I don't really know how to talk to women."

"You don't?"

"I just . . . I never had any friends. Not really. And I'm afraid I'm going to say something insensitive or mean. Because women care about that more."

"You don't care about that more."

"I think that's a bug and not a feature."

"Maybe. You don't know. Fia is a spitfire. Believe me. She gave my brother hell for years. And rightfully. We all found out eventually."

"What do you mean?"

It wasn't really his story to tell. But it was public lore of Four Corners at this point. "When they were in high school, Landry and Fia had a baby. They didn't tell anybody, though. Fia put the little girl up for adoption, and Landry spent the years after that pissed about it. As if they could have parented a baby when they were sixteen."

"That sounds horrible. And you know, I can tell you in that situation what you'd get is my life."

"Not always," said Daughtry. "But given the state of the ranch at the time, I don't blame Fia at all." The truth was, he was damned empathetic to his sister-in-law. Because he knew how it had been. The adults around them had been nonfunctional. He understood not being able to imagine a scenario in which bringing a baby into that with a couple of toxic teenagers would be anything but a disaster. "But the point is, things changed for them. Their daughter's adoptive parents died. They ended up taking her in, and they found a way to rebuild all the bridges between them. But when I tell you Fia can certainly handle your brand of being a sticky wicket, I mean it."

"What is a *sticky wicket*?" she asked.

"I don't know. It's something my mom said sometimes." He didn't know where it had come from. Why it had come forward from the recesses of his memory.

"It's weird," she said.

At that moment, they were pulling up to Sullivan's Point. The farmhouse was as bright and cheerful as ever. Lila was running around in the front yard with a couple of other kids from the schoolhouse, and her dog, Sunday, was leaping about with them. He watched Bix's expression as she looked at the children. At the dog.

"You like dogs?"

She nodded. "Yeah. I think so anyway. Never had one. If you can't take care of yourself, you can't go dragging another creature into your problems."

"Fair enough."

But that was another thing that made him feel regret for her. Not that he had any pets. Other than all the cows that lived on the ranch.

They went around the back of the farmhouse, and pulled up where there was a line of other trucks in front of the large barn where they held their meeting every month. There was already a big bonfire going, and there were tables laden with food. Pies and cakes, steak and potato salad. Sides provided by the ranch hands. A whole spread of great food. He saw Bix's eyes get bright.

She did still get very excited at the sight of food. Every time. It was almost charming.

Hell. That's your problem. You're charmed by her. In spite of yourself.

They got out of the truck, and she moved closer to him, which he thought was interesting. But then, she hadn't spent much time away from the ranch since she had showed up. In fact . . .

"Until earlier today had you actually left King's Crest since you got there?"

"Unless it counts that we went to the van to get my stuff, no."

"Oh. I don't think I realized."

"Well, we're hardly in each other's pockets. You go to work every day in a different place than I do."

That was true. He realized he hadn't asked her. It made him feel guilty. The same kind of guilt he'd felt when he'd realized she only had the same clothes that she'd come with. That her room still didn't have furniture. He had been waiting for her to leave; that was the thing. He hadn't gone out of his way to make things permanent, because he'd kept expecting to wake up and find her gone. But she was still here. And when he had invited her to the town hall meeting, he'd realized that that was a step toward things feeling more official. Really involving her in ranch business like this. It was common for the employees to come to the town hall meetings. Expected, even. But she had held herself at a distance, and acted like she was going to walk out at any moment, so he hadn't really considered her part of the regular employee base.

He did now. But also, she was something different. Because every ranch hand didn't eat dinner at their house most nights. And she did. Every ranch hand didn't get along with his brothers like a house on fire. And she did.

"Well, I'll introduce you to everybody."

"Oh," she said.

That, he realized, was also a little bit out of the ordinary. She occupied a strange place. But . . . she was singular. He had never met anybody quite like her, and maybe that was at the heart of the issue. People just didn't surprise him very often. But Bix surprised him daily.

He had seen her rap sheet now, of course. He had done a background check before putting her on payroll. Shoplifting, that was the big one. But always under a certain dollar amount. Always food. Basic necessities. One time she had stolen a tube of Neosporin and a box of Band-Aids. He had gone digging for the different reports so that he could see the details. To him, her rap sheet didn't paint a picture of a hardened criminal. It painted a picture of a life that was just regretfully sad.

Of a person trying her best to be resilient in the face of a whole lot of obstacles.

They walked past the tables of food, and into the barn. His siblings were already there, the large space jam-packed. Each family had their own section, and the hands that worked their particular ranch usually sat in the chairs behind them.

Like a very strange wedding.

But he took Bix and marched her right over to the Garretts. "Sawyer, Evelyn, Wolf, Violet, this is Bix."

Bix's eyes widened. "Hi."

"Bix, this is the Garrett family. They run Garrett's Watch. This is one of our new ranch hands. She's been with us about a month, but she hasn't really gotten out into the ranch yet."

"Nice to meet you," said Evelyn warmly. They made small talk for a few moments before he marched her over to the McClouds, where he made introductions to that whole group. They already had a concept of who she was because of Alaina, who was married to Gus, and was Fia's younger sister.

After that, he took her to meet the rest of the Sullivans. They already knew who she was too. And it was clearly a relief to her that he didn't go saying he had found her in a van down by the river, and that she was making moonshine on the property. Whatever anybody else knew about her, he couldn't control that. Fia might've told her whole story, and he wouldn't blame her. But nobody had said anything. It was clear Bix was happy about that.

After that, they took their seats. She sat next to him, and he knew that there were people in the barn who would find that somewhat remarkable, but he didn't care.

He didn't want Bix to feel uncomfortable. And yes, she could've sat with his brothers, but she hadn't. She had sat with him. She was his . . . project. Anyway.

She was his.

Not like *that*. It was just that he did feel a little bit possessive of her in this bigger environment, and clearly, she felt the need to stay close to him.

So, who was he to deny her that?

Everybody got up to say a piece of their business. There was an update on McCloud's Landing, and the work they were doing with horses there. An update on Sullivan's Point, and their farm store. The Garretts were moving along as they ever had, much the same as King's Crest. In many ways, they were set to have easier profitability. Beef was mainstream, and valuable. But he didn't think that they could rest on it forever. And that was where the expansion was coming in. There were more of them; that was the thing.

While Sawyer and Evelyn now had two children and another on the way, and Wolf and Violet had two kids, Wolf and Sawyer's youngest sister, Elsie, had married into the McCloud clan, and was working there. The McClouds also had a lot of people to sustain. Five brothers, their wives and their children. The Sullivan sisters were all married now too, and as Landry had married Fia, his base was more Sullivan's Point now than it was King's Crest.

But Landry took very seriously that both ranches were a legacy for his daughter, Lila, and for the baby he had on the way.

And while the King family wasn't as prolific as far as marriage and children as the rest of the ranches were, Arizona and Micah were planning on having children, and they had their teenage son.

The fact was, they had to keep making money.

Keep making the place profitable.

It was Landry that got up to speak about the expansion work happening at King's. Everybody seemed on board. They'd had everyone go in on investing in the project pretty early. Much to Fia's chagrin at the time. It had created a bit of conflict between her and Landry, but then, at that point, what didn't?

When the meeting was done, Bix leaned over. "That was interesting."

"Really?"

"I think it's fascinating the way you all run the ranch like a business. That was like a board meeting."

He thought about her self-help books. He wondered if she had read about corporations and businesses and the way they ran.

"It's not unlike that."

"It's kind of like a publicly traded company," she said.

"Kind of," he said. "Except of course, we don't really have a stock market that we're involved in. But everybody here is kind of a shareholder."

"It's smart," she said. "Because of course there's always going to be dips in the market. And you can all cover each other."

"That is the idea."

She looked pleased that she understood it. And he realized how hungry she was for information. That was probably the root of those kinds of books. Of nonfiction.

She wanted to learn things. She had been denied that.

"Have you ever thought about going back to school?"

"Yes. I have also thought about going to the moon."

"There's financial aid available," he pointed out.

"Great. I know about as much about how to get that as I do about going to the moon."

He hadn't really thought about that before. But he supposed she was making an interesting point. That

that sort of thing was only helpful if you knew how to navigate the system. And Bix made it very clear that she didn't. That her dad had put her in a position where she knew nothing about the system, and was in fact barely in it.

"I could help get you some information on that if you want."

She waved her hand. "It's not necessary."

"Okay."

But he decided that he was going to anyway.

"And I would get to go eat," he said.

She looked happy about that, and they walked out of the barn, and everybody was already making their way down the tables, filling their plates.

Bix started with pie. He appreciated that about her. She was unorthodox, even when she was being human. "Dessert first?"

She shrugged. "I don't play by the rules."

"No. Of course you don't."

His family naturally gravitated together; he knew that they had a reputation for being insular. And maybe they were. Most people would say that they were assholes. But he didn't think that was true at all. Their dad had been an asshole. And they understood each other in a very particular way. He thought it was one of the more amazing things about his family that they had banded together and made something that looked functional in light of what they had grown up with. He supposed that was true of everybody on the ranch.

The Garrett family patriarch had been weak more than anything else. A charming man who was able to get women to procreate with him, but couldn't get them to stay, because he was just such a neglectful, unpleasant son of a bitch. Seamus McCloud was infamous. He had been cruel. He had beaten his wife; he had beaten his children. He had very nearly killed his oldest son, Gus. For years, the rumor had been that Gus had actually killed his father, and that was how they had finally taken control of McCloud's Landing. But Daughtry knew that wasn't the truth. They all did now. Because his wife, Alaina, had made it very clear that she didn't want her husband being tarred with the same brush as his father.

Fia's father had simply abandoned them. He had been like the light version of the Kings' dad. He had scammed a neighboring rancher when he'd been vulnerable, but luckily, that guy had been able to land on his feet. Some of the people that Daughtry's father had swindled hadn't been so lucky. Like Dan Patrick, who had gotten embroiled in his shady practices, and had gotten shot trying to go to collect a debt from someone else.

Denver, Fia, Sawyer and Gus had all banded together to make this when their parents had left. And if the Kings stuck a little closer to one another, that was just because they were making the most out of what they had.

"What do you think, Bix?" Denver asked.

"Amazing," she said, taking another piece of pie and eating a couple of bites.

She looked down the table longingly.

"Go off and get more food," said Daughtry.

She did, a near hop in her step as she went back toward the tables.

"I'm surprised she's still around," said Justice.

"Me too," said Daughtry honestly.

"She looks good," said Denver. "Much better than she did when she got here."

"She looked like a half-grown piglet," said Landry.

"Mean," Fia whispered.

"But true," said Arizona. "It isn't her fault. She was clearly going through a really hard time."

"I think she'd like to get to know you better," he said, directing that at Arizona and Fia. "She told me she's never had friends before."

Even Arizona softened at that. "Oh. Poor thing."

"Don't look at her like that," said Daughtry. "She's liable to scratch your eyes out. She's too prickly to want anybody's pity." It was strange, because he pitied her more often than he didn't, but he also wanted to protect her from that in some regards. He couldn't quite explain it.

Bix returned then, her plate piled high full of food—dinner food rather than pie—and they returned to talking about the running of the ranch.

That was when the band started playing, and people began to circle the bonfire, dancing and laughing. This was when the alcohol started flowing. It was better than any bar in his opinion. He didn't have much use for Smokey's Tavern, since the hookup scene wasn't really his thing, but this was where Daughtry let himself have a good time. Because it was exactly the opposite of anything his father would have ever been involved in. It was sharing. Sharing food, sharing success, sharing joy. The things that they had created at Four Corners, because they all worked together rather than working against each other. Because they engaged in honest labor, rather than trying to cheat anybody.

And so this was the one place that he let himself be a little bit more loose. Be a little bit more free.

He noticed that Bix was looking wistfully at the dancing. And he remembered what she'd said. About the prom she would have gone to, and the boy she would have dated. The regular old teenage mistakes she wished that she had made.

"Care to dance, Bix?"

Her eyes went wide. He reached his hand out toward her, and she looked down, then back up. "Yes."

BIX *DID* WANT to dance. Because she had been so looking forward to being at a party. And this place was the best party she had ever even imagined. It was filled with people, and everybody was happy. There was so much food, and the barn and the bonfire were amazing. But the minute she reached out and her skin touched his she realized that she had made a very strange mistake. Because her stomach flipped. Turned right over on its head, and damn near went inside out.

She hadn't expected that. Because it had never happened to her before. She had felt hints of it, when she had seen Daughtry wandering through the house without a shirt. She did her best to ignore it. To pretend that it hadn't happened.

But then her hand touched his. It was rough. Surprisingly rough. And it was a strange time to realize she had never held hands with another person before in her life. Well, it was entirely possible that when she was a child one of her parents had taken her hand to keep her from running off. To keep her safe. But she almost doubted that. Because it showed a level of care that she certainly hadn't experienced in her memory from those people.

And now Daughtry was holding her hand.

Leading her toward the bonfire. She knew that it was casual. A lot of different people were dancing with each other at the bonfire, and it didn't carry any significance. But it did to her, because she had never done it. It did to her, because she couldn't remember being skin to skin with another person before, even if it was just their palms touching.

It opened up the cavernous ache in her stomach, and it made her feel small. Ashamed, in a strange way, because couldn't all the people around her see that? Couldn't he see it?

Oh, if he knew the truth about her, he would just think she was the saddest thing on record. Lonely. A virgin.

Having a strange moment of . . . was this lust?

Was that what the feeling inside of her was, this restless pounding of her heart, the twisting of her stomach. The awareness of her breasts. Normally they were just there. She did not think about them that much. Right then, she was thinking a lot about them. And her lips. Her lips felt strangely present. She could only blame him.

She couldn't look at him. She was looking at his throat as they moved to the bonfire and he wrapped an arm around her waist.

And she nearly died then and there.

He was hot. It wasn't the bonfire. It was him.

His hold was strong, and she shouldn't be surprised by that. He was a very big man. Just broad, arms heavily muscled. She knew that. She had observed all that. She had seen him without a shirt, after all.

And she was very aware just then of the condoms in the drawer of his bedside table.

She also knew there hadn't been any women at the house since she had come to stay. So they weren't something he used a lot.

He had come home every night since she had gotten there. And she supposed it was possible that he did things during the day while she was gone, but she didn't think so. Still, she knew they were there. She knew that he wasn't just this benevolent presence in her life. He was a man. A full man, with a life that was fuller than hers had ever been.

With family, friends and lovers.

This meant nothing to him. Asking her to dance, taking her hand, had seemed like nothing to him.

She could see that in the casual way he had approached it.

But her? It felt like everything.

It felt singular.

She was desperate to make sure he didn't see that. Because how embarrassing.

They were moving, but she was only dimly aware of the movements. She was doing her best to follow him. But then, that hardly took any skill. He was just so strong. The way he held her was so secure. So . . .

Amazing.

She looked up, and she did look at his face this time, and her mouth went dry. Oh no. Oh shit. She could not afford to have a crush on this man. She was way too cynical to have crushes. She knew better than that.

Bad boys had never appealed to her. Because they smelled like cigarettes and alcohol, and dead ends.

Because she was way too smart to hitch her wagon to a man who was only headed to prison. She hadn't chosen to be associated with her father, and had been. She didn't see the point in expanding her convict network by choice.

But apparently, she was susceptible to this. To his innate goodness. Maybe that was the problem. He was a cop. And what could be more forbidden to somebody like her? Everybody wanted that, right? Good girls wanted bad boys. Apparently she wanted him. This man who stood in stark contrast to everything she'd ever known. This man who represented a system that she had been trained to be afraid of.

That added up.

Because people were dumb like that.

And apparently so was she.

She didn't want to stop dancing with him, though. Because it was fun. Because he spun her in a circle. Because her dress swirled up around her thighs, and it made her feel feminine and pretty. Because she felt small and protected when he held her in his arms, and she couldn't think of a time that she'd ever felt that before.

Because it was different. And in that moment, so was she.

She didn't want it to end. And she was desperate for it to. Because it felt like her body was waking up.

That made sense.

Normally she was cold. Normally she was hungry. Normally she was worried about survival, so how could she think about this? But sometimes she did. Like when she had read *The Wolf and the Dove* and she had wondered what it would be like. To be forced to be comfortable. Chained to a bed. Vulnerable, but protected. Warm. Safe. But the dangerous thing, the barbarian, would become your greatest ally because of love. Because of desire.

That had definitely stirred a lot of things inside of her. And this felt . . . like that. Except it was dangerous, because he was real. And so was this moment.

The fire sparked, flecks of orange on a black sky.

Stardust.

And then finally, the song ended. She wanted to cry. And then she wanted to hide. Because it had to be obvious to everybody around her what was going on. That her heart was threatening to burst through her chest, that she felt dizzy, and not just from being spun.

How did anybody get anything done with him around? She supposed that his brothers were handsome too, and she spent a lot of time with them. But they weren't him. How come nobody else seemed immobilized by that? By his magnetism.

She had never known anybody like this.

Nobody had ever made her want to throw caution to the wind.

But she couldn't. She could imagine what might happen if she stretched up on her toes and kissed him. She could imagine those strong arms taking her and pushing her back. Holding her away from him. Worst of all, she could imagine pity in his eyes. That such a pathetic creature would think that a man like him would want to kiss her.

Because he wouldn't. Of course he wouldn't. It was . . . unthinkable.

So she moved away from him. "Thanks," she said. "For the dance."

"No problem," he said, his eyes completely unreadable. And anyway, she couldn't stand to look at them for another second.

She went back to the food table. She wasn't hungry, but she ate another piece of pie, because she didn't know what to do with herself and she thought that might do something to quiet the blood in her veins. He felt loud. Hot.

She was worried that everybody could hear it.

And without his touch, without his hold, she suddenly felt cold. She shivered, and fought off a wave of irritation. She didn't want him to see her shivering.

But it was like there was an invisible string bonding them together, because in the next moment, he was there.

"You're regretting that you didn't bring a coat now, aren't you?"

Her heart did a little shimmy in her chest. "I'm fine."

"Are you?"

"Yeah. I'm not dying of hypothermia."

Then he shrugged his jacket off his shoulders, and held it out toward her. "Put this on," he said.

She could only stare at it.

"Won't you get cold?"

"No. I'm a gentleman, anyway. Mainly, I only bring a coat in case a lady is in need."

Dimly, she thought she should protest that characterization. Down way deep somewhere at the bottom of her soul she thought maybe she should be offended. But nobody had ever called her a lady. And no one had ever had occasion to behave like a gentleman around her. So she decided that she was going to accept it. She decided that she was going to hold it close to her chest. Relish it.

Because next to the dance, this was one of the nicest things anyone had ever done for her.

So dramatic. *Nicer than actually giving you a job? Feeding you? Giving you shelter?*

Well. Maybe this felt more personal.

It felt like something. She knew it wasn't. It could never be. Not with a man like Daughtry. He was just very good.

Yeah. Very good.

So much so that it nearly hurt.

They only stayed for about twenty more minutes, and then he was ready to go, and she . . . wished they didn't have to. But she wasn't going to suggest they stay. Not after he had been so extra nice to her. They got into the truck and drove quietly back to the house.

"I need a shower. Then I'm going to head to bed. I have an early shift." He nodded once. "Good night, Bix."

"Good night, Daughtry."

She stood there in his living room for a long moment, wearing his coat still. Trying to come to terms with the very strange situation she found herself in. It had been a month, and it still didn't feel real.

And it wasn't going to feel real. Because it wasn't real. It was temporary.

She repeated that to herself as she walked into her bedroom. And stopped there. The nightstand. Her books were on it in a little stack. The bed looked so inviting. Made with matching sheets, and a bedspread over the top of it. Matching pillowcases.

She sat down on the bed and smoothed her hand over the blanket. Then she tightened the coat around her body and smelled it. Woodsmoke, and pine. The earth. The way that he was, just him.

She curled her fingers into fists.

She was going to have to leave.

CHAPTER TEN

BIX HAD DECLINED to come to dinner that night, and Daughtry was almost relieved. He needed the reprieve. He always felt like he had to watch her, keep an eye out for her.

You make it sound like she's a chore. She isn't, and you know that.

He felt hyperaware of her, though, and it was a strange sensation, and not one that he liked all that much. He sat down in the living room with Denver and Justice after everyone else had cleared out.

He'd love to pretend he didn't know what it was. Sadly, it was the all-too-familiar ache of being attracted to a beautiful woman. And he couldn't afford that. Not with her. She was under his care, and he wasn't that guy.

Worse, though, had been her reaction. The heightened color in her cheeks, the way her breathing had gotten faster.

She'd felt it. The same thing he had.

The pulse of electricity when their hands had touched. And her eyes had gone all bright. Her attraction had been . . . naked. Like she hadn't known how to hide it or hadn't wanted to.

And something about that was appealing to him, even if it shouldn't be.

Because it was like an invitation to wildness. To something deeper than the arrangements he'd always had. These very clear-cut sexual agreements that had no risk, and no real spark.

Sparks start wildfires.

And only you can prevent forest fires, dumbass.

"Where's your little shadow?" Denver asked.

He gritted his teeth. "*My little shadow* isn't actually my shadow, and she is at home."

"Home," Denver said.

"Yes. That is where she lives."

"I thought this was all just temporary."

"Well. It is. But for now, it is what it is."

"Sure," said Denver.

"How is she? As far as work goes."

"She's great," said Justice. "She does the work of two people easily. And when she doesn't have the know-how, she definitely has the enthusiasm."

"You mean like the willingness to climb up on top of the barn roofs?"

"Exactly that," he said.

"Great," said Daughtry.

"You know," said Denver. "I'm wondering about something."

"What is that?" Daughtry asked, feeling irritated with his brother.

"When are you going to stop playing cops and robbers? You're half in and half out of the ranch. And it isn't like you're gunning for a top-level position in law enforcement. So . . . what is the game?"

"What the hell is that supposed to mean?"

"Exactly what I said." Denver straightened in his chair. "Sometimes I think maybe you took Bix on because she's acting as your surrogate. Living in your house, coming to work for us every day. But it's not you, Daughtry."

"No," said Daughtry. "It's not. But I put work into this place whenever I'm not on shift."

"But you're on shift full-time. And like I said, you're kind of half in both. That's what I don't understand."

"Because it's not about being the top of anything, or the head of anything," said Daughtry. "I didn't know that you cared about this. I didn't know you felt like you needed a greater understanding about it. Because let me make it clear. Let me give you the rundown. Our dad was a miserable human being. He probably still is. He caused damage in this town, Denver, you know that. And I know you feel a sense of responsibility for it. Or you wouldn't be off trying to pay for all of his mistakes—literally. I know you give Sheena Patrick money. That you sent her sisters to school."

Denver's lip curled. "It's different."

"The hell it is. It's not different."

"Yes, it is," Denver said.

"All those people aren't the surrogates for your redemption? Because actually, it seems like it's the same thing. And if Bix is anything, then she's that. It has nothing to do with me sending somebody to do my work on the ranch in my place."

"I don't understand the need for the job."

"I didn't ask you to understand it. You're right about one thing, Denver. I'm not in charge of any other

place, but you and I both know that I'm never going
to be in charge here. I don't want to be. I care about
it. You handled it all your way, I handled it mine. We
were both there, Denver. We both saw Dan Patrick die.
We both have that feeling of . . . blood on our hands."

"You don't have to tell me about it," Denver said.

He looked at his brother. He loved him. There was
no doubt about that. And he knew Denver loved him
too. But after the scales had been torn from their eyes,
after their dad's empire had crumbled and they'd seen
it for what it was, there had always been a wall between them.

Landry and Justice seemed beneath their dad's notice most of the time. Arizona had been the object of
contempt. Daughtry and Denver had been his boys.
There was an inescapable feeling that his bond with
Denver was somehow tied to that and he knew they
both rejected it completely.

It made things a little complicated sometimes. They
worried about each other. They didn't really know
how to fix each other. Mostly they left each other alone
when it came to deep emotional wounds or whatever.

Why Denver was choosing to get in his grill now,
he couldn't say.

Daughtry gritted his teeth. "I have done my level
best to make sure that I do better, that I give better,
since then. But I have to be careful. You know that. I
have to . . ."

"What? You think if you quit being a police officer
then you're going to forget how to not be a criminal?
You're not going to forget how to not be a narcissist."

"You don't know that. And anyway, it's my business."

"We all have our own ways of dealing with this," Justice said quietly. Justice rarely opposed Denver. Hell, none of them opposed Denver all that often. "If that's what works for him, then it's what works," Justice continued. "It's not up to you to tell them what to do, or how to do it better."

"Well, that's nice," said Denver. "My little brothers forming an army against me. When I'm the reason that this place got pulled up out of ruin."

"And I'm appreciative," Daughtry said. "But you can't tell me that you want to share the crown with anybody. We both know you don't."

"The whole point of expanding all this is to give everybody their own niche," he said. "But the truth is, Daughtry, you don't have that kind of time."

"You're right. I don't. And I don't especially care but I . . ." Suddenly, he remembered what Bix had said to him. "What do you think about beer?"

Denver gave him a look like he was insane and raised his beer bottle in the air. "I like it pretty well."

"That isn't what I mean. I mean what do you think about brewing beer? There's my contribution."

"Brewing beer?"

"Yeah. I mean, I'm not going to actually head it up, but that was an idea that Bix had. And I think it's a good one."

"Not doing much to make me think she isn't your surrogate."

"That's your hang-up, not mine. I think it's a good idea. And I think it's something that she could manage."

"If she does that, then you're looking at a much more permanent position."

It was true. He was looking at needing to get her a place of her own, as well. He was looking at . . .

For some reason, his brain just quit working. He wasn't sure he wanted Bix to find a different place, and yet the idea of having her on a more permanent basis was . . . strange. A little bit jarring. But definitely less jarring than the idea of her leaving. And anyway, the beer thing was a good idea.

"It is a good idea," said Denver. "Four Corners beer?"

"Yeah," said Justice. "There can be a type for each ranch. I mean, assuming everybody else wants to chip in. They don't get fancy beer for nothing."

He could sense the irritation coming off of Denver in waves, because Denver couldn't deny it was a good idea. And Daughtry could see that he wanted to.

"Okay. Find out some more information about that. Or get your critter to do it."

"She's not my *critter*. Talk about her with a little bit of respect. You said she was a good worker. So give her the full credit that you would give any good worker."

"I do. In front of her," Denver admitted. "It's only in front of you that I'm this big of an ass."

"Lucky me," said Daughtry.

He rounded out the night with his brothers without having another fight or coming to blows. Not that they ever did that. He was a little bit surprised at Denver's commentary. Mostly because they didn't tend to get in each other's business like that. Their father had been so manipulative, and they were all pretty wary of that sort of behavior.

But there it was. Resentment, bubbling up beneath the surface. He wasn't that thrilled about it. He pondered it as he drove home. The lights were on in the front of the house, but he could see through the windows that Bix wasn't lingering in any of the front rooms.

She had been a little bit scarce since the town hall meeting.

He thought back to those bright eyes, her pink cheeks . . .

Shit.

Good thing he had a lock on control.

Good. Damn. Thing.

He opened up the front door, and went inside, closing it heavily behind him.

He paused, and listened. He couldn't hear any movement. He went over to the fridge and opened it up, taking out a bottle of beer. He closed the fridge door, and then he heard a sound from the hallway.

"Bix?"

Soft footsteps started to head his direction.

"Bix?" he repeated.

"No," she said. "It's the Golden State Killer."

"That would be a surprise."

She held up her hands like claws. "Death is always a surprise, Daughtry."

She lowered her hands, and looked embarrassed. He stared at her for a long moment, stunned again by how much she had changed. Not so much in personality. She was still prickly. And insincere at first. Every single time. Sincerity had to be dug out of her with an ice pick. And even then, it was tough to manufacture.

"What did you have for dinner?" he asked.

"Leftover pizza," she said. "How was . . . everybody?"

"It was a reduced crew tonight. But good." He opted not to tell her about the fight that he had with Denver. Because he and Bix weren't friends. It was funny; she had told him that she didn't know how to have friends. He wasn't sure he did either. He had his brothers, and they bumped along just fine until they had a little dustup like tonight, and then they pushed it only so far before letting it go.

Justice had a friend. She was a woman, and he wondered if that was something to do with . . . Hell, he didn't know. He didn't have an explanation for that. Landry had Fia, but that was it. Denver sure as hell didn't have anybody. Arizona had an expanded network these days. She and Rue bumped around just fine. And these days, Arizona even got along with the Sullivan sisters.

But Daughtry had no idea how to have friends. And it had never bothered him. He had colleagues in the state police, but the way it was structured, they didn't really have to talk to each other much if they didn't want to. And mostly what he wanted to do was clock in and clock out. That was it. That was what he did. His job had always been about service, not brotherhood or any other such thing.

So he could tell her about it. It would be interesting. An exercise in friendship.

But instead, he just looked down at the beer bottle in his hand. "My brother is interested in beer. Our own beer."

She frowned. "Okay?"

"What do you know about brewing beer?"

"Oh, plenty. I haven't done a whole lot of it, but I have before, on special request. And I know how to get a setup together."

"You don't need to make anything out of buckets. We can buy actual equipment. But I would like your help pricing it out. And it would be great if you could walk me through the process a little bit."

"Sure. I can do that."

"How would you like to head up the endeavor?"

She blinked. "What?"

"If Denver ends up agreeing after we present him with a plan, would you like to be in charge of Four Corners Beer?"

She looked like she had been slapped with a wet fish. "I . . . I don't know. I really don't. I . . . What does that mean for me?"

"It would be something of a permanent position."

"Permanent. Here."

"Yeah."

"I have . . . I mean I was going to . . ."

"What were you going to do?"

She looked up at him with wide blue eyes. "I don't know."

BIX FELT EMBARRASSED, standing there looking up at him. Daughtry, who was too perfectly formed for her to bear. And who seemed to just be. As easily as putting on a uniform every day. A man with purpose. A man who knew who he was, and what to do about it.

A man who made her feel.

Because it was maybe the most honest thing she had ever said to him, other than that outburst about everything she would've done with her life if she'd had a normal upbringing.

Because she didn't know.

She had been lying to herself this whole time. In her head, she had thought it made sense to go to California because her dad did have some contacts there. She had been planning on setting up a still. Planning on getting the product out there, where her father's name and reputation might mean something.

She had been planning, dimly, on trading on her father's sketchy reputation down in a rural part of California where she didn't have any friends or family.

The truth was, no one was waiting for her.

She had planted a seed inside of herself, a little white lie. An idea that there were people there she knew better than she did. A vague notion that they would be appreciative that she had showed up with product. It had given her a feeling like she was heading to a destination. That she had a goal.

She didn't. She didn't.

Nobody was waiting for her. Her father was imprisoned, and so was her brother.

Her mom might not even be alive anymore, and if she was, she doubted she even remembered she had a kid.

The only people who really had a sense of who she was . . . were the Kings. Daughtry King was offering her more than any other person ever had. And she would be an idiot to turn them down. That was the bottom line. That was the truth.

"What about . . . ? I mean . . ."

"What's worrying you?"

She laughed. "Only everything. Nobody has ever offered me a permanent position before. Nobody has ever offered me anything close to . . . Where am I going to live?"

"Here. For now. But you're right, there should be some other housing."

"I mean, you should probably let me pay for my own housing."

"We're lousy with land. If there's one thing we're not short on it's places to stay. It doesn't actually make any sense to have you paying for your own place. Because you don't need a lot of space. It can be part of your compensation. We can continue with room and board. But I agree, you want to have your own space."

"That's . . . nice of you."

"I'm not being nice. This is a good opportunity for you and for us."

"Yes, you are," she said. "You're being nice. You have been, from the minute that you met me, and I really don't know why. I just . . . I can't believe that you're being this . . . You could find somebody with experience."

"I could. And I would have to pay them more. I'll pay you something fair, but something that represents that this is your first gig. But also, there will be room and board. And you don't have to stay forever. Get it set up and then . . . go to college."

Her chest hurt. It was the hope. That was the problem. It was so foreign, so painful, it was the reason that she turned away from all of this most of the time. Because it was just . . . It was hard. It was just so hard. She wanted everything that he was offering.

She wanted everything she had found here.

The sense of camaraderie, the food, the . . . the family.

But it scared her too. How could it not? This was nothing like her life. Nothing like the life she had known previously. Her own family treated her like she was disposable, and Daughtry was giving her something real. It wasn't a handout. He was actually giving her job experience.

If she stayed here long enough she would be able to get work elsewhere. And he was right; if she stayed and saved enough money then she could go to college. She could probably start online classes.

She would be able to buy a computer. And they had Wi-Fi on the ranch.

Her heart was pounding, but she was smart. She knew how to survive.

She wasn't sure she knew how to do this, though. It felt like something bigger than survival. Something more. And that was something she didn't have any experience with. Not beyond the last month.

"So what's the plan? We have to present him with information?"

"Yes. We need to get together some information on projected costs."

"Well, I'm familiar with all the supplies. For brewing, bottling and distribution. I imagine you're going to want real labels, and there are companies that can do that for cheap, and there are companies that can do it good. My recommendation would be to do it good."

He chuckled. "Okay. Whatever you think. You give me some ideas, and we'll work them into a proposal for Denver."

The absolute terror of the hope that was rioting through her was better than any cigarette. It was intoxicating, and she was worried that it might be addicting. Just like he was.

Her feelings for him were anything but straightforward. And she had a feeling she was a special project to him. She was going to prove that she was worth the investment.

She would make sure that Daughtry King was not sorry that he believed in her.

Because he was the only person on this green earth who ever had.

And that was worth more than whatever strange sensation she got in her stomach whenever she looked at him. This was worth everything.

"I'm going to get something together tonight. And . . . I can give it to Denver in the morning."

He nodded. "Great."

She wrapped her arms around herself, and they looked at each other for maybe a minute longer than necessary. Not a whole minute. Just a heartbeat. A breath.

She cleared her throat. "I'll see you."

"Yeah," he said.

She went back to her room and closed the door, leaning against it, trying to calm her rapidly beating heart. He was giving her a chance to make something of herself. He was giving her a chance to plan for her future. That was worth more than anything else ever could be. It wasn't stardust. It was something more concrete than that; it was what she needed.

It was a brick. And she would be damned if she was going to waste it.

CHAPTER ELEVEN

EARLY THE NEXT MORNING, Bix presented her plan to Denver. "This looks good," he said.

He passed the paper to Justice, who looked it over. "Damn good."

Arizona grabbed a page and skimmed it quickly. "This is great."

Landry took it last. "I'm in," he said. "What's your time frame?"

"Well, we need to determine a formula. So we're going to have to consider what we think the signature should be for King's Crest. Assuming that's how you want to go. A beer for each ranch."

"Let's start with King's. I think we'll wait and see if anybody else wants to invest," said Denver.

She nodded. "Seems fair. So, what do you all like to drink?"

She spent the next hour listening to them talk about their favorite beers. She put it all together, synthesizing it and trying to figure out the right direction. She wanted something hearty. Not an IPA. A stout. Maybe wheat ale. Yes. That was what she wanted to do. She felt a surge of excitement. No, she wasn't really a beer drinker, but she understood the clientele. And that was the key anyway.

"Bix," said Denver, right before they began construction work for the day. "I might have Daughtry take you into town to buy the supplies for brewing."

"Oh, that's . . . I mean, I do know how to drive. I could do it."

Though she realized she hadn't done much of that recently.

"Yeah, I know. But he knows the place. He's off again in a couple of days. So work on getting your list together."

"Sure," she said. She felt jittery, and excited about spending time with Daughtry, and she really shouldn't, considering they lived together. But they often passed each other, not actually spending a significant amount of time together.

And she was still stuck on the town hall meeting. On the way his hand had felt against hers. When she should be thinking about her future. And brewing beer. So she shook that off.

"The other thing is I need to know if you need a crew."

"I will. Eventually. If we're going to bottle on-site then we are going to need some help. And managing different equipment . . . is just helpful. And if I can get a space in one of the unused buildings . . ."

"You've got it."

They went back and forth, talking about what she would need. He offered to dedicate a crew of five to the beer-brewing endeavor. And she would be the boss.

She felt completely undone by that. Being somebody's boss when she had barely been able to get a job until recently.

It was crazy.

When Daughtry came back from work that night, they ended up eating at his house. And over barbecued chicken, she excitedly told him about his siblings' buy-in for the venture.

"Thank you," she said. "He's actually giving me a team."

"Did he say how much he was going to pay you?"

She was stunned to realize that she hadn't actually secured payment. It was very off-brand for her. Normally, that would be the first thing on her mind.

But it was the opportunity that was getting her now. Not the money. Yeah, she'd been able to put a lot away, but actually having work, having a purpose, that was worth more.

"He was saying that maybe we should go to town together and pick up everything on my list."

"Sounds good," he said.

Her palms got a little bit sweaty.

"Great."

"But he should tell you how much he's paying you."

"Don't you have the authority to mandate that?"

"I do. But I'd rather see how much he's willing to give. It might actually be more generous, and in fairness, Landry is actually the one who knows more about the budget than anybody else. So, it's probably going to need to be Landry."

"Right," she said.

"Denver got a little bit annoyed with me the other day," he said.

"He did?" She couldn't imagine being annoyed at Daughtry. Which was strange, since she had begun their relationship being pretty annoyed with him.

"Yeah. I think he doesn't believe that I have a big enough commitment to the ranch."

"He doesn't? How can he think that? Everything that you do is . . . I mean, you . . ." Well, in fairness, he didn't really work that much on the ranch. But she felt like his presence was an essential part of it.

Plus he was . . . amazing.

She blinked. She was beginning to hero worship him a little bit, and it was ridiculous. She needed to remember that he was just a human man. She needed to remember the condoms in the bedside drawer. He wasn't any better or any worse than a normal dude.

No. Okay. Maybe thinking about the condoms in the drawer had been a mistake. Because that made her feel a little bit warm, and she couldn't afford to go feeling warm.

"I disagree," she said.

"That's nice. But, he is my brother, and he does run the ranch. So, I think that his opinion on it might be a little bit more important."

"No," she said. "His opinion is based on his own bias. I think that people respect you. And I think that you being part of the family, part of all this, I think it matters. I know the way that everybody talks about the family here on the ranch."

"What did they say?"

"Just how . . . great you are. How fair. Some of them remember working for your father, and I think everybody is very impressed with how you have handled yourselves. The people say all the time what a great man you are, Daughtry."

He looked uncomfortable at that. Hell, she was uncomfortable saying it. But nobody had ever said such glowing or nice things about her. If they did, she would want to know. Someday, maybe she would earn it. Someday.

"Well. Thank you."

"Plus . . ." She scrunched her face up. "If it wasn't for you, I would still be making moonshine in the middle of the woods. Starving . . . I . . . Thank you." She needed to say it. She had avoided saying thank you, and really meaning it for a long time, because it made her feel like she was beholden to him. But the truth was, she was beholden to him. And she should be. Because what he had done for her was more than a little bit wonderful. It was more than a little bit of amazing. It was life-changing.

All the books in all the little free libraries hadn't quite done it.

But a hand up from Daughtry had given her this.

"Bix, I really appreciate that, but the truth is, if it wasn't for how strong you are you wouldn't be here. You took the opportunity you were given and you proved yourself twenty times over. You don't owe me."

She understood what he was doing. That he was trying to be nice. But actually, it hurt a little bit. She was okay owing him, she decided. Because he had done something great for her. There wasn't anything wrong with acknowledging that. And a month ago, she would've said there was. A month ago, she would've said that she didn't want that.

"So, when will we go shopping?"

"Two days. We'll take a truck and a trailer so that we can haul it all. Congratulations, Bix. You've got yourself a business venture. One on the right side of the law."

"Wait a minute. Does that mean we're actually going to . . . get a license?"

"We will indeed be getting a license."

Her heart stuttered. "I probably won't be able to get one. I have a record."

"The ranch will be able to get one."

He said it with such certainty. So much trust. That things would work just the way they were supposed to, and not even a little bit different.

What must it be like, to be able to trust in things like that?

"I . . ."

"You should bring your ID. We can go get you a bank account as well. You're going to need one."

She blinked. "A bank account."

"Yes. So that you can have your checks deposited. You can even use one of those newfangled debit cards to buy your things."

She knew that he was teasing her a little bit, but it made her throat get scratchy. "My dad would be . . . Well, if he was that he would be rolling over in his grave. As it is, he just sat bolt upright in his prison cell and screamed into the void."

"What did your dad ever do for you?"

It was an uncharacteristic moment of him looking absolutely grim.

She frowned. "Well, he did keep me alive for the first several years of my life."

"That's not a gift. That's the bare minimum. I know that you care about your dad. I know that part of you even admires him. But trust me. From the child of one narcissist to another. He doesn't deserve your loyalty. He doesn't get to hold you back, not anymore. You said you would do all those things if you were free to do them, if he hadn't chosen your path for you. So choose it now. And let go of all his bullshit. You deserve better."

"How do you know?" she whispered. "I mean, seriously, how do you know? What have I ever done to indicate that I deserve better? All I've managed to do is the job that you gave me, and then, I guess I didn't steal from you. That's not . . . that's not exceptional."

"That's not true."

"How can you say that? Look at you."

"Look at me what?"

"You . . . you didn't have to try at your dad's lifestyle before you decided to be a decent human being."

"You don't know what I did or didn't do," he said. "Because we haven't talked about it."

"But you know about me."

"I found you in the middle of what we could both agree is maybe a low moment."

She recalled herself then. Skinny. Scabbed.

She lifted her chin up. "I don't know that I would call it a low moment. It was a teachable moment. It was a moment rife for problem-solving."

"And that is why you're exceptional," he said. "Because that's how you see things. And that's pretty amazing. When your dad, and the world in general, hasn't given you much of a reason to be persistent, to be hopeful, you are. You have been. I'm proud of you for that."

She despised herself for feeling so warmed by that. Knowing he was proud. It mattered so much, and she wished it didn't. Because caring about the opinions of other people was kind of a dead end. At least, in her experience.

She hadn't done it much. In fact, she had always felt that it was best to do it as little as possible.

If you didn't care, you couldn't be disappointed when they were disappointed in you.

She paused. "Wait a minute. So what is it about you that I don't know?"

"A lot of things," he said.

Like who he used those condoms with.

She did not say that. She felt flushed all the same.

"Like what?"

"My dad was kind of a loan shark."

"A loan shark? I was unaware that small towns had such things."

"Doing the kind of work that you do, you're surprised about it?"

She wrinkled her nose. "I guess . . . No, I think I've seen people that are like that. You're right, those are the sorts of people who hover around the edges of businesses like my dad's."

"My dad charged extortionate fees to loan people money, and then . . . he took everything. But he liked to trade in favors, plots of land. He cheated and hurt the people in this town. He would come in all charming, acting like he was offering to really fix something. But often, he would make sure that the situation and the terms of the agreement were impossible. He was good at that. There were other things he was into. Drug dealing and all that." He cleared his throat.

"Oh hey," said Bix. "Twinsies."

He smiled ruefully. "Yeah. I didn't know about the drugs."

"Oh, I did," she said, cheerfully.

"Anyway I was his . . . I went with him. I was there to be muscle. Just in case."

"How old were you?" She tried to imagine it. Tried to imagine Daughtry being intimidating, being there to take things from people. A menacing presence rather than someone who radiated . . . well, not menace. Yes, she had been a little afraid of him right at first, but not because she actually thought he was bad. It was because she was . . . well, because she was doing things that weren't entirely aboveboard, so she had reason to be uncomfortable around him.

But the idea that he had been . . . something other than the man that stood before her now rocked her.

"I was old enough to know better. It went on until I was about seventeen. I was big for my age."

She could believe it.

"What changed for you?" She found herself desperate to know. Because something had turned the whole world on its head for him, and she wanted to know what that moment was. Since she herself was in the midst of a come-to-Jesus, she was curious what had led him to his.

"We pulled up to the house one day, and there was a little girl at the place. She saw us coming. She ran away. I knew that if we were the kind of person that made little kids run away, then we weren't the good guys. And I had never put a lot of thought into that." He cleared his throat. "It was after that when Dan Patrick was killed, by somebody he went to collect from. At the behest of my dad. So basically, it was a combination of things. But that little girl's face really stuck in my head. It changed things for me."

He looked grim, and she found she wanted to reach up and smooth the lines that had appeared on his forehead. She also felt like she didn't have the right to. They lived together. He had taken care of her. She still wasn't quite sure what they were to each other. And he was telling her this now. This thing that seemed personal and real. She wanted to hoard it like food.

The corner of his lip tugged upward. "I wanted to be a good guy. But it was also my first real understanding that my dad was a bad guy. He wasn't like your dad. I feel like your dad had a certain amount of pride in going against the law."

She laughed. "Oh yeah. He loved to grandstand on why he was actually sort of a hero. Fighting the man and all of that."

He shook his head. "My dad was never one to grandstand. He spoke with this very real conviction that made you feel like he couldn't be anything but right. It was why when he showed his true colors it was always a bit of a shock. Arizona was in a terrible accident when she was seventeen. She had injuries, scars on her body—it took a long time for her to recover. He was horrible to her. He just said the most poisonous things. It was painful because there were other times when he seemed nice." He stared at a point just past her head. "He was like a snake. Slithering in and out between the rocks. Sometimes he would catch the light and you would think he was pretty. But at the end of the day, he was a pit viper. And he was poison."

"My dad had all kinds of justifications for what he did," said Bix. "But I always knew. When you have to be secretive about what you do, when you don't have any friends, when you're not allowed to go to school, when you can't tell anybody what your dad does for a living, you know that you are the ones that are wrong. I have clung to a whole lot of what he taught me because I didn't want to feel like I was a bad guy either."

But she didn't know what else to be. Didn't know what other move to make. Except now she did. Maybe that was what mattered. Maybe they were more alike than she had realized before.

"You're not a bad guy," he said.

Warmth bloomed in her chest. "Well. I appreciate that."

The days flew by until it was time for them to go on their shopping trip, and she found herself fretting over what to wear. She had never done that in her life. But Daughtry always looked . . . well, like Daughtry. And she wanted to look like a woman who ought to be walking with him.

She chose another one of the dresses that she had bought. It was short and pretty, with buttons all the way down the front, and a flower pattern. She had bought a few dresses like this because they were frivolous. Because they were something she never would have picked in her other life, and she was working on making something new.

She felt a cracking sensation in her chest. Like something old and calcified was beginning to loosen. Beginning to ease. It was terrifying, and she wanted it. In spite of the terror.

They were going to buy supplies to brew beer, and she had put on her nicest dress. She rolled her eyes at herself as she looked in the mirror, and wished that she had just a little bit of makeup. Just something. A little bit of brightness to make him look at her and see that she was different.

What exactly do you think is going on?

Nothing. She wasn't foolish enough to think that . . .

She shut down that train of thought. This was what she had always been afraid of. Cracking the door on hope. Because then all these other dreams would push in. And that was exactly what was happening. She had food and shelter, so she'd begun to think maybe she could have stability too. And then she'd started to think if she could have the job brewing beer maybe she could also go to college. And then she thought if she could begin to make friends here at the ranch, maybe Daughtry . . .

There was just a limit to how much she could put herself through. To how much she could test this new, fragile hope that was blooming within her.

She reaffirmed within herself that she was absolutely fine without makeup.

Because she didn't need Daughtry to see her different. She needed to keep on trying to see herself different.

That thought pulled her up short, and as she walked out of her bedroom and into the living room, where she was waiting for him, she let that settle. She saw herself as a fighter. But more than that, she realized she saw herself as an underdog. It was something that had fueled her. The idea that she had an enemy, somewhere out there. She had gotten that from her father.

The idea that everything she did wasn't just about surviving, but was about opposing someone who was pushing against her. For her dad, it had been the system. She had taken on a bit of that herself, but she realized that a huge part of how she functioned was fashioning weapons against imagined enemies.

What if she didn't need enemies?

What if all she needed was to want something better for herself?

It was a radical idea. Something that made her feel off-kilter. She wasn't sure she was going to accomplish it in a day. But someday, she hoped she could feel that way. That she could do things just for her. For her own well-being. For her own improvement. Her own happiness.

Happiness.

That had never been a goal of hers. Another thing that seemed desperately out of reach due to the budget of her own personal economy.

She had aimed for survival, and very little else.

But what if she could have more?

She heard Daughtry's bedroom door open, and he came walking down the hall. He had traded the black T-shirt for a white one, white hat on his head.

"I didn't really think cowboys were real," she said, not meaning to say that out loud. But she had.

"And now you're here with a whole mess of them."

"That I am."

She felt lightheaded as they walked out to the truck.

"What are you thinking?" he asked as they began to drive away from the house, down the dirt road that would take them to the main road.

"Just that I can't quite believe that now I do live on a ranch with a whole bunch of cowboys, and I'm about to start heading up a beer-brewing operation. One that's legit."

"Shocking. I know."

"I mean, do you?"

"Sometimes when I think about my life. When I think about what I've done, where I've been, when I think about my father, I can't quite believe that I put on that uniform most days and go out and enforce the law, rather than my father's terrible loan terms. So yeah. I get that."

She didn't think he did, though, because for her it came with a whole bunch of other feelings that she never had before. This desire to plant roots. To stay. To get closer to the people around her rather than building a wall around her. After digging a moat around the place where the wall was meant to go.

And then there was him.

This fluttering that she felt when she looked at him, and the fascination with the condoms she knew were in his bedside table.

It was all bad. And yet it was also good.

It was like she had been a paper-doll version of a human being when he had found her. Thin and one-dimensional. Needy for food, shelter. Warmth. Not understanding that there was a fuller, deeper human experience out there.

She'd had tastes of it through reading. But it was hard to say which parts were fantasy, and which were actually obtainable. She certainly had never been able to work it all out. She was wondering about it now.

They made casual conversation about the area, the weather and brewing plans on the way to Mapleton, and when they arrived at the outdoor store which had all the supply, he got a big flat cart and pushed it through the aisles while she managed finding all of the equipment. They were an efficient team.

People stopped and talked to Daughtry, and he chatted with them easily. They knew him because he was a police officer.

She wondered if any of them knew him as his father's son, or if this new thing that he had done had entirely replaced that image in their heads.

She was just wondering for a friend. Who was her. How long it took to be defined by your own actions, and not the reputation of a sketchy family member.

The tab for all the items left her nearly gagging, because it was more money than she'd ever had in her life. But Daughtry didn't seem shocked by it at all. He pushed the flat cart out to the truck and lowered the bed. She rushed to bend down and pick up one of the metal bins, and he grabbed it at the same time, his hand going over the top of hers. Her eyes flew to his, the breath exiting her lungs in a sharp gasp.

His face was still. If he felt anything over the contact he didn't show it. She jerked her hand back, and stepped away.

"How about bank account next?" he asked.

She flexed her fingers, curled them into a fist. "I still don't know about the bank account."

"Why not?"

"It is very traditional. Very *in the system*. It kind of freaks me out."

"Bix," he said. "I hate to break it to you, but you are now gainfully employed. You need a bank account."

He finished loading everything into the back of the truck, and shut the tailgate. She just stood there staring as he rounded to the driver's side and got in. Her fingers were still burning. She hustled to open the door and get in, feeling a strange rush of relief when she was. Because riding shotgun in his truck was normal, at least. And what had just happened a moment ago had not felt normal at all.

He drove them both to the center of town and parked against the curb. The bank was housed in a historic old building, and something about that made her feel a little bit more calm. But this was weird.

"Will you come with me?" she asked, looking up at him as they stood outside the front door of the bank.

"I'm about to walk in with you," he said.

"No, I know. But will you . . . ? I can't talk to a banker by myself. I can't . . . I need you to go with me."

He nodded slowly. "Okay. I'll go with you." They waited behind two people before they were able to see the banker at her shiny wooden desk in the center of the old-fashioned room. There were gold posts with thick velvet rope delineating the lines to the different tellers. It was such a strange thing. Velvet rope.

The kind of thing Bix was always behind.

But she felt like she was crossing over.

Was this a betrayal of everything she had been raised to believe? And was that actually a bad thing? Or was it something that needed to happen?

They sat down at the desk, and Bix swallowed hard. She looked at the woman's name plastered on the desk. Hope Berkey. It was a very fancy thing, to have a nameplate like that. And that was one reason Bix noticed. The other reason was that the woman's name was Hope. In context with what she had just been thinking earlier, it seemed a pretty big coincidence. Bix didn't especially believe in signs from the universe. But she did believe and trust in her gut. Listening. Paying attention.

Right now it definitely seemed like she was being told to have a little bit of hope.

"I need to open a checking account," said Bix. She frowned. "The problem is I've never had one before."

"Well," said Hope. "Let's go over our different products and see which one is right for you."

Bix was entirely sold on the free checking account option and didn't need to hear about anything else. And there was the option to add a high-yield savings account if she had more than two hundred dollars to deposit. A special offer to a new bank customer. And she did have more than two hundred dollars.

It was strange, depositing all her money.

She sat in the seat and waited while Hope went to get papers for Bix to sign, and waited for her debit card to print.

Daughtry leaned in, and her heart fluttered. "That's not all your money, is it?"

"I'm not an idiot," she said. "I've got some stashed away too."

She hadn't been able to imagine sending all of her money to this weird theoretical place, where it would just be a number on an ATM screen, theoretical as she swiped her card. No. It was too weird. She couldn't bear it. She felt like she had to have real, concrete backup.

The woman came back, and Bix signed the papers, and then found a shiny debit card with a picture of a mountain being slid toward her.

Bix Carpenter.

It had her name printed on it.

She ran her fingertips over the top of it, just staring. And then she felt Daughtry's gaze on her. "What?" she asked.

"Nothing," he said.

Bix shook Hope's hand, and she and Daughtry walked out of the bank and back onto the street. Bix clutched her packet to her chest, her debit card safely in her purse.

"Are you okay?"

"I'm fine," she said.

"You looked . . . wistful."

"I guess I am. I've never had a card with my name on it before. It feels very official. I feel very official in a way that I never have."

"You're doing great," he said.

She wondered if he would ask her if she wanted to have lunch. She would like that. Sitting in a restaurant having lunch with Daughtry. She didn't want the afternoon to end.

"Thank you."

"We better head back," he said. "If we're quick the food will still be out on the tables. We can eat, and then you can start getting your space set up."

Disappointment made her stomach bottom out. Which was stupid. There was no point being disappointed that Daughtry didn't want to have lunch. That he couldn't read her mind. It was a workday, and this had been a work trip.

It wasn't personal. That was the thing. She had to remember that. But it was getting harder and harder to do.

CHAPTER TWELVE

BIX TOOK TO her new job as head of their brewing arm with relish. While she worked on getting the practicalities set up, he applied for a liquor license for the ranch. They were projected to have their barn done as an event space in the next two months. They wanted to be ready also to serve alcohol and food, and it would be even better if they could serve their own alcohol.

And of course, since Daughtry was involved everything was going to be aboveboard. He didn't know what it was about Bix that made him confide in her. Because that was what he'd done last week. When they had spoken about the way he helped his dad collect on debts, he had pretty well told her more about it than he ever had another person. He saw himself in her.

She was younger, angrier. But he had been both of those things at one time.

He was in a different place now. Settled.

She would have that eventually too.

She was getting it. And he was proud that he was playing a part, even if a small one, in that.

The way she had looked at her debit card at the bank . . .

It made his chest sore to think about it. He couldn't explain his connection with her. The only way he could explain it was by identifying the ways in which they were alike. The ways in which he saw himself.

A kid without a chance.

That's what Bix was.

She's not a kid.

Yeah. Well. He walked across the gravel in front of the outbuilding where Bix had set up her brewing station. He could hear voices, talking and laughing. She had a whole crew assembled to work with her. Four men, and a woman, and they all seemed to get along great.

One of the guys was young, close to her age. He had been doing basic labor work, but he knew a lot about beer, and Bix had been keen to have him on the team.

When Daughtry opened the door, he saw Bix standing close to the young guy, and the two of them were laughing.

He looked up at Bix, a glint of humor in his eye. Flirtation.

Daughtry's stomach twisted.

He didn't like that. That guy was a player. He had it written all over him. And Bix was not to be played with.

Mine.

He pushed that thought to the side. That was caveman shit. She wasn't his.

Yes, he felt an attraction to her, but that wasn't anything he was going to act on. It was . . . nothing. It was just a side effect of them being a man and a woman in proximity to each other and . . .

And he wanted to punch that guy in his fucking teeth.

"I'll see you tonight then," the guy—his name was Michael; Daughtry did know that—said to Bix.

"Yeah," Bix said, her cheeks turning a shade of pink Daughtry had never seen before.

"I'll swing by and pick you up at seven."

"Okay."

Michael tipped his hat to Daughtry. "Afternoon, boss."

"Afternoon," Daughtry said, curling his lip, the word coming out more like a growl than he intended it to.

If Michael noticed, he didn't indicate it. Instead, he kept on walking out the door.

"Daughtry, is there a place in town where I can buy makeup?"

That killed the *What the hell was that?* that had been on his lips.

"I . . . don't know." He blinked. "I assume you can get some down at the general store. Maybe."

He couldn't rightly say if it would be any good, but he had no idea about that sort of thing.

"Maybe I'll just find out if I can borrow something from Rue or Arizona."

"Why?"

"Oh. Michael asked me on a date. We're going out to Smokey's tonight?"

She looked giddy. And he thought about what she had told him. She wanted to dance. She wanted to have a boyfriend that she could break up with, so that she could let him go for the greater good of her education.

Maybe she saw Michael as potentially being that boyfriend.

He didn't like it. At all.

"Bix, how well do you know him?"

"As well as I know anybody."

Well, that was bullshit. She lived with Daughtry. She knew him better than that. "I see. And what is your plan?"

She blinked. "To go on a date with him?"

"But to what end?"

Her face got pinker. "I don't know, Daughtry. I hadn't really thought it through. Maybe a kiss. Maybe sex."

"Oh. Great. Are you just going to put a tie on the door of your bedroom?"

"I don't know. What's your plan if you ever bring a woman home?"

His blood felt too hot. He didn't like it. He didn't like any of it.

She's Bix.

She's like a stray dog.

Well, that was both bullshit and insulting bullshit all rolled into one.

"I don't have to make a plan. It's my house."

"Oh. Really? You have to make a plan. Great. I guess maybe someday I'll just walk in and find you having an amorous liaison on your living room floor."

Her face had gone to scarlet.

"That won't happen, because I'm not irresponsible like that."

"Excuse me? Are you implying that I'm irresponsible? Because I'm going to a bar with a man that I—"

"You're his superior. His boss. It's inappropriate."

Bix looked at him, her blue eyes flat. She spread her hands wide. "Are you concerned that I'm taking advantage of him, Daughtry?"

"Well, you do have to be mindful about these things," he said, barely getting the words out around his gritted teeth.

"Oh. Well. Thanks for letting me know. I will be sure to be extra mindful. Is there a form I should submit to human resources? Oh wait. You don't have a human resources department, you just have a dumb fucking attitude."

"Wait a second," he said. "Why am I the bad guy just because I want to take care of you? That's what I've been doing since you got here, and you've been fine with it as long as it was in the form of food and shelter."

"I was fine with it as long as it wasn't high-handed and unreasonable. This is about my personal life. I'm allowed to have one. I'm not . . . I am not a stray dog that you took in. I'm a woman, and if I want to go on a date . . ." Her eyes filled with tears, and it made him want to retreat. Because that was just weird as hell. "Why am I not allowed to go on a date? I'm not a raccoon. I'm not a child. If he wants me, then why can't I go out with him?"

It was a good question. And there was no reason. Except that he felt absurdly possessive of her, and he had no call to it. It had nothing to do with attraction.

Ever since that dance Bix hadn't seemed fazed by him in the least. Like it had passed with the moment—and it sure as hell should have.

He just didn't like Michael. That was all.

"He just strikes me as the kind of guy who does these things casually," he said.

And that was true.

"Maybe I'm not in the market for anything but casual," she said.

"Bix, I worry about you."

"*Daughtry*, I navigated a whole scary world without you in my life for twenty-three years. Do you think men never hit on me?"

And he could see that there was definitely a wrong answer to that question. "I . . ."

"They do," she said.

Hesitation was apparently wrong.

"And here I am. Just fine. Do you not remember when you found me? I was willing to stab you. And you wouldn't be the first man that I've stabbed."

"I wouldn't?"

"No. I can take care of myself. I appreciate . . . I appreciate everything you've done for me. But now I work here. I have a job. I am earning my keep and pulling my weight and all of that. You'll get to treat me like . . . you'll get to treat me like that."

"I'm sorry . . ."

She shook her head. "Just forget it."

She stomped out of the barn, and left him standing there, feeling like a villain. Which wasn't fair because he wasn't being a villain; he was being protective.

He let out a hard breath. She was impossible. That was the problem.

And she didn't make any sense.

He stood there in the doorway, looking at the blank space where Bix had once been.

She was the problem. She didn't make any sense.

He repeated that to himself all the way back to his place, and then back to his brother's place.

"I didn't know you were intending to come for dinner tonight," said Denver, sticking his wallet in his back pocket, and grabbing his keys off the table.

"I . . . I usually do," he said.

"Not tonight. Anyway, Justice and I were going out."

"Where?"

"To Smokey's," said Denver.

Daughtry never went to Smokey's. But that was where Bix was going to be tonight. That little asshole was picking her up at seven o'clock.

"I'll go with you," said Daughtry.

Denver looked at him with deep skepticism. "Why?"

"Because I want to," he said.

"No offense, Daughtry, but I don't know that we need the police around tonight."

"Maybe I want to have a good time," said Daughtry.

"Why don't I believe that?"

"I don't know. Maybe it's because you're bound and determined to misinterpret everything that I do."

He was being dishonest. He knew it.

With everybody.

He gritted his teeth.

"Great. Come then."

"I will."

"Put on something nicer than that."

Well there. Maybe Daughtry would meet somebody tonight. Maybe he'd bring somebody home. It would be perfect. Especially if Bix went off with Michael.

Mine.

"Great. Come around the house in about ten minutes," said Daughtry.

"I will."

She wasn't his. Maybe tonight he'd find someone else, and remind himself of that good and well.

BIX WOULD HAVE felt entirely giddy if not for the interaction she had with Daughtry earlier. She was just so mad at him. She didn't understand why he had to be that way. She had been . . . blindsided by Michael asking her out. Mostly because while men definitely did hit on her, it was rare that they were cute, age appropriate and didn't seem like what they really wanted to do was plant drugs in her car.

Michael checked a lot of boxes. Handsome. Not trying to make her an unwitting mule.

Maybe they were low standards, but she was okay with that.

She would've thought that Daughtry would be . . . maybe not happy for her, but proud. Wasn't she doing something functional? Normal?

You have condoms in your bedside drawer, Sheriff.

That was what she wanted to shout at him. She would have too, if she had thought of it. It had occurred to her later, when she had been getting dressed, and had punctuated her soul with a glorious *So there*. Except, too bad she hadn't actually said it to him.

She groused to herself as she went out to the front porch to wait for Michael.

Daughtry hadn't come home.

She shouldn't care what he was doing.

She was hurt. More than she had a right to be. It was just . . . she had wanted him to be proud.

Maybe that was weird. It was definitely weird. But he was this unobtainable thing. A man who had woken up a loneliness in her. A need too. And she wasn't foolish enough to think that he could actually fill it. Or that he would want to. Now, she wasn't even dumb enough to think that Michael was going to do that. She just had wanted to go on a date. Because it was normal. And she wanted to be normal. Wasn't that okay? And wasn't that what he was encouraging her to do?

She paced a small length of the porch, and finally, Michael appeared.

She grinned, and hopped down the steps, making her way to the truck.

Her heart gave a strange dip. She was going on a date.

It was absurd. And kind of neat.

She was wearing a dress; she felt like just a normal twenty-three-year-old. At least, what she imagined a normal twenty-three-year-old might feel like—she didn't really know where she could get confirmation on whether or not her experience was normal.

She opened the passenger door and got up into the truck. "Hi," she said, overly cheerful.

"Hi yourself," he said, smiling.

This was going to be fun. She was pretty sure.

Except, as they started driving away from the house, she realized that he didn't really know anything about her, and he would probably think she was weird if he did. Were they going to talk about themselves? What sorts of things was she supposed to ask him? What were good date topics?

She didn't want him to ask where she had gone to school, or what she had studied in college. She didn't want him to start asking questions that—if she were honest—she wouldn't have very good answers for.

"How long have you been living in Pyrite Falls?" he asked.

Okay. That was a pretty innocuous question.

"About a month and a half."

"And you live with Daughtry," he said.

"Yeah," she said, wondering if he was . . . jealous. "He's kind of like an older brother."

"I see. So he's the one that brought you to work at the ranch?"

"Yes," she said, feeling slightly relieved. "He told me there was a job opening, and so here I am."

It was definitely evasive and for sure sidestepping the truth of the situation, but it was necessary. Because he could fill in the blanks with something made up for now, something that was a little bit less weird than *Daughtry found me squatting in the woods*.

And then later she would be able to remind him that she had actually never lied to him.

Good plan.

"How about you?"

And that had been the right move, because the minute she asked about him, the floodgates open. By the time they got to Smokey's she knew that he was from Redding, California, and that he had dropped out of high school. She chalked that up as a point to her, since technically she hadn't graduated either.

He had an ex-girlfriend who had broken his heart, and had decided to come to Oregon to see if things would be better.

His ex was crazy.

Him saying that made Bix flinch. But, she supposed everybody had a dim view of their ex. She didn't think that that particular phrasing, and the fact that it was volunteered without her asking, was a pink flag.

But again, this was much more about having the experience than actually believing that Michael was perfect in some way. So there.

He parked, and they got out. She looked around the parking lot, which was relatively full, and felt a sense of accomplishment. That she was doing something so normal. This was clearly where the people of Pyrite Falls hung out. And she was part of the hanging out.

She'd never been in these kinds of parking lots. Never been on the outside about to go in. She'd lived on fringes her whole life. And the truth was, even living with her dad, she'd been alone.

Even when she'd been with her dad and her brother, there had been no loyalty. No trust. No . . . love.

She'd never ached for it, because she'd been too busy aching for food. She'd been too busy aching for security and shelter and safety.

Now she was about to be part of something. Something normal.

She wanted it.

Felt full to bursting with it.

Bix from a month and a half ago would've rejected this. She would have curled in on herself and said she didn't need it. She would have hidden away and said she didn't need community or to fit in. She felt like she was learning different things about herself. But it was amazing how much more expansive her feelings were now that she wasn't simply in survival mode.

He grinned, and reached his hand out to her, taking it in his. She blinked, looking down at where their palms touched. With their fingers locked together. Not that long ago, Daughtry's hand had touched hers as he led her out to the dance floor. And it had ignited a flame in her gut that hadn't gone out.

She was hopeful, for a full thirty seconds, that this might stoke that fire. That maybe she was just starved for touch in general, and this would help her out.

That Michael would be just as good as Daughtry. And some other guy down the line would be just as good as Michael. Normal, casual dating, casual touching and kissing. For a moment, she had a brief fantasy of that life. Of something breezy, that you might see on a TV show. A single woman cycling through a series of easy dates, learning how to navigate relationship waters without ever getting hurt too badly—or at least getting her deep enough that it couldn't be solved by a pint of ice cream.

Except she didn't feel anything. Except his skin. And just like that, the fantasy vanished.

How inconvenient.

Still, she didn't pull away from him. She let him lead her into Smokey's Tavern.

He pushed the door of the old wooden building open, and they went inside. It was dim, with a surplus of neon lighted signs, a big old-fashioned jukebox in the corner. There were bright red vinyl-covered stools in front of a rough-hewn bar. It was like a nineteen fifties diner had crashed into a country outpost. And somehow, she found it . . . well, fascinating. It smelled like alcohol, and people were dressed their best.

There was a woman behind the bar with an ornate flower tattoo on her arm, her makeup strong, her dark hair teased big. She was stunning and intimidating and looked like she'd cut someone if they messed with her.

Bix loved her instantly.

There were women in the corner with big curly hair and rhinestone belts. Cute tie-front T-shirts that showed off their belly button rings and cleavage. Glittering cowgirls there to find a cowboy.

And right then, Bix felt drab. She didn't have fake eyelashes or shiny lips. She didn't have their easy confidence or easy, seductive smiles.

She glanced at Michael. He was definitely looking at the group of women.

Her eyes adjusted to the dimness of the bar, and she looked around more broadly. There were just cowgirls on the prowl. There were cowboys.

Tall, broad and handsome, some less tall, less broad. Quite a few that were less handsome. But pretty much every single man in there was a cowboy.

Either ranch hands from Four Corners, or the nearby ranches, and she had a feeling some had even come from elsewhere, since she didn't get the sense that the population of Pyrite Falls was quite this robust. But the whole area was rural, so it would make sense that this would be a gathering place for people from neighboring communities as well.

Bix had never gotten to go to college. Hell, she'd never been to a day of real school in her whole life. But she felt like she was in a sociology class right now. Studying a foreign culture that she knew nothing about.

There was flirting and talking and dancing. And she almost didn't know where to look. "I'll get you a drink," said Michael. "What do you like?"

She blinked. "Oh. A Coke."

His eyes lifted. "A Coke?"

"Yeah. We deal with beer all day," she said. "I don't need any more."

He laughed. "Suit yourself."

Bix felt the back of her neck prickle, and she turned. At the corner to her back right were the King brothers. And right in the center was Daughtry.

He was looking at her, his gaze intense.

What was he doing here?

Stupid question. *He has condoms in his bedside table.*

Yes. She knew that. Of course she did. She was, in fact, relatively obsessed with it. Was that why he was here? To hook up?

Was that . . . ?

It made her feel small. Nervous and upset. And mostly, she found herself wanting to drift over to where he was. Wanting to stake a claim. Wanting every woman in there to know that she . . . Well, she lived with him, didn't she? She knew him. Maybe.

"Awkward."

She turned at the sound of Michael's voice.

"What?"

"Boss's here. Also, like you said, he's a bit like your brother. Not the best to have your brother in residence when you're trying to have a good time."

Oh right. That lie. Like a brother.

"Let's get a table." He thrust her soda into her hands, and she followed him to the opposite corner from the Kings. She looked down into her drink. "You want to dance?"

Immediately, she flashed back to dancing with Daughtry. She'd loved dancing with him. She'd always wanted to be asked to dance, and now she was being asked two times within a month. But she didn't feel giddy over Michael asking.

She felt happy, though. That had to count for something.

"Yes," she said. "I would. Thanks for asking."

She took a big sip of her soda, as if it was a source of liquid courage, and not the benign drink she had chosen for herself.

Then she took his hand again and let him lead her to the dance floor. The dance was fast, and fun, even though she didn't know what she was doing. And she found herself letting go of her worry about attraction and flyers and anything connected to Daughtry. Because there was one thing she hadn't really even thought about. That it was fun to just go out with a friend.

She realized that she was firmly of that mindset after only ten seconds of the song. Michael could be a friend. And that would be fine. But as much as she wanted to experience dating and the normal parts of being twenty-three, she also didn't want to kiss or sleep with a guy she wasn't into. She had let herself feel grim for a moment about the fact that Daughtry had stoked something in her that Michael didn't. But every man wasn't going to be attractive to her. Every man wasn't going to make sparks go off in her stomach. It didn't mean that Daughtry was the only one.

Daughtry was, in many ways just a training ground.

He was *safe*. That was the thing.

He was the first man she had been around while feeling secure. Daughtry was probably more a casualty of circumstance than anything else.

And he's hot.

Sure. There was also that. It was a fair enough observation, and one that she couldn't deny. But again, not necessarily the only element of chemistry. There were plenty of good-looking men in the bar. And she had a pretty good instinct about people. Michael was nice, friend material. He wasn't a dick. Dancing with him was a good time.

He didn't try to put his hands anywhere he shouldn't, and she felt safe the entire time. The song tripped over to something slow, and Michael closed his hold, spinning her around so she was facing the other direction. And there was Daughtry.

Her heart slammed into her breastbone. Daughtry was dancing with one of the pretty, glittery women. She was older than Bix, obviously, her hair cherry red, and so were her lips. She was wearing so much makeup. And her boobs were spilling out of her top.

And her good, right and proper sheriff let his eyes dip, and looked straight down her top.

She felt appalled. Like she had just heard a priest swear in a church. At least, that was how she imagined she might feel if she heard a priest swear in a church. Bix herself had never even been in a church for any reason other than to collect food from one of the pantries. *He has condoms in his bedside table.*

The little voice inside her head was getting insistent and annoying.

I know that.

But knowing that and witnessing him looking at a woman's breasts were two different things.

In spite of herself, she looked down. Her dress had a fairly demure neckline, but even if it didn't, she wouldn't have cleavage. The woman that he was dancing with was like a two-scoop ice cream cone, and Bix was a child's serving. If that. It was maybe more fair to say that she was one of those little sample spoons.

She was very familiar with those. When she couldn't afford ice cream she would just go in and sample flavors as long as they would let her.

Yeah. Maybe she was just one of those.

"Bix?"

She looked up at Michael. "Huh?"

"You okay?"

"Fine. Just fine."

Thankfully the music was loud so it was almost impossible to talk, but she did her best to keep her eyes more on Michael than on Daughtry and partner.

They finished dancing, and went back to their table. Daughtry and his mysterious redhead kept on the dance floor. Michael and Bix ordered fried pickles and a basket of JoJos. They made shallow conversation about the beer, and Bix had a hard time not staring at Daughtry.

And then Daughtry took the redhead's hand and they walked out of the bar.

Bix felt like she was going to be sick.

"You okay?" Michael asked her for the second time that evening.

She tried to hold back a snarl, but she ended up sounding like a feral possum. "Why wouldn't I be?"

"Because Daughtry just left with somebody else."

She curled her fingers tightly around her glass. "Well, so what?"

"Bix," Michael said kindly, but a little bit like she was a child. "You have a crush on him."

"I do not," said Bix, but even she could hear the lack of conviction in her own voice.

"It's okay. I mean, it makes sense. And makes me feel a little better about how not into this you are."

She let out a low, hard breath. She felt like an asshole. And she also felt a little bit proud. Because she had never been on a date with anybody, and she didn't think she was what anybody could ever consider a heartbreaker. And here she had done something a little bit . . . It was terrible to be pleased she was the one in the power position. The one who was wanted, not doing the wanting.

But she was.

"I don't want to have a crush on him," she said. That was honest. "In fact," she said, "I'm not entirely convinced that's what I have. I just . . . He helped me out during a really hard time. I think I might just be grateful."

"You're stuck on him either way, does it really matter why? You could make all kinds of arguments about that. Maybe I only have a crush on you because you're the first new woman to show up at the ranch in over a year."

"That's not very flattering," Bix said, frowning.

"In fairness to me, neither is watching your date moon over another man the whole time."

She grimaced. "Sorry."

"The point is, it doesn't really matter why. If the feelings are there, they are."

"I'm sorry," she said. "I like you. I wanted to feel something."

He chuckled. "I appreciate it."

He was being surprisingly decent, especially for a man who'd said his ex was crazy.

"What . . . did your ex girlfriend do to you?" she asked.

He frowned. "Why?"

"Curious."

"She drove through the garden at my parents' house and took out all of my mom's flowers."

"What did you do to her?"

"She thought I cheated on her because I talked to the checker at the grocery store for more than ten minutes one day."

She blinked. "Did you?"

"She was sixty-five," he said.

She cleared her throat. "I mean . . . did you?"

"No."

Well, okay, she could see why he'd led with the info about his ex.

"Nothing is going to happen with me and Daughtry," she said. "Here is the thing. He's . . . Well, he's older than me, first of all. Second of all, he's a police officer. I think he feels duty bound to help me. To be nice to me and all of that. He's a caregiver. It's not like that for him."

She felt so . . . small and sad. Here was a perfectly nice guy who liked her, and yet again, her dysfunction was making this difficult. Because she had probably imprinted on Daughtry or something because he was the first person who was nice to her, and that was probably the biggest reason that she felt all these things for him.

And she couldn't take the nice, normal thing right in front of her because she was fixated.

"We can still hang out, Bix."

Damn. He was nice. He wasn't even getting creepy and being mean.

"Thanks," she said. "I . . . Thanks. At least for listening to me. When I say that I'm from difficult circumstances, I mean I don't even have any friends. I don't really know how to have them."

"I do. So . . . I can help you with that."

She was pretty sure that she sensed a little bit of relief in him all of a sudden. Like he finally got the sense that she was kind of a project, and he didn't actually want to be saddled with a huge project.

Well. Bully for her. She was able to make him feel good about her rejecting him. Not that she had actually even rejected him. He had just been able to pick up on the vibes. Which were not settled vibes, in fairness.

They stayed for a while longer, and then left. The other King brothers were still there. Daughtry wasn't.

She suddenly got tense as they got close to the house.

"What if he's *there*? With *her*."

Michael shrugged. "If there's a tie on the door or something, then I'll take you somewhere else for a bit."

"Thanks. I . . . Is that a thing? The tie on the door?"

Daughtry had said the same thing to her earlier, and she did not get the reference but she'd been too embarrassed to ask him what it meant.

He frowned. "Yeah. It's kind of a joke, but I think it definitely originates as being something serious."

She made a small sniffing sound. "I see. Just a pop-culture thing that I am not entirely up on." She got that sense of relief from him again. "I am a bigger project than you want," she continued. "Seriously. I never even went to a regular school. I don't know a lot of things. I'm trying to become a real girl."

"You're real enough, Bix," he said. Though, he did still seem a little bit relieved.

She held on to that, though.

Daughtry's truck was in the driveway and she decided, with a burst of anger, that if he was there and there was no signal, she was just going to go in.

You're real enough, Bix.

Michael had given that to her. As a friend. And she really appreciated it, because she felt a little bit bruised, and it was nice to have a friend.

"Are you sure you're fine to go in?"

"I think so. I'll wave you on unless they're boning in the living room."

He nodded. "Sounds good."

She walked up to the front door and stopped, peering around. She didn't see any clothing strewn about on the floors. No clear and obvious signs that Daughtry had a woman in there. But then, it was possible they had just taken themselves back to the bedroom. In which case, she was completely clear to walk into her own place of residence. Except of course the problem was, it didn't really feel like hers; it felt like his.

And she didn't really feel okay; she felt tragic because whatever the reason, she wanted him.

She curled her hands into fists, just for a second, then she turned and waved Michael off.

He waved back, and pulled out of the parking area. She opened the front door and slowly went inside.

She crept down the hall, listening. She heard water running. The shower.

Were *they* in the shower together?

She felt a strange, heavy sensation between her legs and a deeply upset feeling in her chest. It was the most confusing experience of her life. She felt aroused thinking about him, naked in the shower, his hands moving over wet skin.

When she thought of that other woman, it made her feel like vomiting, and that was just awful.

She stomped into the kitchen and flung the fridge open. She took out the last piece of leftover pizza from the other night and nuked it in the microwave. She had a moment where she paused just for a second to feel grateful that there were leftovers in the fridge that she had access to. That she could easily reheat in the microwave. She wasn't fishing and scaling a fish and gutting it, trying her best to preserve it until she could start a fire.

Her chest cramped painfully when she thought of that fish.

When she thought of that *girl*.

That girl who was now . . . perilously close to weeping over what? A man?

A man.

What had men ever done for her?

Well. The King men had done quite a lot for her. It was true. But in the general sense, men were so much more trouble than they were worth, and what the hell was the matter with her?

She gritted her teeth, blinked hard, fighting back angry tears.

He is nothing to me. Nothing. A friend at best.

"Bix?"

"Argh!" she screamed and turned around, and there was Daughtry standing in the doorway. Shirtless, a pair of gray sweatpants low on his hips. Barefoot.

"Should I heat some more food up for you and your friend?" If she had been a raccoon she'd have been baring her teeth.

"What?" he asked.

"Are you done with her already? Didn't realize you were a Minuteman, Daughtry."

He frowned. "What the hell is that supposed to mean?"

"You don't know what it means?" She held up her finger, pointing erect and straight at the ceiling, and then slowly let it droop.

His eyes narrowed. "The hell, Bix?"

"You left with her."

He looked confused for a second. "No, I didn't," he said. "I walked out to the parking lot at the same time she did."

Bix blinked in confusion. "You didn't . . . I mean . . . It looked like . . ."

"No," he said. "I was just ready to leave and so was she."

She felt enraged. Betrayed. Because she wasn't crazy and he'd definitely left with her, and now he was acting like she was making things up when she had been very upset and torpedoed her date that was already sucking. But she could blame him.

"You were holding her hand," she pointed out.

"We know each other," he said, with a maddening lack of real explanation.

"You know each other?" she echoed.

"Yes," he said.

"I . . . You . . ." He didn't casually hold *her* hand. Or any other woman's. And for some reason she felt doggedly determined to prove she just wasn't wrong. "You've slept with her before, haven't you?"

He frowned. "What does that have to do with . . . ?"

"You *have*," she accused.

"I haven't—" she nearly breathed a sigh of relief "—in the last year."

Of course he'd slept with her before. She thought of how he'd held that woman when they'd danced. She was right for him. Tall, confident. Closer to his age. The way he'd looked at her, and where he'd looked at her, had spoken of attraction. Certainly an attraction he didn't feel for Bix.

And why would he? He probably sees you as a rescue animal.

Her own thoughts wounded her.

"Right. So why didn't you sleep with her tonight?" she asked.

"Just because you *can* doesn't mean you always want to," he said.

She was under the impression men always wanted to. And he wasn't making any sense.

"Whatever," she said, jerking the microwave open and taking out her pizza.

"Where's Michael?"

"We're just friends," she said, picking up the pizza and taking a vicious bite. Dammit. It was too hot. The cheese stuck to the roof of her mouth, and it was like having a red-hot coal held against her flesh.

Argh.

She did her best to keep her face stoic.

"Is that a good thing or bad thing?" he asked, leaning against the kitchen doorframe.

"Fine. My decision," she said.

"Really?"

She shrugged. "Just because you can doesn't mean you want to, Daughtry."

She leaned against the counter and stuffed the rest of the pizza in her mouth, her eyes watering from the heat. She was determined to not act bothered. But she had a feeling she only seemed more bothered as a result.

Bix felt itchy.

"So she's your ex-girlfriend?" she asked, trying to make her tone casual.

"No," he said, coming into the kitchen and jerking the fridge open. Her eyes slid to his body, to the play of muscles in his biceps. The movement of his chest.

He was hot. He was so hot. And now she felt terminally distracted by it. By the glorious way his body was constructed. The way his skin played over his muscles. His pants rode so low she could see that deep-cut mark that seemed to form an arrow pointing down to . . .

She started breathing a little bit too fast. She couldn't help it. He reached into the fridge and took out a beer.

"Just a hookup then?" she pressed.

"Not really. She was somebody that I used to see sometimes."

"But not a girlfriend."

"I've never had a girlfriend," he said.

Her eyes went wide. "You what?"

"Never had one. I don't do relationships."

This was an out-of-body experience. Talking to him half-naked, in sweats while he was drinking a beer. About the kind of guy he was when it came to relationships or the lack of them.

Not in uniform. Not above reproach.

"You don't seem like that kind of guy," she said.

"I'm not the kind of guy my brothers are. I don't go out to the bar and pick up a different woman every night."

"You just have . . . arrangements."

"Yeah. I don't know why this is of interest to you, but she sells vitamins. She used to come around to the ranch every few months. We were part of her route that she was on. So she and I . . . used to see each other."

"Fuck," she said. "Used to *fuck.*"

"Yes," he said.

And she could honestly say she had never been quite so aware of what that word meant as she was right now. She threw around hard language because it was a way for her to blend in. A way that she became part of the group with her dad or her brother and all the other men. But the truth was, she was blessedly, physically innocent, and because of that she had never really had to ponder the meaning of that word.

But when she said it in connection with Daughtry, it created a distressingly graphic series of images in her mind.

"We were friends too," he said. "We *are*. As you can see, we are on good terms still."

"So then why didn't you sleep with her?"

"Why do you care?"

She was jealous. She was miserably, smally, horribly jealous.

It made her want to lash out.

So she did.

"I'm curious," she said. "Only because you seem so sexless. It's like when I found the condoms in your nightstand drawer. It was just weird."

That earned her a hard stare. He looked angry, and so sexy she had to press her knees together to manage the pulse that radiated through her. "I'm *sexless*?" he asked.

"Yep." She wished she had more pizza so she could take another bite and stop herself from talking. "Like a cardboard cutout of Captain America. Pretty but . . . you know. Cardboard."

"Okay," he said, turning and heading toward the doorway. He lifted his arm and tipped his beer bottle back, and the muscles on his back shifted. A mockery of what she had just said. And he didn't stay and argue with her. He just left her there. Marinating in her misery and arousal. Her knowledge that he had arrangements, and that she was hopelessly, miserably attracted to him. And that he was completely out of her league.

Because what did that even mean? She had never kissed a man before. She had never wanted to.

"Can't afford it," she whispered to herself.

And the truth was, she still couldn't.

CHAPTER THIRTEEN

DAUGHTRY COULDN'T PRETEND he didn't know what had happened last night, no matter how much he wanted to.

He hadn't invited Andrea back to his place because he'd been thinking about Bix.

And Bix thought he was a Captain America cardboard cutout.

Bix was a liar, though.

He knew that.

She resorted to lies when backed into corners, and relented only when she realized she couldn't wriggle around the truth.

Evil little possum.

It was just that when he had seen Bix with that guy, he hadn't been able to think about anything else. Everything he'd been trying to suppress had gone up to a boil and once his mind had been firmly fixed on that, there was no way he was going to . . .

"Lord Almighty," he growled, grateful that he had a full shift of work to get to.

Of course, then work was boring. He waited for calls, parked on the side of the road and pulled over a few idiots who were driving too fast, and then it was all over before he was ready to head back to the ranch.

The sun was still shining, even though it was getting late. And somehow, it stood in stark contrast to his mood and it annoyed him.

He decided to take a walk down to the river to do a little fishing, like he had done the day that he had found Bix. Something to get his mind off of her seemed like a pretty good idea. He ignored the fact that she seemed inextricably linked now to this location and activity. He walked through the woods, his pole slung over his shoulder. He stopped for a moment, and listened to the sounds.

Smelled the pine heavy in the air.

There were birds, calling to each other. Sunbeams shone through the pine needles, fragments of light reflecting on the forest floor. It was a strange thing, that this place, where he had been a bad man, and had done his best to become a good one, had stayed the same.

That across the river a month and a half ago had been a skinny, half-starved woman who was now enmeshed in his life in a way that he would never be able to explain. And yet it was all the same. The sky, the trees, the scent in the air.

He was the same.

No matter that the day-to-day sometimes felt different.

That was what he had to remember.

No matter how things seemed like they might be different, they were actually the same. He came through the trees to the edge of the river, and looked down a few feet from where he had emerged.

There she was, standing on a rock. Her blond hair was flowing around her shoulders, and she was wearing a short dress that came just midthigh. She had a fishing pole, and she cocked it back over her shoulder and let the bait fly out into the center of the water.

She shook her hair out, and the sunlight caught the golden locks, shining.

It hit him then. Like a ton of bricks.

It wasn't possessiveness.

That would've been too easy.

It was *jealousy*. Pure and simple.

When another man had been with her, treating her like a woman, it had been far too easy for him to tell himself that what had happened when he'd danced with her had been a trick of the firelight, but then he'd seen that man holding her . . .

He'd known it was more.

It was like every moment of seeing her from that first time collided with this one. Her brilliance. Her sharpness. The humor and the ferocity. Her climbing up on the barn. The triumph of her succeeding. Her books. Self-improvement and a romance novel.

The way she had told him about what she wanted.

He had never known anybody like her. When he thought about it, he wasn't exactly sure he knew anybody. Not as well as he knew her. They had talked about a lot of things. And he admired her.

More than that . . .

She was beautiful.

And feral as hell. And he was angry that some other guy had been dancing with her.

He didn't want Andrea, because he wanted Bix.

His stomach went tight.

No. Hell no. Bix was . . .

She was his to protect. She wasn't his to . . . to possess like that. Suddenly, it was like she sensed him standing there, and she looked in his direction.

She startled for a moment, and looked like she might run. It was a reminder. Of the way they had met. Of how she had been when he had found her.

She had pretended to be afraid. But deep down, he suspected that she was a little bit.

"Hey," he said.

He lifted his fishing pole.

"Oh hi," she said. "I guess technically I'm fishing on private land without permission."

"Are you?"

She sighed. "No. I even got a fishing license down at the general store last week." She looked distressed. "My street cred is irretrievably damaged."

He couldn't help himself. He laughed. He felt, for a moment, like he was back on even footing with her. But then she smiled, and his world felt rocked again.

He pictured her like she'd been then. With that scab on her chin. He could still see that woman, there beneath the healthier, smiling one now. But it wasn't who she was.

It never had been.

It was what life had done to her. And the person she was now, was the woman who had dug out of it.

It would be tempting to feel a certain level of triumph over that. To take credit for it.

But he and his father had been responsible for ruining more lives than intervening in this one could ever make right.

"My condolences over your inability to poach."

She snickered, then started to reel her line back in. "Thank you."

They hadn't spoken since last night. That moment when things had been charged. He knew he wasn't imagining it. He knew it, because he was standing in the bolt of lightning that had resulted from it. Cardboard-cutout Captain America.

And he had been shirtless, and in the shower thinking about her while he was naked, and even if it hadn't been a sexual fantasy, it had still been a step over a line he hadn't been aware he was so close to.

For somebody who thought it was cardboard, she had an awful lot of thoughts about his sex life.

Unfortunately, so did he, since it had been nonexistent for close to a year now.

Maybe there was some truth to what she'd said. He had become a cardboard cutout.

He had forgotten that he was a man.

Right now, she was reminding him of that.

"So how are things going with the brewing?"

"Good. Getting antsy for that next meeting. Denver is thinking that it might be good if I am present."

"Are you comfortable with that?"

"I don't know. I've never presented in front of people. I've never been treated like I was an expert in anything. Well. Except petty crime."

"Yeah." He realized that they had never talked about that with any real seriousness.

"You know I read your record."

"Yeah. I do."

"Mostly taking food and first-aid items."

"Yeah," she said, casting her rod again. "Listen, I like to pretend that I'm a hardened criminal, but mostly I was just sad and desperate. With some distance from it, I feel like I can admit that." She looked down.

It was still hard for her to come to terms with. That was for sure.

"Why do you need to be hard?"

"Because it's the only thing that helps you survive. When everything is hard, what's the point of being sad about it?"

"I can relate to that," he said, setting his pole down so that he could bait his hook. "When Denver bought the ranch out from my dad, he was really clear with all of us that our dad was toxic and needed to be out of our lives. I knew that. I knew that I didn't like who I was when I was with him. But I didn't know what to do about it. I still cared about him. And I was angry that Denver sent him away, even though I knew it was the right thing to do. That was when I decided to go to police academy."

"I don't get how those two things are connected," she said.

"Because I didn't trust myself to not just become my dad if I didn't have a very rigid framework to live my life in. And that's all I've done. Ever since then. You asked me what my dreams were, and I guess it's just to do more good than harm. But I don't trust my-self to do it outside of . . . the system."

She chuckled. "Well. In that way we are very different."

"Yes. We are."

He sidled up to where she was, keeping a healthy amount of space between them so that when he cast he wouldn't hit her with his hook.

They stood there, bathing in the last little bit of sun, their lines in the water.

"I'm going to catch the fish before they make their way downstream to you," she said.

"I can handle that."

"I don't want your charity fish, Daughtry."

"Too bad."

"Is that why you took me in? Atonement?"

He firmed his jaw, trying to figure out how to answer the question. Because there was honesty, and he had a feeling it would hurt her feelings. And also, the honest answer was complex, and he didn't know if he could give it without exposing pieces of himself that he would rather keep private.

"Maybe. A little bit at first. But primarily, all I could think was . . . if my dad found you on our land, he wouldn't have helped you. And sometimes, when I don't know which way is north, I can find south by figuring out what my father would have done, and do the opposite of that."

"I want to do that," she said. "I want to . . . change the way that I see things. I want to do more than just survive."

There was something about her words that echoed inside of him. He felt drawn to her. There was something in her, and it was more than just beauty. It was the spirit that she had. That fight that she carried with her. For no real reason. Because everything in her life had been difficult. He had his siblings. He had this ranch.

She was right. He had a brick. Hell, he had more than one. Sure, there were some things that were difficult, but it was nothing compared to what she had been through.

"How much time have you actually spent in jail?"

She scrunched up her face. "The longest time was three weeks. Quite a few overnight stays. Mostly in the drunk tank. I wasn't drunk. Just holding on to me until they decided whether or not to let me go. But I've had a couple of six-week sentences that ultimately got reduced."

"The threat of prison never deterred you from doing anything?"

"No," she said casually. "I really wouldn't have been stealing things if it didn't feel necessary. So the threat of prison always felt like a more abstract worry than not having what I needed in the moment. And you have no idea how many times I got away with it versus how many times I got caught." She cleared her throat. He could have sworn he saw tears shining in her eyes. "The worst thing that I ever did was there was this old woman, and she had twenty dollars sticking out of her purse. I walked slowly by her shopping cart, and I snagged the twenty dollars." She cleared her throat again. "About ten minutes later the old woman caught up to me, and she handed me another twenty-dollar bill. She said if I needed the first one that bad I probably needed a second one too." She tried to laugh, but it sounded forced. "I told you, I've heard basically

every version of the good news out there. That was the
only version of it that felt all that compelling to me.
There was no reason for her to be that kind to me. That
was about six months before you found me. It was
right before my dad and my brother went to prison. I
kept the forty dollars for myself. I didn't share it with
them. The way that woman treated me made me want
to be different. But then they went to jail, and I was
left by myself, and I didn't feel like I had the choice.
But every time I would get tempted to steal something,
anywhere, I remembered her kindness. And I just . . .
I would rather be her than my dad. But I've never gotten to a place where I felt like I could be." She took
a shuddering breath. "Scarcity makes you so mean.
Even when you wish you could be kind."

"It's not just scarcity for some people. My dad never
had that excuse. He was just mean. You know how you
can tell you're not that person?"

"How?"

"Look how different you are now that you don't
have to worry about where your next meal is coming
from."

She said nothing for a while. "Do you think that
you're different?"

He grunted. "The problem with me is that it was
never about desperation. It was about trying to please
the wrong person. It was about having an entirely
wrongheaded view of the world."

She shrugged. "Many people would say that I have
a wrongheaded view of the world, Daughtry. Anti-
paperwork as I am."

"Listen, I don't agree with you, not on everything. But when you talk about the way that life has worked for you, and why, I can definitely understand why you don't like how certain things function. I can certainly appreciate how difficult it is for you to try to earn money when you don't have it."

"Well. Listen. I might feel justified in brewing moonshine still. Even if I know I can't justify stealing money out of old ladies' purses."

"Fair."

The breeze flared up, and her dress tightened around her hips, coming up on her thighs. She was a lot more shapely now that she had regular meals. It looked good on her. Everything about her looked good.

He practically wanted to get in a fistfight with himself.

He didn't know how to reconcile his desire to protect her, his admiration for her, with the attraction that now had him in a choke hold.

And he realized that all of his hesitance when it came to her was about trying to minimize her.

Trying to make her less than a woman. Trying to treat her like she was a charity case, always and forever. Because if he had met her in a bar and he had thought she was this beautiful, he would want to do something about it.

Well. There was that. There was also the fact that she lived on the ranch.

And when he had told her he didn't do relationships, he had meant it.

And whatever decision he made, it could be about his own issues. But it wasn't fair to make it about her. She was strong. And if she knew . . .

Well, if she knew that he was checking her out she might reiterate that she thought of him as cardboard.

But if he told her that the only reason he wasn't making a move on her was because he was afraid that she couldn't handle it, she would probably pull a switchblade on him.

"So if you give the speech at the town hall, what are you going to say?"

"You should invest in this beer because you'll be an idiot if you don't?"

"Listen, I think it's excellent," he said. "But maybe if you don't call everybody idiots . . ."

"I was under the impression that was how Denver handled things."

"We try not to encourage it."

"Are you and Denver still in a fight?" she asked.

"No. We had a disagreement. But that doesn't mean we're in a fight."

"My brother doesn't love me." She looked at him and wrinkled her nose. "I'm sorry. This is just kind of a whole list of all the things about me that are sad. My brother, Chip—"

"Chip and Bix?"

"You'd think they charged by the syllable for baby names, I know." Bix rolled her eyes. "He is honestly the biggest asshole. And I think he always resented me. And was angry that my dad took me in. We have different moms. And he's thirteen years older than me. One time we went into the woods to check on one of my dad's stills, and he left me there. And I mean, he didn't leave me by the still, he tried to get me good and lost so I couldn't find my way back."

"What?"

"Yeah. That was the first time I really knew . . . that I was on my own." She shook her head. "But the thing is, I never have been. Not really. Because sometimes there are old ladies who give you the extra twenty dollars out of their purse. And then sometimes there are policeman cowboys who find you in the middle of the woods and give you a whole new life." She looked up at him, her blue eyes dewy. "I'm never going to be able to pay you back."

And that right there was the reason. It wasn't underestimating her; it wasn't not giving her credit. It was that as long as she felt like she owed him, he could never make a move on her. Because he would never, ever treat her like that. He would never be one of those men who acted like a woman's body was a collection against a debt. Even if it wouldn't be that for him, if she felt even slightly coerced he . . .

He could never do that.

"I don't need you to pay me back."

"And I come back to *why*."

"Atonement. Is that the answer that you need?"

She looked hurt. She turned and looked at the river, and then her fishing pole jerked. She pulled back on it sharply. "Fish on," she said. And she spent the next couple of minutes reeling in the fish. Not long after he caught one of his own, and when they had five on a string, they walked back to the house together.

He had hurt her feelings. And he didn't have answers to much of anything. So that had been a productive trip.

At least there was fish.

BIX WAS EFFICIENTLY cleaning fish at Daughtry's kitchen sink while he warmed up the pan, and she was trying to process why she was irritated with the conversation they just had.

Why she felt prickly.

It had felt, for a minute, like they were getting closer, and she had valued that. Especially after what happened last night. She had been mean. Which was completely ridiculous and uncalled-for when he was being so nice.

But then . . .

Atonement.

Why was she even mad about that? She had always known that was why he was doing it. He had *tortured do-gooder* written all over him.

"Fish," he said.

"Here you go," she said, giving him the cleaned trout.

He fried them up in the pan with butter, and they ate them with rice and salad. He had a beer. She had a Coke.

"I'm sorry about what I said last night," she said. She was trying to decide if she was being nice or provocative. She wasn't really sure which.

Because sometimes it was hard for her to say exactly what she was doing. She just wasn't experienced enough with people. With friendship. With men.

And he was all of those things. He was people, in the general sense.

He was a friend, kind of.

And he was definitely a man. A man that she was attracted to.

"Which thing?"

"Well. I feel that it was unladylike of me to bring up that I saw the condoms in your bedside drawer. I also feel like it was a bit churlish of me to say that I thought you were sexless."

She looked down at her food and tried to keep her expression mild, while he made a choking sound. "Did a trout bone get caught in your throat?" she asked.

"I think you know it didn't," he rasped.

"I don't know," she said, pushing her food around her plate. "I was maybe a little bit jealous."

Why are you saying these things, Bix?

His expression looked cool, unreadable. "Don't be," he said.

"Why not?"

"Did you hear what I said about not doing relationships?"

"Haven't you heard anything I've said about me not planning too far ahead for the future?"

"Bix . . ."

"I'm not innocent," she said. "I have had a really hard life. And you are not part of the hard."

He looked at her for a good thirty seconds. "I don't want to be," he said. "I never want to be a part of the hard things that have happened to you."

"You couldn't be."

"Bix, one time, my dad took a man's whole ranch as collateral. It was all legal, all the paperwork. I watched that man come apart when my dad came to collect. Elias King unraveled the men in his debt, and he enjoyed it. And I didn't feel sorry for him. I felt like my dad was amazing at his job. At what he had set out to do. I thought my dad was a hero. That's how wrong I can be. That's how much bad I can be in somebody's life."

"Okay, but counterpoint," she said. "You can't know what you don't know. And you can't unknow what you know now."

"What does that mean?"

"Well, I didn't know how to get a bank account. And maybe half of the reason I was so angry about some of the things in the system was I didn't know how to use them. Now I know how to use a high-yield savings account. I can collect interest on my money. That's just making money doing nothing. I didn't know that. I can't be angry at myself for not knowing that. But also, I know it now. So I'm never going to view banks quite the same as I used to." She picked at a piece of rice in stuck in her teeth. "Still pretty skeptical about fishing licenses."

She looked at him eagerly, trying to gauge his response to that. She didn't know if she should be embarrassed that she made it kind of obvious that

she was attracted to him. Because she had never told
a man she was attracted to him before. Because she
had never been attracted to a man before Daughtry.
And suddenly, she was seized with a very desperate
need to act on that attraction.

To feel something normal.

That's what it was. Daughtry had given her this
beautiful, normal life. And she wanted the other things
that came with that.

And somehow, she had a feeling that it was contin-
gent upon him understanding what she was trying to
get him to understand.

"That's if you think it's about knowledge. And not
about an innate lack of empathy," he said.

"You think that it's excusable that I didn't have
empathy because of my situation. But I'm not sure if
yours was as much different from mine as you think
it is."

"It is, though. I always had food. I always had
shelter."

"Your dad controlled it all, though. And I imagine
that he made it really clear that your position in the
household was based on how happy he was with you.
Right?" Daughtry looked uncomfortable then. "What?
I can't be the only one in the hot seat all the time. You
know so much about me because of how it was when
you found me. But I don't know that much about you."

"You know as much as anybody."

"The way that your family has rallied around each
other is honestly one of the coolest things I've ever
seen. And one thing that kept me at the ranch, even

before the beer brewing, was all of you. But I can tell that you didn't grow up in a happy house."

"Gee, what gives you that idea?"

"I have a nose for dysfunction," she said, tapping said feature. "Considering it's my natural state."

"I'm not looking for absolution."

"Because atonement is different somehow?"

He nodded once. "Yes. In my mind, atonement requires an action. Absolution is just given to you. I don't have any interest in that."

She nodded slowly. "So you are also not interested in the good news." When he didn't say anything, she sighed heavily. "You don't need to protect me."

"But I want to."

She pushed against that. "I really don't need you to protect me. Because the thing is, no matter how well this goes, no matter how long I stay here, it's just a pitstop in my life, Daughtry. I don't need you to go projecting permanence onto me."

She suddenly felt like it was really important that she say that.

"I will always have to take care of myself. But the beautiful thing about this is I can't unknow all the things that I've learned here. I will never go back to being what I was. Because I know too much. And that is the real beginning of something new. Because you gave me enough space to have hope. But you've given me enough space for other things too. I don't need you to protect me, because the truth is, I'm going to have to go back to taking care of myself. To protecting myself. So as grateful as I am for the rest but, I can't . . . I can't be sheltered by you. Not completely. So whatever your reasoning for things, whatever you're thinking, just don't."

She looked down at her plate again, then back up at him. "I'm sorry. I am half-feral. Not *completely*, not anymore. But I just . . . Sometimes I feel normal. And sometimes I feel like I finally get to want things the way that normal people do. And then I remember I'm still somewhere in the middle of all that. Because at the end of the day, I don't have family. I think that's why I admire yours so much."

She pushed back from the table. "I'll leave you to finish your dinner."

"You never told me what you were going to say in your speech," he said.

Sidestepping the whole thing. Sidestepping her attraction, sidestepping everything else.

"I was going to say that over the course of the last two months this has really started to feel like home. And I've never had one of those before. I'm honored to contribute something to this ranch. To leave a piece of myself. For whenever I do leave. And I hope that everyone will join in. That I can make a beer that honors every corner of this place. All four of them."

Then she walked down the hall and went to her room. She sat on the edge of her bed, and she leaned over and took her copy of *The Wolf and the Dove* out of her bag. "You could chain me to the bed," she whispered.

She didn't know what she wanted. Not really. She had no idea how to process this deep desire to be closer to him. This intense attraction to him. Because it was just so completely different than anything she had ever experienced before. She knew what it was.

She had read about it.

But why didn't he want her?

The only real answer was because it wasn't just that he wanted to protect her, it wasn't just that he wanted atonement, but it was that he still saw her as being less. An object of pity.

"Well, I'm not pitiable," she said out loud.

She wasn't. She had a job now. She had some dreams.

And she was going to leave. Once she got the beer formula down, once they got the whole thing set and ready to go, she was going to go get herself an apartment, and she was going to go to school. She was going to take her experience and she was going to get a job at a brewery. She had to remember that she wasn't staying here.

It wasn't her place. It wasn't her life. She couldn't be dependent on him forever. She had to find her own path.

It was a good reminder, that conversation she had with him in the kitchen.

She had tried. She had voiced her attraction, and it hadn't gone anywhere.

And you couldn't unknow things. Now she couldn't unknow how uninterested Daughtry was. So she was going to have to scrape up that pride that she had left and try to move forward.

CHAPTER FOURTEEN

IT WAS THE day before the town hall meeting and Bix had worked tirelessly to get everything ready. They had sample bottles packed and ready to go, and she had her suggested recipes and mock-up labels for the other ranches. Profit projections and every other thing she could think of.

She stood back in the old outbuilding and surveyed all the progress that had been made and felt a sense of accomplishment so deep and true it nearly knocked her over.

Denver had trusted her to do it herself, more or less. She'd never been in such an important position. When she'd made moonshine for herself, she supposed she'd been in charge of everything, but it wasn't like this.

There were so many people depending on her. And knowing that what she did mattered—not just for herself, but for others—was revelatory in some ways.

Bix had never felt indispensable.

Bix had never even felt much more than expendable.

But in this venture she'd been made into an integral part of it all and it was like she mattered. Like it was good she was here, and not just a favor to her. That was how she'd felt when she'd been doing construction work, because she knew there were other people on the ranch who could do the things she did.

But this was something she knew.

They could have found someone else, but not as easily. She'd always struggled with certain parts of her favorite self-help book. She liked the ideas in it; she always had. But it suggested that to be effective you had to think ahead to an end goal, and she was always so busy playing catch-up that she could never get to that place.

Then there was that word. Synergy. Which she'd really never understood. The way you could work with people around you and make something bigger and better than you could alone. That had never been her experience.

But she'd felt that here. With the team she was brewing with, with the King family.

Not as much with Daughtry, who so resolutely had his own life.

But there was something she got from him too. A weird sort of stability. If she got charged up during the day, her mind spinning with everything that came next—because that was the thing about being able to think ahead; now she did it obsessively and anxiously sometimes—he was the calm presence at the end of the day that closed all that down.

He brought her to the moment.

He made her feel calm.

The way he made her feel was scary sometimes. He was a rock. Firm and steady. But he was also more.

There was something electric and sharp she could feel radiating from under his skin sometimes, and she knew he didn't want her to feel it. Didn't want her to see it.

The truth was, she was really beginning to want him.

More than a crush.

Which she didn't like or trust. Because where the hell could that possibly lead? Nowhere. And also apart from a few weird clashes—which had felt more electric than others, like that charge inside him had escaped—he didn't seem like he was . . . hopelessly, desperately admiring her physical beauty in the way she admired his.

The truth was, she still couldn't get the image out of her head of herself standing in the mirror looking like an escaped prisoner. Skinny and tragic and injured.

She had been a prisoner, she supposed.

A prisoner of her own inability to imagine a life, a future, that was different and more than the one she'd have if she stayed on the same path.

But she still felt tied to that girl. The one in the mirror. The one with the scab on her chin and the pitifully sunken-in stomach. The one whose body had been like a bag of sticks. A body that was built just for dragging her on through life, not enjoying things.

She didn't let herself anticipate the taste of food in case she wasn't going to get it.

She didn't let herself have favorite foods because who knew when she would be able to have them.

She didn't let herself feel lonely because there was no guarantee there would ever be a person that she could trust, a person who would care for her, a person that she would care for in return.

And she definitely didn't let herself feel desire.

Well. Apart from reading fiction. And there was a reason she was very spare on letting herself pick up any romance novels, because they did open up an ache inside of her that felt unbearable sometimes.

Because at the core of the ones that she had read was always this idea that love was inevitable. No matter how hard the situation you were in, no matter how seemingly unlovable you might be, in the end, it would be there for you.

And nothing in her life had ever demonstrated that to her. Nothing in her life had ever given her any indication that could be the case.

So she could only read them when she wasn't tempted to trust them. When it was a nice thing to let herself hurt, because some days it was.

She didn't trust herself to touch that book now. Not with Daughtry so close. Not with that keen need much more focused than it ever had been.

Because now it was personal. Now she understood what it was to want somebody.

Now that she didn't have to ignore the feelings in her body—because when all you had was hunger, discomfort and bruises, why would you ever focus on what you felt?—she knew that she wanted him.

And that was the other place that romance novels had helped her and hurt her. Because she had read how it could be. Because even though she had never done it, she could feel, really feel what it would be like to be held tightly by strong hands, to have a firm masculine mouth on her skin, to get lost in the sensation of being held.

She'd had a taste of it when they'd danced. The promise of all that pleasure in his touch.

Stardust.

That extra thing.

She'd only ever had survival. She had never had extra. The ability to just feel something good. To indulge in it simply because it was there and she wanted it . . . That had never been available to her.

Now she wondered if this was the sort of crossroads normal people stood at all the time. And if like her, they were a little bit afraid that it was a path to ruin.

Because at some point, her father had stood there with temptation in front of him. A life stretching out before him that had been unbearable to him in some way. Whether it was because of poverty or a lack of control, and he had decided to step over a line. He had decided to discard the rules of the system because they didn't serve him, and create a system of his own. To gain power. To gain more money. What was that if not self-indulgence?

She had been caught in the middle of it, unable to make a choice. For her, it had never been self-indulgence, but survival.

In this, she had a feeling, was in some ways her own version of that.

Except it wasn't breaking the law.

So what did you do when things were great like this, and you were trying to see the end result—that all-important tip for being a highly effective person, which she was doing well at when it came to business—but you couldn't see where all this might go?

What did you do then?

She could see why Daughtry liked certainty. Why he took comfort in being a police officer.

Suddenly, she felt a kick of something in her breast. A burning, bright conviction.

She wasn't Daughtry. She wasn't her dad.

She was Bix, and she always had been.

She had carried herself this far. And no, it hadn't been without help. But maybe she had to stop giving every achievement away.

The Kings were wonderful. Daughtry in particular had given her something spectacular. But she hadn't wasted it.

Suddenly she felt . . . filled with energy. Filled with joy. Because when standing at a crossroads, when being given the chance to do better, she had taken it. And whatever her feelings for Daughtry meant, the real crossroads had been back there when she'd had to make the decision to stay or go. To actually work, rather than continue to hustle in the margins of the law.

She had made good choices. Choices that had brought her here.

Because that was the real gift. The real gift of being in a place that was beyond survival, was being in a place with choices.

And when presented with choices, she had made some pretty good ones.

"Good job, Bix," she whispered to herself as she looked around the room. "Good job."

WHEN BIX HADN'T come home, he felt compelled to go looking for her. Not for the first time, he wondered if he should get her a cell phone so she would be easy to track down. But he had a feeling she would lecture him on tracking devices, and the dangers of hooking herself up to satellites.

Because that was Bix. And he enjoyed that about her as much as he found it annoying. He heard her voice before he opened the door to the outbuilding where they did the brewing, and he had expected to see her there with someone. In fact, he expected to see her there with Michael, and he knew a moment of extreme irritation.

But he wasn't there.

It was her. Standing in the dark, illuminated only by shafts of moonlight that came through gaps in the wooden planks.

"Bix?"

She whirled around. He expected her to say something threatening. Tell him that she could've taken his eyeball out before she realized it was him. But she didn't. Instead, she smiled.

"Daughtry."

"I got worried when you didn't come home."

"Worried? I haven't had a home for any number of years. It's funny that you should be worried I didn't come in right on time."

"Well," he said. "I was."

"I appreciate that. I don't think anybody's ever worried about me before."

There was something about her tonight, something joyous, but with that kinetic, untamed energy that always radiated from her. She was glorious. A little bit wild.

Beautiful.

"I was just out here feeling very proud of myself. All of these things . . . I made them. I made this beer, and we actually get to sell it. With a license and everything. It's like being a pedigreed dog instead of a stray. I never thought . . . I really never thought that I would ever get to do anything like this. I really never thought that I was going to . . ." She frowned. "I never thought about the future before. Not really. And you have to, if you want to be a highly effective person. You have to look at the end in the beginning. You have to think about your goals."

"Is that from one of your books?"

"Yes. I used to read those books, and I used to get angry, because I wanted to do the things in them, but I didn't know how. I didn't have the tools. You know, I didn't have a brick." She let out a breath. "But I get it now. And not only that, I'm just really proud of myself. I did it. I made this."

And then she did something unexpected. She twirled in a circle, her arms stretched out wide, her blond hair swirling around her.

And he could only stare. At her joy. At her enthusiasm. It echoed inside of him. In a place where he'd once felt things that big. That deep.

He had always focused on the ways that he recognized himself in Bix.

And this . . . It was an old thing. But it wasn't anything he carried with him anymore.

It felt dangerous. To even stand this close to it.

"I think we need to try the product."

"I didn't think you did that," he said.

"Normally I don't. Because in my life, alcohol has been associated with either greed or a need to forget. But that's not what this is. I don't need to forget anything. And this isn't about greed. It's about making something people actually like. It's about building something new in the ranch. And I will always have been a part of it." She glowed with that. Her eyes luminous. "Even when I'm not here anymore, I will always have been a part of this. It's not just . . . a still in the woods that I'll have to tear down and pretend it never happened. Do you know how much of my life I've spent doing that? Erasing any evidence that I was ever there? But that's not what I'm doing now. I just . . ."

She took two beer bottles out of one of the crates sitting at her feet. But then rather than handing him one, she scampered to a ladder that extended down from the ceiling. And with the two bottles in one hand, she began to scurry up the rungs.

"Hey," he said. "I didn't say that I was going to . . ." He looked up after her as she disappeared, past the loft, and then up through an opening that led out of the ceiling. "Are you kidding me?"

But his stomach tightened as he went to the ladder, and began to chase after her.

And there she was, up on the roof, beneath the star-light, beneath the moon.

Her hair was all silvery in that light, and her smile was radiant. Then she extended her hand toward him, holding out the bottle. And he crossed the space and took it, then sat down beside her.

She fished a bottle opener out of her pocket, opened her own, then opened his. He let her do it, because it was her beer.

She tilted it back, and he watched her profile as she took a long sip of the beer. It reminded him of some-thing. And yet, it was entirely new also. It was an echo of what it had been like to be younger.

"I think this is freedom," she said, resting back on her elbows. "Can you feel it? Can you taste it?" She lifted up the beer bottle and took another sip.

"Is it that good?"

"No," she said. "I really don't like beer that much. But that isn't the point. I feel like I . . . I did it. I did it, Daughtry. I'm not pathetic anymore. I'm not mak-ing decisions just to survive anymore. I am something more. I am expansive." She grinned. "I am large. I con-tain multitudes."

"Are you quoting poetry?"

She nodded. "Yes."

"How did you come to know all that poetry? Your different references to things. Free libraries?"

"Yes," she said. "My father was never going to edu-cate me in any way past what he saw fit. He was never a reader. He didn't understand all the things that were contained in books. He didn't understand that I could find secrets to all the world, to myself, on white pages with black text. To him, that was all boring. To me, the secrets of the universe. But it's only now that I feel like I finally know what to do with them. It's only now that I feel free. Hunger, scarcity, fear. Those are chains."

She took another sip of the beer, then set it beside her. And she stood, there on the roof.

"Hey," he said. "Be careful."

"Daughtry," she said. "You're always so concerned."

Her words twisted around his throat, echoed inside of him. Because it was true. He was always so concerned. Always. Because he had to be.

And right now the thing he admired most about her was the thing he feared the most in himself. This need to be free. This wild thing within her. He was a police officer, because he knew it was the only way to be sure that he kept an accounting of right and wrong. Because he lived his life in black-and-white, and Bix was shades of color. All the rainbow in between. Not gray, everything golden and bright and glittering.

He had been mistaken. Thinking she was growing more and more civilized.

She was growing more and more into herself. The woman he had met had only been a sliver of the Bix that she became. And even all the stages after, there had been fear. Uncertainty. Insecurity. But this woman right here, this was *her*.

Certain and sure in a way he wasn't entirely certain he'd ever been of himself.

But then, when Bix made mistakes, she didn't hurt people.

When she tasted freedom, it wasn't a sick, twisted joy in power.

And as for himself, he simply couldn't trust it.

Then Bix scampered up to the ridgeline, and grabbed hold of a low-hanging tree branch.

"Bix . . ."

"I'm reaching for the stars, Sheriff," she said, grinning at him, and then she hefted herself up into the trees, and disappeared.

"Dammit, Bix," he muttered as he set his own beer down and went to the tree. Went up after her. Compelled to do so, even as there was something in him that demanded he not do it. That demanded he get back down immediately.

Instead, he followed her little ass right up the tree. He looked up, and saw her a few branches above. She peered down at him. "Well, look at you, Sheriff."

"Look at you, you feral little beast."

She smiled. "Born and bred. And . . . proud. Of where I've managed to get myself to."

His heart hit the front of his breastbone. He liked hearing that. That she acknowledged her own achievements here. Her own triumph. That she truly understood that she herself was great. That she wasn't just saying she owed him. There was something different about her tonight, and it was stunning.

She was proud of herself.

Bix would always be whiskey in the shape of a woman, poured out and lit on fire. A shot of something far too strong for just anybody to handle.

She would always be this.

And he would only ever bring her down to earth. He didn't want that for her.

More than that, he knew he couldn't spend too much time up here with her.

He knew himself.

And what he didn't know, what he had never known, was when you crossed the line so far that you could no longer look at the face of a terrified little girl and feel guilt.

He had been his father's muscle.

He had thought that they were smarter than everybody else. That they were better. That they inherently deserved the money that they had because they had outsmarted the idiots who had agreed to do business with them. The arrogance that came from something like that was astonishing. If you had too much confidence in your own moral compass, it could be pointing due south, and you wouldn't even know anymore.

Wouldn't know that you'd lost north so many miles ago that you were off course so damned far you were about to walk into the sea.

The water would be up over your head before you ever realized it. Before you ever admitted that you had taken a wrong turn.

Bix had a compass inside her that worked just fine.

He admired it.

She had said something about him. That he was innately better than her or something because he hadn't followed in his father's footsteps the way that she had.

But Bix had only done what she'd done because of her own fear. Her own insecurity.

What he had done had been about power.

Those were poles apart. North and south.

Bix had been following her true north. She had just needed to keep herself going. To keep herself alive.

And so she had moments where she dipped and weaved off course just a little bit. East or west. But never completely contrary to what was right.

There were justifications. There were reasons.

The King family had never been on the verge of being down-and-out. The King family had no such excuse. And neither did he.

He and Denver had handled coming to terms with their part in their father's games in different ways.

But it amounted to the same thing.

They kept themselves on short leashes.

They kept themselves focused on what was right in front of them.

And even if Bix was right in front of him now, he knew she wasn't anything he could reach out and grab. Not for keeps.

Freedom. That's what she'd said.

He never wanted freedom. He had to keep himself in chains. But he didn't want to spoil her moment by talking about any of his nonsense.

"I never dreamed. Not really," she said. "It was too hard. And then, right at first when I was here I just felt like I was never going to be able to leave who I was behind. But I don't have to, do I? Because who I am got me here. She was scrappy. And she was strong. I think I can be grateful to her."

"You should," he said. "Because you're right about that. That's what got me. From moment one, Bix. You have to know that. I didn't look at you and see somebody different than you could be. I didn't look at you and see only potential. I looked at you and saw somebody strong, right then. I looked at you, and I knew they were something. Special. Strong. Spirited. I admire the way that you lied to me, right to my face."

She laughed. "I still do that. I lie first, don't I? Captain America."

His stomach went tight. He climbed up another couple branches, bringing him to eye level with Bix, his elbows rested across a branch about three feet away from hers. They had a healthy amount of space between them, but still, he felt drawn to her. Like there was a magnet between them.

"Sometimes a lie isn't such a bad thing," he said.

"When?"

"When it's constructed to protect something."

Wasn't that his whole life? His uniform. It was a lie. In many ways, she hadn't been wrong about the Captain America thing. He put on a costume every day, trying to make himself into a superhero. But whether or not it was true, he couldn't say. He wanted it to be. But it was the gaps, the unknowns that got him. His inability to be entirely certain when his father had simply embraced that villainous part of himself. When he had gone completely off the deep end into something that you couldn't come back from.

Bix would never be that.

She might not have a brick, or at least, she didn't think so. But she had a compass in her soul. And it didn't take a genius to see that. At least, not in his estimation.

"Right," she said softly. "To protect a little pocket of happiness, I suppose. Because if you change things, who knows what will happen?"

Maybe she did mean them. He wanted to change it. He wanted to wreck it. Destroy it. To kiss her until neither of them could breathe.

Because she wasn't untouchable. She wasn't a fey, golden creature. She was a woman. Wholly and completely. And she held an indomitable spirit that sparked something in him he had forgotten ever existed.

Something he had forgotten about on purpose.

But with her, it was easy to tell himself that maybe he didn't need that anymore.

That leash.

Short and sharp, keeping him contained.

So he would just turn Bix into his compass? That wasn't fair.

She had already been dragged down by too many terrible men.

"Yeah," he said.

"You know, you could set me up in another house."

"I could," he said.

"You like having me around." It wasn't a question. It wasn't even an accusation, just more of an observation.

"I do," he said.

She was the only new, lovely thing he'd had in his life for a very long time.

She had become the focus of everything. Over the last two months, there was very little in his life that didn't orient around Bix.

He was obsessed with her. That was the truth of it. He couldn't pretend it wasn't, not anymore. He had tried.

He had tried to keep the truth of his feelings for her held at bay. And now they were here, laid bare in front of him. He wasn't sure that he liked it. Hell, he knew he didn't.

Because it would be a mistake. He didn't make mistakes anymore. But the truth was, he hadn't wanted to make one in a long damned time. He hadn't felt anything for a long damned time. Everything had been dampened down. Everything had been muted. Not with her.

That riot of color shone through.

It colored all that black-and-white in brilliant, glorious prisms. And it made it hard to tell what was right and what was wrong.

He couldn't afford that.

But he wanted her close.

Because being near her, being near her like this, it reminded him . . .

The truth was, he hadn't been truly happy in years. He hadn't been truly angry. Truly sad. Not really much of anything.

But he had been righteous. And didn't that count for something?

Being near her was like being close to happiness. It reminded him of all the things that could be.

Of the capacity he had to feel.

But he had made the decision to stop feeling very intentionally.

That she was a temptation was ample evidence that he needed to stay the hell away.

"I spent all my life being untethered. And in many ways, it kept me from freedom. But I don't know that that's any different than anyone else. I mean, we are all essentially what our parents want us to be. At least right at first, right?"

"I suppose that's true," he said.

"And then we grow up, and we have to decide what we are going to be. And some people get to start out with . . . you know. All those bricks. And some of the bricks are very fancy. And they help you build something really nice really fast. But at the end of the day, we all have to decide who we want to be. I feel like I finally get to decide that."

"Good," he said.

"I think I want to go to college," she said. "You asked me that. A while ago. If I ever thought about going to school. And I asked you if you had ever thought about going to the moon. It doesn't feel like it's on the moon anymore. Thank you. Because yeah, I give myself a lot of credit for this. But I owe you too. In a good way. Not a bad way. Not in the way that I think my dad or your dad would look at owing somebody."

She didn't know. Not really. That he had looked at it that way at one time too. And maybe that's why he was so resistant to it now. Why it made him feel wary of the growing connection between them.

"Is there a good way to owe somebody? In my experience a debt is only bad."

"Gratitude, then," she said. "I guess I don't have very much experience with that sort of thing. Not any more than you do. I don't think. Or maybe I just like you, Sheriff. And I'm free to do that. And that feels pretty magical all by itself."

He wanted to touch her. In that moment, looking at her felt like moonlight had burned through a gap in his own chest, and shone a light down on his soul. Right now, in the dark, with stars above them, it almost felt possible.

Almost.

Except he thought about what she had said. Looking at the end, right at the beginning. And the truth was, there could only ever be an end. And if he hurt Bix, he would hate himself for the rest of his life. He wasn't his number-one fan as it was. But . . .

If he hurt her . . .

Well, there would be no point to much of anything.

"When you leave, promise me you'll go to college," he said.

"I will."

"Promise me you'll go on a lot of dates. Go to parties. Dances. Get a library card."

She laughed, but it was trembling. "Sheriff . . ."

"I mean it. Check out every book you want."

"What if I don't want to kiss a lot of guys?" she asked him, her expression going serious.

She didn't have to ask the rest of the question.

"You don't have to, but you could. I think that's more the point. You can do whatever you want. Hold on to this. Feeling free. Trust herself."

"Okay, thanks. I will."

They sat there, up in the tree, in silence. He looked at her, his body on fire. But it was more than that.

She set him on fire in a very specific way. An all-encompassing way. It didn't just make him want to kiss her. It didn't just make him want to touch her. He wanted to be like her.

"We should probably go," she said. "I have to give a speech tomorrow and all of that."

"Yeah," he said. "You do."

"I've never been the authority on anything. It's weird, to be the authority on this. But I actually feel like I am. Like it's real."

"It is," he said.

She had said that she was doing something permanent here. Something good. And he realized then he could too. He could do something good, something permanent for her. Before he sent her on her way. He wanted to be part of the good things that happened to her here. And he definitely never wanted to be a bad thing. Which was why he didn't move nearer to her now. It was why he didn't touch her.

Why he didn't kiss her.

Even though he wanted to. It would be tempting to believe that meant he had found north in him.

The only north he'd found was her. The direction she was going. He was just a stop along the way.

But that reoriented him. Grounded him. Gave him purpose.

Gave him black-and-white back.

And it might not be the magic that he felt a moment before, but it was more important. It was something.

They climbed down from the tree. Collected their beer bottles and climbed down the ladder.

She had two more steps to go, and he couldn't help himself. He reached up and grabbed her by the waist and lifted her down. Turned her toward him.

She looked up at him, her eyes glittering, her lips parted.

He wasn't going to kiss her.

So he just reached out and put his thumb on her chin, traced a line along her jaw and back to the center again. "You're something else, Bix. Don't ever forget that."

After that he took a step back, and turned away from her. Because he had to leave quickly. Before he lost the intention he'd just set.

Tonight had been something different. A little step off the straight and narrow. It had been a little bit magic too.

But magic was for other people.

And Bix was magic entirely.

CHAPTER FIFTEEN

THE DAY OF the next town hall meeting saw Bix careening around King's Crest like a windmill. And Daughtry wishing that he could calm down his physical reaction to it. She was . . .

She was really something.

And he had already made his decisions about her last night. When they had been shrouded in moonlight.

When they had been wrapped in magic, and the kind of need that he had never experienced before. But then he'd found sanity at the end. Maybe.

Because then he had gone back home, and out the back to dig around the yard and find a present just for her. One he wanted to give her today, but not until after she had given the speech.

And now all he could do was sit back and watch her exploding with energy as she breathed new life into this place. Into everything she did.

"Can I help you with anything?" he asked, going into the outbuilding, and bristling when he saw Michael there.

"No," said Bix. "We've got it."

He didn't like that. He didn't want Bix to be beholden to him, but he also wanted to be the only one that helped her. And that was pretty ridiculous behavior.

He didn't act on it, though, and that was the crucial thing that made him a little bit less of a dick. Maybe.

So he went back to some of the finish work he was doing on the barn, and did his best to pretend he wasn't mostly watching Bix.

She ran across the parking lot in front of the out-building she was using to brew, her skirt flying up and revealing more leg than he imagined she realized.

No, it wasn't only her physical beauty that held him in thrall. But sometimes, for a moment, it was.

She had great legs. She had great everything.

And he knew that he wasn't in a great space to put himself in proximity to her today.

But when it was time for them to all go over to the town hall, he found himself claiming Bix as his passenger a little bit more aggressively than necessary.

She was in a dress again, and if he wasn't mistaken, she had on a little bit of lip gloss and some shimmering eye shadow.

"I got some makeup from your sister," she said. "I thought that it made me look a little bit more . . . serious or something."

She looked glittery. Shiny and far too pretty.

"Is that so?"

"Yes," she said. "How do I look?"

He couldn't look directly at her. That was the thing.

"You look good, Bix."

"Thanks, Daughtry. You could try and make it sound like I'm not torturing you."

He'd like to pretend nothing tortured him. Being tortured would require . . . caring.

Sex for him had always been casual. And there was nothing casual in how he felt for Bix; that was the problem. She was special, and he didn't know what to do with special. Particularly because the feelings he would need to handle her well and proper were also feelings he felt the need to build a fence around.

But she wasn't a symbol; she was a woman. And it was impossible for him to deny that now.

"You're going to do great," he said, deciding to sidestep the tension that was building between them.

"I know that, Sheriff," she said.

They pulled up to the barn, and Bix hopped out, and he watched her skirt along the edges of the different people there. He could see her confidence growing, but it wasn't all the way there yet.

He moved to join his own family, and had the strangest feeling creep over him.

They weren't really any different. They didn't know how to join people. Landry was the closest to figuring that out. Arizona was a close second, though she was still prickly as hell.

Justice, Denver and Daughtry didn't really know how to do anything but stick to themselves.

And apparently adopt strays. He was struck by the parallels between himself and his brothers. He hadn't really noticed them before.

He wondered if this was their twisted attempts at making a new family. He knew why Denver felt beholden to the Patrick girls. He'd been there when their father died.

He didn't quite understand the connection between Justice and Rue.

It was some kind of deep caring that had started back when they were kids.

As for himself? He had wanted to help Bix, because he felt like his work as a police officer functionally meant nothing if he didn't move to help a person in need too.

It was more than that now. It wasn't about atonement, really. What he'd said to her hadn't been honest.

Maybe this was friendship.

Except he was attracted to her.

One thing he knew: he was just as feral as she was.

That much was clear.

They all were.

And then Michael came over to stand next to Bix. He grinned, and was saying something encouraging to her. And Daughtry wanted to punch him in the teeth.

What the fuck is wrong with you?

For all his sense of law and order, for all he carried a badge. For all that he was Daughtry King, he didn't want that guy being nice to Bix. He wanted to be nice to her. He wanted to be the one encouraging her, and he wanted his encouragement to be the most important encouragement.

You're a dick.

His father's lingering narcissism made him feel like he'd been punched in the gut. Because that was exactly the kind of thing his father would've thought.

It was exactly what he wanted. For his children to revere only him. For his wife to want only him.

It was disgusting.

And he didn't want to be that.

He also wanted to break Michael's teeth.

Because Bix made him the most feral version of himself, and if that wasn't reason enough to keep distant, he didn't know what was.

He had a gift for Bix, anyway. The kind of sentimental bullshit he wouldn't normally do.

But he knew her. And that was a hell of a thing. Different.

He liked Andrea, but he didn't know her.

Not really. Bix had shared things with him, and he had watched her grow and change.

And now that asshole was talking to her.

She said they were just friends.

That could change, though. It could. And if it did, then what the hell did that mean for him? For her?

You should be happy about it. It's the kind of normal that she thinks she wants.

And that was when he realized, really, truly, that this wasn't altruism for him. Not anymore.

He'd wanted it to be.

But it wasn't.

That was just a fact.

He was a hell of a lot more complicated than that.

It was longing and possession; it was this intense desire to understand somebody, to feel close to them when he never had before.

It was admiration. The kind that went down bone-deep.

Something he wasn't entirely certain he understood.

And it was important to him that he understand his motivations. Because they'd been lost before, and so had he. Because for a lot of years, he'd been absolutely certain of everything he did, and why. And with her, there were things he couldn't explain. He didn't like it. He also knew there wasn't a damned thing he could do about it. Because here he was. Right then, everything felt uncertain. The whole damned world. And it made him wonder if he was wrong. About himself, about everything. About the facade of certainty that had surrounded him for all this time.

Right then, he felt like he didn't know anything.

All because he was watching Bix talk to some other man. He'd never been jealous a day in his life. Not until the other day. Had he had stayed in his gut and grown and changed and lingered, in spite of what she had told him.

It made him feel like . . . like an asshole. An out-of-control asshole. And he hated every single thing about it.

But she was his. How was it fucking fair that Michael got to come in and—

What the hell is wrong with you?

They all got seated for the meeting, with Bix by his side, and he was grateful for that, but Michael was on her other side, and he didn't like that at all.

He knew that Michael was part of the brewing initiative, and therefore it was actually reasonable, but he didn't care for it.

Sawyer Garrett got up and gave an introduction, along with the minutes, and then they got an update from Fia on the farm store, followed by a good report from Gus McCloud on the goings-on at McCloud's Landing.

"Elizabeth is training three new therapists at the ranch, getting prepared for her maternity leave, and we have a full roster for the summer."

He looked over at Gus's sister-in-law Elizabeth, who was sitting there next to Brody holding his hand, with his other hand resting protectively over her stomach. Brody was raising Elizabeth's son from her first marriage, and this was the first one for the two of them. It was amazing to him, the domesticity all around him. But even for Landry, who had his child now, and who had gotten things together with Fia, it wasn't typical.

It hadn't been a smooth road.

Not at all.

But then, everybody else was a little bit different than the King family. The way that they had managed to make connections with each other even before they were all in relationships spoke volumes. As did the continued isolation of his own family.

Denver had a point about Daughtry being the only one to work off the ranch. He was actually the only person in any of the families to have a job away from Four Corners. But the thing about Denver was that he didn't have any alliances within their alliance. Yes, he had been part of putting the collective together, but even while he tried to improve the image of the King family by working with best practices and building a better reputation as a rancher—and not a loan shark—he didn't have close friendships on the ranch. They kept to their own.

It was the stark difference between the Kings and everybody else.

And, he supposed, it was a stark difference between *him* and everyone.

But this ranch, this place, it was the source of nothing but feeling. And it was better for him to spread some of that out, rather than consolidate all of it here.

He'd loved this ranch once. With everything. Had wanted nothing more than to follow in his father's footsteps. To carry on the legacy of the King family until he'd understood that the legacy was broken.

Then it was Denver's turn to speak, and he knew that Bix would follow shortly after.

She began to vibrate with barely contained energy beside him as Denver went up to the front of the room. He put his hand on her knee, to still her movements, but a crack of electricity went between their skin. She looked at him, her blue eyes wide. Color stained her cheeks. She had made it pretty clear she felt that all too. That she'd been jealous. And he was doing his level best to throw barriers up in the way of it. He wasn't sure why. He had a lot of pretty excuses, but while he was looking into her eyes just now, he couldn't quite figure out what they were.

But his brain didn't let them get to that place. Maybe because there were too many revelations rolling around in there already.

And anyway, then Denver was talking.

"My new brewing manager, Bix Carpenter, is going to give a presentation about her plans, and has a business proposition for all of you."

Bix stood up, a folder clutched to her chest. And he didn't care that everybody was watching. He reached up and took her hand, and squeezed it once. "You're going to do great."

She let out a slow breath, and released her hand from his without any real urgency, and then she walked up to the front of the room, and took her position on the stage. "My name is Bix, and I've been working on King's Crest for two months now. I've met a lot of you. What you probably don't know about me is that Daughtry found me in the woods. I'm not kidding. I was homeless, and he gave me a job. He is maybe the first person ever to believe in me."

He felt blindsided by what she was saying. He hadn't expected that.

"The whole family has been so supportive of me, and of my taking on this venture. And because of them, because of the way they believed in me, we ended up getting together this brewery. We are in the process of making a custom beer for King's Crest. And inspired by all of the hard work that goes into this ranch, what I would like to propose is that we also make a beer for each of your ranches. Now, we would need an investment from each of you. And I understand that we've already asked for that recently. I was here at the last meeting. But I think it's going to be worth it. I really believe that it's going to make something special. Something different. And I know that I opened this by letting you all know that I'm a rescue. But I do know a thing or two about making alcohol. That's actually what I was doing in the woods.

You can't arrest me for it, Daughtry. You don't have any proof."

In spite of himself, he laughed, and so did everybody else.

"This is what we would need as a starting investment." She went on to make her presentation, and he felt . . . bizarrely proud. Not so much of himself, because no matter that she tried to give him credit, it was her. He was proud of her.

"We'll invest," said Fia King—formerly Sullivan—and it surprised him that Fia was the first to put her hat in, even though she was with Landry. She liked to remind Landry of the time he had told her that the budget was the budget, and there was nothing that could be done to move it.

She'd felt personally attacked by that, considering she was the one asking for a budget increase. But then, at the time, everything between her and Landry had been a full-on personal attack. Things had cooled down, though she was still opinionated, which was why he was surprised she hadn't made them sweat a little bit.

"I'm in," said Sawyer.

"Count us in too," said Gus.

Well. That was the kind of thing that made him wonder . . . Made him wonder if maybe everybody else felt a little more connected to them then he realized. Or maybe not. It didn't really matter. Or maybe it did.

Because it had made this venture a bigger success than it would've been. And it was giving Bix a win.

Though, who could possibly fail to be moved by Bix's story, he didn't know. And hell, maybe that was the real genius in her sharing it. Maybe it was about her, and if it was, he was glad enough of that. Because she deserved it. She really did.

He could see her draw up with triumph. Her joy at winning palpable.

There was no more business after that, and she swept down from the stage, and right to him.

"I did it," she said.

"You did," he said.

He wanted to take her in his arms. He wanted to pull her up right off her feet and spin her in a circle. But that was the kind of thing other people did. People who indulged themselves. People who let their emotions lead. And that could never be him. Not ever. But Bix was beaming, and he wanted to capture part of it. She was like a sunbeam, and he wanted to bask in her.

Wanted to keep that joy rolling. Because . . . as frightened as she'd been when he'd first met her, she burned bright now.

It was all things that had been there already. He knew that. "I'm starving," she said.

He laughed. Because that was Bix.

"All right. Go get your food. After that I have a present for you."

"A present?" She looked so excited that he felt a little bit bad. Because as presents went, it was a lame one. But he had thought that it might be meaningful. Or maybe it wouldn't be. She would do with it exactly what she'd said she would. But, that would be fair, he supposed.

"Get your food first."

"No," she said. "I want my present."

"You are a little brat," he said. "It's in my truck."

"All right. Let's go to the truck."

They walked out of the barn, and to where he had parked, just on the outskirts of the gathering. They could hear the din of conversation, the pop of the bonfire. Their makeshift ranch band was beginning to play, jugs, banjos and lap steels going strong along with some pretty decent harmonies.

He reached into the bed of the truck, and took out a hefty, large brick. He had painted "Bix" across it in white paint. "Here. It's a brick. Because you have one now."

She held it in her hands, stared at it. She looked up at him. "Thanks." She sounded stunned.

"Yeah. Well. You have that now. To take with you wherever you go."

She nodded. Her eyes were glassy, and he could see that she was trying to push the emotion down. Hell. He wanted to push his own emotion down. And he wanted to reach out and hold her. Wanted to pull her against his body and tilt her face up so that he could look at all that emotion in her eyes.

He wanted to drown in it.

He wanted to let go of this new lifetime of restraint, and give it all to her. Everything. Everything he'd ever felt, everything he hadn't let himself feel.

And that was some dangerous shit.

"Thank you," she said. "I really appreciate it."

"What I want you to know is that I'm not actually giving you the brick. You made the brick."

"With ingredients that I got from King's Crest."

"I guess so."

"Listen, I know I'm amazing. But if I can acknowledge that, I need you to admit you helped."

"That sounds a fair trade."

"Thank you, Daughtry." She held tightly to the brick, looked from it to him. He felt scalded, inside and out.

"You can put it back in the truck."

She laughed. "Thank you. Because I didn't want to carry a brick around for the whole rest of the night."

"I didn't figure."

She opened up the truck door, and put it firmly on the floorboards on the passenger side. "I don't want anyone stealing my brick. Bastards be everywhere."

He wanted to laugh. He found he couldn't. "That is true."

They walked together back toward the party. "You're a liar, though," he said.

"Am I?"

"Yes. Because a while ago you told me that if you had a brick you would smash my face with it."

"Things change. People do too."

"I guess so."

"Yeah. Now I think I might just use the brick. You know to build things, rather than as a weapon. I'm tired of fighting. I really have been enjoying living."

She looked up at him. "Dance with me," she said, her voice a whisper.

He knew that it was an invitation to more. He knew that it was up to him to say no. But he couldn't think of why, not now. And he didn't especially want to.

So he took her hand, and led her to the bonfire. And spun her beneath all those showers of sparks. He held her close, and it felt different this time than when they had danced a month ago. She felt soft and warm in his arms. She felt like a woman.

Strong and vital and filled with color and life. Not a fragile creature, or an object of pity. But wholly herself.

Not mired in the difficult things she'd been through, but transcendent.

She was the kind of feel-good story that everybody wanted to hear.

But she was more than a feel-good story. She was complicated. And he liked that about her.

Maybe you're allowed to be complicated too.

With her beneath his hands, he sure as hell wanted to be.

He wanted to forget every safeguard he'd installed in his soul. He wanted to change the rules he'd made years ago. Rearrange it all so he could justify what he wanted from her, with her.

He could remember so clearly how he'd decided to help her that day because he'd wanted to make a difference.

He hadn't counted on her making a difference in him.

"Let's go for a walk," she whispered.

She took his hand, and this time she was the one that led him away. They melted into the trees, walked in the darkness. Her skin was soft, warm.

"I don't need a lecture on all that you can't give me," she said. "All I need to know is if you want me or not."

"I don't think it's that simple."

"It can be. Thank you for the brick. But you know eventually I'm going to have to lay it down somewhere else. Like I said to you, I know that I'm going to have to take care of myself someday. I'm not asking you for anything permanent. But I want . . ."

Just then, they came out from the trees, to stand in the middle of the field. The sky was velvet black, the stars glittering up ahead.

"I want stardust, Sheriff. Just a little bit. A dusting for right now. Because when you finally have a brick, you can start wanting something more." She turned to him. "I've always just wanted to survive. That's it. I didn't worry about what felt good, I worried about what sustained me. I was wary of men, because I knew that in the wrong situations they could have too much power over me. But that's not you. And I knew that, from the beginning. When I clocked you as a whole big sexy problem, Daughtry King. Because I certainly didn't want to have feelings for a cop. For a man who had so much power over my situation. But you never took advantage of it. I trust you. And I think more to the point I trust myself. Because I have seen some things. And I have known some really shitty men. And you're not one of them. I'm not sure you know that. Not really."

He touched her cheek. "I've done some pretty shitty things, Bix."

"Me too. Remember the time I robbed an old lady?"

"You didn't exactly rob her."

"Whatever. The point stands." She took a hard breath. "I think we should have a little stardust, you and me. A handful even. Something magic. Because this feels magic to me."

She looked up. He could see the stars reflected in her eyes.

He was done fighting. Himself, and everything else.

And he didn't need to be asked again. Right there beneath the stars, he pulled Bix Carpenter into his arms, and kissed her with all the feeling he pretended he didn't have.

CHAPTER SIXTEEN

BIX THOUGHT SHE was drowning. He was finally kissing her. She had never really dreamed about her first kiss. It had seemed silly. Abstract. She was still stuck on dreaming of school dances and other things that she had never experienced. That first flush of attraction, and crushes.

Daughtry blew through all that. It wasn't just that his mouth was sexy; it's that it felt necessary. His lips were firm and insistent, and she loved being held by him. He was so strong and hot, and . . .

He had been holding her for the last two months. In all these ways that mattered. But now he was holding her for real, and it made her feel like she might be, herself, entirely made of stars. Glimmering, burning, shining out in glory.

She clung to his shoulders. They were so broad and strong. And the way that he held her, pressed against his body, made her feel . . .

She had never in her life been appreciative of being small. It felt like a weakness. It felt like losing.

But not now.

Because she felt powerful, the way he was kissing her, the way he was holding her tight like he didn't want to let her go.

And it felt nice to be small. To be able to be co-cooned entirely in his arms.

Her heart was pounding so hard she was nearly dizzy. Need gathered between her legs, her breasts feeling heavy. And when he moved his hands down a little bit lower and tightened his grip, she could feel an answering hardness pressed to her.

"Do you want me, Sheriff?" she asked, wrenching her mouth away, needing to ask the question.

"God forgive me," he said, his voice rough. "I do."

"Not an act of charity," she said.

He huffed a laugh. "I'm not egotistical to think that my dick is an act of charity, Bix."

She couldn't help it; she grinned wickedly. Because her gorgeous sheriff had occasion to talk about his penis with her, and that felt perhaps like the biggest win of all.

"I don't know about that. It might be."

"I need to know," he said. "Do you want me? Or do you feel like you have to make payment. Because I get what you're saying. About shitty guys. You told me right in the beginning that you expect that I wanted a blowjob in return for what I was given, and I need you to know that I don't."

"You don't want a blowjob?"

He narrowed his gaze. "Not as payment."

"I don't think I have to pay you."

He held her face steady and looked into her eyes. "Did men ever do that to you?"

He was looking at her, so earnest and handsome in the dim light, and she didn't want to talk about other men.

Even though there were no other men, so it was all theoretical. It was just that . . . she didn't exactly want to tell him that she was a virgin. Because she didn't really . . . she didn't care about it. All she had ever wanted was to feel like she was free to give it to somebody when she was good and ready. Somebody she wouldn't regret.

She didn't believe in forever. She'd never seen it.

But she knew that there were versions of this that she could still walk away from with her head held high.

Daughtry King would be the first.

And she would always be glad of it.

So she supposed she needed to suck it up and be honest.

"No. I never let anybody close enough for them to do that."

"I know you go to prom or . . ."

"I've never dated anybody. I've never . . . I've never done this before. I just want to be normal."

"Hold on," he said. "You've never done this . . . You've never done *this*?"

"No. Not any of it. Not kissing, the touching. I know all about it. I'm not innocent. You know me, I've made moonshine and smoked cigarettes. I think not giving men access to my body felt strong. Not falling into a pattern of letting some guy have me just because he was around and he wanted me. I just didn't want to be more stuck than I already was. I had too many ties to all of that without introducing someone that I was sleeping with into the mix."

"Shit," he said. "I should . . . I should take you home, and send you to your own room."

"Why?"

"Because you want normal, and I don't think the Kings are normal. I don't think I am."

"But wanting somebody, wanting them so bad that it's all you can think of, that's normal, right?"

"I don't know," he said. "I've never had it quite this bad before."

"Really?"

"Yeah, really." His voice was rough. "I wanted you even though I felt like it was wrong. Or like it should feel wrong. It should, right?"

She looked into his eyes and saw a desperation there that made her chest hurt. He didn't know? She would have said the man could write a self-help book on how to be a better human being when you were raised in a trash heap.

But he looked so earnest just then, and she wanted to be the one to tell him everything was okay. He'd been making everything okay for her for months now.

She wanted him. Damn everything else.

"No," she said. "I have been sleeping down the hall from you for two months. If you wanted to take advantage of me, you would've done it. You never did. You gave me my first dance. My first kiss. I want it to be you. Because it doesn't matter where I go, where I take my brick, it's always going to matter. This place and you."

He was going to be her brick when it came to relationships. He was going to be the one who gave her a standard to measure everybody else by. He was going to be the one she remembered fondly as her first. And whether they actually slept together or not, she realized that would always be true.

Every man would be measured against Daughtry King. They would probably be found wanting. That, she supposed, was a part of life too.

But she could handle it. As long as she got to have them now, she could handle it.

She didn't want to ruin her chances by laying herself bare like this, but she also knew that she had no choice. Not really. He had given her honesty. The talk. Even when she didn't want it. She owed him honesty too. He was so good. She couldn't give him her virginity without him knowing that's what was happening.

But instead of something concerned or overly caring lighting up his eyes, there was something wicked there.

Something that made her stomach turn over, anticipation and need tightening through her.

"I should tell you now, you realize that, right. Because I'm no virgin, and if you are, then you need somebody who can offer you more. More than a little bit of stardust, Bix. You deserve the whole damned sky. I can't give you that. But I want you. And I am . . . I am thrilled as hell to find out that no other man has ever touched you." He took a step toward her, dragging his thumb along her lower lip. Desire arrowed down between her legs.

She had wanted this. Last night, when they'd been up on the roof, she had climbed the tree to keep herself from kissing him. Because she would have. Because she had wanted him. Had needed him. And she had been embarrassed to put herself out there. But this was the culmination of everything. Of her growth over the time she had been here. This wasn't simply about confidence in the way she looked—though she did know that she looked better now that she was healthier. This was about whole acceptance of herself.

The woman she'd been up to this point, the woman that she wanted to be. The one she was now.

Pride in herself. An understanding of who she was and why.

And that woman deserved to have what she wanted. To have Daughtry. To kiss him, to be held by him.

She deserved to be in his bed. Even if she wasn't chained to it.

She deserved everything.

She had so much compassion for herself then. And so much excitement for her future.

But best of all, she was happy right now. Looking at him. Knowing that he wanted her. That she had driven him to this.

"You do want me, don't you?" she asked.

"Bix, you have no idea how long it's been since I let myself really want anything. And I know that I'm crossing a line here."

"Why? Because I'm a virgin?"

"No. Because I keep myself more controlled than this. And I'm not right now. I'm not making good decisions. But I want you. And I need you to know that. That this is in the same kind of thing for me. I'm *not* a virgin. But this is new. Something different. I can't tell you no. I don't want to. Maybe I could refuse you, but

I won't. It amounts to the same thing. But somehow it feels . . ." He sifted his hand through her hair. "You're extraordinary. No one has ever made me want to burn everything to the ground quite the way that you do."

"It's because we are fire, Sheriff," she said.

She wrapped her arms around his neck, and paused for a moment. All she could do was luxuriate in the moment. In the feel of him. The way it felt to push her fingers through his hair. To feel the hot skin on the back of his neck. She smoothed her hands over his broad shoulders.

He really was just so beautiful. She kissed the corner of his mouth, his chin. Then she took his lips, moaning as he parted hers, as he slid his tongue against her own.

It was so good. He was so good. His large hands moved down her back, over her body.

To feel desired like this was something entirely new.

And maybe that more than anything was why she'd never done this before. Because the kind of sexual desire she'd been exposed to had felt mean. Selfish. Being touched by Daughtry felt expansive. Every brush of his hand over her body spoke of a mutual need. The way that he held her was possessive, it was true, but there was something else. A desire to give to her. She felt it. She relished it.

"You're not going to go on a date with Michael again, are you?"

She shook her head. "No. I already told you. He's just a friend."

"I'm jealous of him," said Daughtry.

He sounded *furious* about it.

She couldn't help herself. She barked out a laugh. Even then. Even right then under the stars, with her body still buzzing from his touch.

"What's so funny about that?"

"It's funny," she said, "because it's ridiculous. You are the most gorgeous man that I have ever beheld. You have no reason to be jealous of anybody."

"I'm jealous of any man you might want, Bix. Because I want to be the only one."

"You are. You will be. For the whole rest of the time that I'm here. It's another brick. Teach me. Everything that I'm missing. Show me what I want. I have all these feelings. I have all these desires, but I don't know what to do with them. And I feel like you can show me. Really. Truly."

He held her close, there in the darkness, with only the moon and the stars as witnesses. "Tell me what you want."

She shivered. His words were filled with sensual promise, and the hot press of his body against hers threatened to be her undoing.

She had been the one pushing this, and now he was showing her that he would take the lead. Down the path that she wanted. It was up to her. Her choice.

She knew that.

He was giving her the opportunity to say what she needed.

What she wanted. He was making it about her, while making it clear he was the one who knew exactly what he was doing.

She thought of her book. Her favorite book.

"I think I want . . . I want you to show me. There are things I think I'd like, but I . . . I trust you. I have trusted you, this whole time. You found me in the woods, and you took me in. You took the lead. That's what I want. I want whatever you're going to give me. Because it could never be anybody else. Not this time. Not for this first . . . It needed to be you. And I need for this to be . . . about you and me. Not about any other things I've wondered about . . ."

That was when he kissed her again. Cut off what she was saying and kissed her. Deep and hard and long. Everything she had ever wanted.

Because he was everything she had ever wanted. All the things she had never known she'd wanted. All the dreams she had been afraid to have. "Take me home," she whispered.

"Gladly."

He took her by the hand and led her back through the trees, around the outskirts of the party. Nobody noticed them as they picked along the outskirts of the revelry.

They got into the truck, and she put her brick in her lap, vibrating with need as they took the slow drive down the dirt road back to the ranch.

"We could do it in your truck," she said, impatience making her giddy.

"No," he said. "I'll have you in a bed. With all the space, and all the time that I want."

She had told him that he got to choose. And what he was promising sounded good. Very good.

When he pulled the truck up to the front of the house, he got out, and for some reason, she stayed where she was. He came around to her side and opened the door, taking her out and into his arms, brick and all.

"Daughtry," she whispered.

"This is a show of trust on my part," he said. "You are holding a weapon."

She grinned. "I am."

"I'm trusting you not to use it on me."

She tightened her fingers on her brick. *Her* brick. It had her name on it and everything. "I promise."

"You did once tell me that death was always unexpected," he said, carrying her up the steps, and there was something extremely comforting about the fact that he was still himself, even though there were aspects of him that felt new. This was still Daughtry, and she was still Bix. Even while he made wildly sexy promises to her, and told her he relished her virginity.

"I *did* say that," she said. "But I promise you, I won't kill you tonight."

"You won't?"

"No. Most likely in the morning."

"Good to know," he said.

"I think so."

He pushed open the door to the house, and set her down. She was reminded of that moment of fear she felt last week when she thought that maybe he brought that other woman home. But also of the fantasy she'd had of him in the shower.

She was glad that they agreed this wouldn't be just one night. That it would be for while she was here. Because that was truly the most realistic way that this could pan out.

Of course, she wondered if that meant she needed to think a little bit more clearly about how long this would be. Because what she'd said to him was true. She couldn't get used to this.

But she also knew she wanted to live in it. For just a while. A little while.

A little while was better than Bix had ever had. Dreaming of forever was a foolishness that she wouldn't allow herself.

That much she knew. She might've changed a little bit, but she would never change that much.

It was impossible.

She prayed it wasn't.

Because she really needed to keep her wits about her. And it was hard when he was standing there looking like that.

When she already knew how he looked without his shirt on.

"You should take your shirt off," she said.

She hadn't meant to say that. It had just sort of fallen out.

"I thought I was in charge."

"Yeah, like in a little," she said. "But the first night that I was here . . . you walked out without your shirt on. And I think it just about killed me. I've never seen . . . I've never seen anything like that. You. Your body. I knew right then that I wanted you. And I've never wanted anybody like that before. The night that we both . . . When we both went out with other people . . . I told you that you were like a cardboard cutout, I was lying. I was completely obsessed with how you look. I thought you were the most handsome man I had ever seen. And I have been dying to see you half-naked again."

"You know I'm going to be more than half-naked, right?" he asked as he grabbed the back of his T-shirt and pulled it up over his head.

She stood there, staring. At all of that broad chest, the dark hair sprinkled there.

"I . . . Yeah. I am. I . . . Please. Be all-the-way naked."

"Calm down," he said, moving toward her. She reached her hand out and placed it flat on his chest, her fingertips tingling as they made contact with his hot skin.

"You said you wanted me to take the lead," he said. "So trust me."

He put his hand on the back of hers, pressing it flat to his skin, and she shivered. "Yes," she whispered.

"Attagirl," he said.

And that made everything inside of her go still. Pleased.

She liked that he was happy with her. She more than liked it. She felt brilliant. Effervescent with his approval.

He wrapped his arm around her, crushing her to his chest, stroking her hair as he leaned in and kissed her. Deep and long.

Slow. He wasn't in a rush. And she wanted him to take it slow. She wanted him to let her enjoy every little bit of it.

Because long nights of being hungry seemed to pass in torturous increments.

Because when you were cold, time slowed to a crawl.

Up from the moment their mouths had met, she had felt like time had raced forward.

So she loved this. This moment to slow it all down. This moment to let it feel different.

To let it feel real. To let it feel right.

To be able to savor everything. The feel of his heart raging under her palm. The sound of their breathing.

The aching, tender way that his mouth claimed hers, before it got rough and hard and delicious.

She wanted this man. And it was a glorious feeling. To be able to want.

To have cravings. To know they could be satisfied. And she would never take that gift for granted. Other people would. Other people would never understand the glory and the joy in simply wanting like this. In the anticipation of satisfaction. Because it had always been a luxury she couldn't afford.

She could afford this.

What an incredible realization. It was bigger than anything.

"I want to make you feel good," he said. "That's what I want, Bix. I want to make you shake and tremble, and scream because it feels so damned good."

"Yes," she whispered. "I would like that."

She wasn't going to let herself cry, because she knew well enough to know that would probably alarm him.

But it was incredible now, to be standing on the edge of all the good things the human body could feel. Instead of just living in the knowledge that it would be nothing but hunger and cold as far as her eye could see.

This was soft beds and rough hands. It was safety and the feeling of edgy danger she knew would only result in good things.

Risk and reward all rolled into a kiss.

Fear and satisfaction encapsulated in a moment.

She had spent so many years feeling tired. Her age had never meant much to her. When she had been a child it hadn't meant that someone was taking care of her, not like it should.

And as she had become an adult, it had meant even less.

But she'd been tired. Maybe more than a twenty-three-year-old should be.

She didn't feel tired now.

This, their connection, it went past time and age and experience.

When she had knelt there on the ground and looked up at him, he'd seen her.

And she'd seen him.

It had been real and honest and this was too.

She didn't have a snarky comment to make. Didn't have a way to make light of the glory she felt around them then.

He held her. And she loved it.

She thought she might even love him. It didn't scare her. It felt sort of beautiful. The idea that she could maybe love another person. Not feel tied to them because of genetics and a sense of loyalty for family that shouldn't have to exist when that family had never been loyal to you.

Bix had never really been loved.

But maybe worst of all, she had never loved.

The idea that she could was beautiful. A flower unfolding at the center of her chest, making something new and pretty and lovely.

She clung to him, then moved her hands down his bare chest, down the front of his flat, ridged stomach. She luxuriated in the way that he felt. In the way this felt.

"Sheriff," she breathed. "You really are something."

"So are you. Something else. Something special."

It was his turn to kiss her. Her nose, the edge of her lips. Her mouth, just tenderly, and it made her knees feel weak.

It was strange how this could feel so pure when her thoughts were anything but. How it could feel right and good at the same time it felt gloriously dirty in the loveliest way.

She supposed if she could thank her dad for anything it was that she didn't have any shame around the idea of sex. She'd only held herself back from it because of her sense of self-preservation.

In the environment she'd been in, she'd known that would have only exposed her to hurt. To maybe being pregnant. To all kinds of things she just didn't want to deal with.

And so now, while she had some concerns, some worries, she at least didn't have any shame to shift.

She could feel some happiness about that.

And mostly, she didn't want to give any credit to her dad. Not for her being here. Because this was all her. And all Daughtry.

She clung to him, let him kiss her. Kissed him back.

Until she was panting, until she could barely breathe.

He moved his hand around to cup her ass, and she gasped, arching against him, rolling her hips forward in an instinctive bid to feel him right where she was most needy for him.

He moved his hands up her spine, and she wanted to purr like a cat, and then he brought his hand around to cup her breasts. Oh, she was very disdainful of her breasts. She thought of them as small and unremarkable. But as Daughtry ran his thumb over one tightened nipple, she had never been more grateful for her breasts. She would never shame them again. Because when he put his hands on them it was like being struck by lightning. Like she finally understood what they were for.

What her whole body was for.

She just wanted to be touched and appreciated and luxuriated in by Daughtry King. Over and over again. Until she couldn't breathe.

"Please," she panted, as he squeezed her, as he sent fire rolling through her veins.

"I have to have you," he said against her lips. The desperation in his tone making her lightheaded. He picked her up again, right off the ground, his strength a damned sensation.

He laid her down slowly on the bed, spread her out before him.

She was still fully clothed, he with his shirt off, and she found herself wanting to cover up her body, even though she was still covered.

She found herself feeling exposed as he stared at her, his eyes filled with heat.

Then he moved his hands to the buckle on his jeans, undid them as he kicked off his boots and socks. Pushed everything down his lean hips and exposed all of himself to her hungry gaze.

"Oh my," she said.

It was perhaps the most demure, pearl-clutching reaction to anything Bix had ever had.

She lay there for a full ten seconds, immobilized by the sight of him.

And then she remembered who the hell she was. Bix Carpenter. Survivor, moonshiner, and no shrinking violet.

She sat up, getting onto her knees, and putting her hand on that rigid abdomen again. She was close now, to that most masculine part of him. The part of him that was making her tremble and quake. Making her wet at her center. Making her internal muscles pulse with need.

She moved her hands down that gorgeous scoop right by his hipbone, down his thigh. He groaned, letting his head fall back.

Curiosity drove her, and she moved her head toward him, and he grabbed her hair. "I'm on a hair trigger, Bix. It's not a good idea."

"But I want . . ."

"Later," he said.

His eyes were filled with molten promise. She was about to argue, but then she found herself flat on her back again, with that big, dominant man on top of her. Making her feel all kinds of things. All kinds of delicious things.

He took her dress up over her head, then her bra. Leaving her needy breasts bare to his gaze.

Then he dragged her panties down her legs, and she gave thanks for the simplicity of dresses.

"You are gorgeous," he said, the words a growl, taking on the same edge as *all the better to eat you with* might.

And that was when she realized. He wasn't Captain America. Not in this one moment. He was the big bad wolf if he was anything, and she wasn't afraid of him. No. She was too turned-on to be afraid.

This man . . . She wanted this man. With every fiber of her being she wanted this man.

And all that he was. All the complexity. It was then she realized that she had awakened something inside of him too.

He had introduced her to this. This feeling of need. Of desire.

But he had been something different when they'd met. Suppressing this. This part of himself. And it was very real. Raw. Beautiful.

He was afraid of it. She knew that. She had listened and collected all the little pieces that he had left for her to grab when he had spoken about his childhood. About his father.

It was her job to make him not afraid of this. To make him see how much she wanted it. How much she loved it.

And so she let her legs fall open, forgetting to be modest or nervous in any regard. Because she was watching his face. Watching the greed there, watching the desire. And she knew that this was about to be everything.

That he was about to be everything.

He moved down, kissing her neck, down her collarbone, all the way to one tightened nipple. He drew it into his mouth, sucking hard. She arched her back up off the mattress. "Daughtry!" she shouted.

"That's right," he growled. "Tell me how much you like it."

"I love it," she said. "I love it so much. I love it more than the first night I was here and I saw all that food, and you let me eat everything. I love it more than that." She was incoherent. She was babbling. As he licked and kissed his way down her body. Over her skin. She cursed and cried out. And when he reached the center of her need, his breath hot against her desire there, she whimpered. She lifted her hips in helpless entreaty, in desperate need of his lips, his tongue.

He put his face between her thighs and licked her. He ate her like she was a glorious delicacy.

She whimpered, throwing her arm over her eyes, moving her hips in time with the rhythm of his movements.

He shifted, pushing a finger inside of her, and the world exploded behind her eyes.

She screamed, gripping the bedspread, a shattering release immobilizing her as her internal muscles pulsed around that finger.

"Holy shit," she said. "I didn't . . . I had no idea . . . I . . ."

"I'm not done," he growled against her slick flesh. Then he continued to pleasure her that way, adding a second finger and moving them in and out of her body. She grabbed his shoulders, his hair. Her fingernails pierced his skin. She wrapped her legs around his back, opening herself even more to him as he licked deeper and deeper.

A second climaxed rocked her. Shook her. Her body was so hungry for this. For release it had never known before.

For pleasure it had always been denied.

She didn't give herself things like this.

She held every good thing back. Because she didn't trust it. She never had.

Tears were streaming down her cheeks. And she was shaking. Lord how she wanted this. Him. He was everything. And this had changed her.

Because now she knew what her body was capable of. The heights. The glory.

Now she knew.

She looked down and watched him, his tongue sliding over her slick flesh. And she felt herself tremble, shatter again, not as drastically this time, but an aftershock, a wave of arousal that overtook her when she watched him take his pleasure by tasting her.

"Daughtry," she said, her voice thin and thready. She felt hollow. She needed him.

"I have to be sure you're ready," he said, his speech slurred. He pushed a third finger into her, and she froze, the stretch of her untried body painful as he worked them in and out of her channel.

Gradually, she adjusted to the feel of him. And when he felt her relax, he withdrew. He moved away from her and straightened, up on his knees. He was fiercely aroused, standing thick and proud away from his body.

She was struck by the sheer physical beauty of him. The hard masculine lines.

And much in the same way she had appreciated her own femininity, her own delicacy, moments before, she appreciated his strength. His masculinity.

Something that had seemed like a threat most days, seemed like a glorious thing now.

Another gift.

The gifts from Daughtry were endless. It didn't need to be forever to matter.

"Please," she whispered.

She felt restless and edgy, needy in spite of the fact that she'd had three climaxes. He reached into the side table drawer and took out the condoms. And she smiled. He opened the box and tore a plastic packet off the strip. She watched with rapt attention as he rolled the latex protection over his length. He was beautiful. She hated that he had to cover himself. To put a barrier between them. But she loved that he'd done it. Because he was keeping them both safe. Because she knew that the consequences for her could be devastating. Particularly on the verge of her freedom. Of her new life.

He moved to her, kissing her mouth as he positioned himself against the entrance to her body. He kissed her deep as he began to move slowly inside her. Filling her. Inch by agonizing inch.

It was almost too much. But at the same time . . . it wasn't enough. It almost never could be. She lifted her hips, encouraging him to go deeper. He moved his hand around to cup her ass, then thrust hard.

She gritted her teeth against the pain as the last bit of her barrier was torn away. He stayed there like that for a moment. And she clung to him. Waiting for the pain to become pleasure.

It didn't take long.

It was different. Having him in this deep. So deep it was like their bodies had become one. And when he began to move inside of her, the pleasure that built was something all-encompassing. Something new and different and wonderful.

She moaned, gripping his shoulders, looking into that face. That gorgeous, familiar face that had brought hope and pleasure and this deep, unending care into her life.

She suddenly felt overwhelmed. The depth of emotion expanding inside of her was something unexpected.

Pleasure was one thing. This connection . . . it transcended pleasure. It was more. More than she had expected. More than she had ever hoped to experience.

His movements were measured, rebuilding the pleasure within her.

Until she was strung out on a glittering wire, suspended over all the stars.

"Bix," he said, her name rough on his lips. And she had never liked her improbable name all that much, but broken, on Daughtry's lips, she thought she might love it.

His movements became hard. Intense. And she lost herself. In the rhythm of it. The intensity of it. The desperation of it. She herself was wrapped all up in that glittering wire now. Everything drawn so tight she thought she might never be able to breathe again.

And then it snapped. And she cried out his name as she fell. Into that endless sea of shining stardust. It was more than a handful. It was more than anything. It was everything. All-encompassing and glorious. A moment of pure, glittering glory.

She opened her eyes and met his gaze as he thrust into her, his breath coming in short bursts, the tendons in his neck standing out. He was trying to control himself. Trying to hold on.

She lifted her head, and whispered in his ear, "Let go. Just let go."

He groaned, his thrusts becoming wild, hard.

Pushing her over the edge again as she clung to him, as his own climax overtook him, and he came holding her hips hard, pulsing inside of her.

She let her head fall back, his name a prayer on her lips as she gave herself over in an endless surrender.

She had lost control.

She had forgotten to protect herself.

She had forgotten to hold any part of herself back.

She was replete.

She was happy.

And for the first time in her memory, she fell asleep entirely, exceedingly comfortable.

CHAPTER SEVENTEEN

HE LOOKED AT Bix while she slept. He waited for guilt to come, but it didn't. He found that disquieting. Concerning. He should feel guilty. For deflowering her in quite such a spectacular fashion.

But he could feel nothing but a bone-deep satisfaction. She looked young, sleeping like that, her blond hair all in disarray. She was curled up like a child, her breathing heavy and hard.

He reached out and pushed some of that blond hair off of her forehead. She stirred. She rolled over onto her back and opened her eyes. She smiled. Sleepily. "I'm the one you use the condoms with."

"What?"

"Oh, I wondered. That first night. I went through your drawer, obviously. And I just couldn't imagine who you were using them with. Because you were just such a sweet, upstanding man."

"I hope I have disabused you of that notion."

She stretched, her arms going up over her head, her hands clenched into fists. Her perfect, round breasts moving up with the gesture.

"Yes," she said. "Any man who can do that kind of wicked stuff with his tongue is definitely not *good*."

He shouldn't like that. But he had definitely been seen as the wet blanket of his family for long enough that it felt . . . just a little bit good. Just a little bit good to have this woman look at him and think he was a little bit wicked.

"I'm smug about it. Especially because I'm sure you usually use it with busty redheads like Andrea . . ."

"Not for over a year," he said.

"Really?" she asked, her eyes going round like tractor gaskets.

"Yes, Bix. Difficult though it might be for you to understand. Just because you can doesn't mean that you always . . ."

"That you always want to. So before that she was . . . this woman that you had an arrangement with sometimes."

"It's all I've ever had. Casual arrangements with women who like the same. It works for me. It always has. I like it."

"Oh. Casual, you mean."

"Yes. Though obviously it's also not a big priority a lot of the time. Since it's been more than a year."

"Yeah," she said. "Why?"

He sighed heavily and rolled onto his back. "I don't know, Bix," he said. "It just didn't seem important."

"But you couldn't resist me." She sounded so pleased with herself.

"No, I couldn't," he said.

"Well, I like that."

"You're being very smug, Bix," he said.

She let out a mean little chuckle. She was so cute. "I am smug."

"All right, so you tell me why there wasn't anybody, then." He wanted to know more about her. Everything. He knew quite a bit, but now they were intimate. Now, they were naked next to each other, and he didn't see why he shouldn't just ask her about whatever the hell he wanted. Especially since she was asking him the same.

"Because. It's too risky. And the guys that were around . . . They were assholes. I could've been with any of them. They certainly wouldn't have protected me from anyone's advances or anything like that. But I think that's part of it. I knew that I was alone in this world. And I knew the sex . . . It wasn't gonna make me any closer to somebody. I think that's the temptation. But I watched all these women . . . Following these men around, these very bad decisions. Sometimes they would get pregnant, but invariably, they weren't the same women that were around within two years. I watched all that. My brother did the same. My dad . . . Hell, my mother was long gone. My brother's mother. I never saw sex do anything but cost a woman. I told myself I couldn't afford it. But now I can. Daughtry, I've never . . . I've never had an orgasm before."

"No shit," he said, unable to help himself.

"Really. I *hadn't* because I . . . I just felt bad all the time. And it was like I was afraid to feel good. I was afraid of feeling lonely. Afraid of wanting sex and not having it."

"But you have a romance novel."

She looked away, her cheeks turning scarlet. "It was this little window into something I knew that I could never have. This secret . . . thing. And it made me hurt all over. It made me want to be touched and held. Rescued. And I knew that I couldn't be. I've had that book for three years. I probably read it six times. But it scares me. It scares me how much I want that. But now it doesn't feel quite so sad. Quite so precarious. Now it feels . . . it feels like I might even be able to just have it all together my own self. And that feels pretty amazing. It makes me feel like I can want more things. And not be quite as scared. That's all."

"What happens in the book?"

"Well, she sort of gets taken captive in order to be rescued. It's a whole medieval Norman invasion thing. He chains her to the bed naked." She sniffed. "She's wrapped in furs. I mean, it was really very comfortable. A comfortable imprisonment."

He didn't know what he'd expected. But it hadn't been that. "Really?"

"Yes. You could ankle chain me to the bed if you want," she said. She looked so earnest he didn't quite know how to interpret the offer.

"Well. That's . . . something."

She grinned. "Don't look so shocked, Sheriff. You're a man who carries handcuffs around. Are you going to tell me you've never used them to restrain a woman?"

"They would be a different set of handcuffs, Bix. Believe me."

"Well, I would appreciate that. I don't need my PTSD to get riled up." She smiled.

"You know the romance novel I get. What about the other things? The self-help books."

She wrinkled her nose. "I just needed to learn something. I mean it. Really. I felt like it was helpful to know what a lot of different people thought about success. Because . . . because I didn't really believe everything my dad said. Because I didn't really think he was the authority. The be-all and end-all about it. And I guess the thing is I just needed a way to learn."

"And when you go to college, what do you think you'll go for?"

"Business," she said without hesitation. "I don't think I'm cut out to be an employee. I would definitely like to start my own business. Maybe I'll start my own brewery. Or my own brewery and restaurant. I don't know. I'm not afraid to work hard. It's just . . . figuring everything out. What I'd like is to be able to do the kind of thing that you've done here. You helped me. And it's that kind of expansive thinking, the ability to be able to care enough to help other people . . . I want that. I genuinely do."

"If you want to," he said, "I believe that you will."

"Really?"

"Yeah. Really. Because you've done more with the last couple of months than a lot of people managed to do in years."

"And I lost my virginity," she said. She looked deeply smug about that.

"Yeah," he said.

"You know, I always thought I was my own person," she said. "Because a lot of the things I think are unorthodox. I'm not saying that I'm abandoning all of my beliefs. I stand by a lot of them. But I don't know that I realize just how many things came from being shaped by my dad. I don't know if I realized how many things I thought just because it was expedient. I mean that's the real truth of it. You turn yourself into a hero so that all the things that don't work for you can be villainous."

"You do what you have to when you need to survive," he said.

"I guess so. So tell me," she said, rolling over to face him. "How come you've never had a girlfriend?"

He huffed. He hadn't expected that question, but with Bix he supposed he had to realize that the unexpected was always a moment away.

"Well, because I don't want to get married."

"How come?"

"Do you?" he asked.

She thought about it for a moment. He could see the wheels turning in her head. "No. I mean, it's silly, right? And at this point, it's a government institution rather than a religious one. Just another way of monetizing existence."

"Right. That goes against your ethics."

"Indeed. And as far as making a commitment to another person for the rest of your life . . . I dunno. I guess people do it. But I think maybe those people were dropped into the kind of environment where it works. Where you have a house, and a job, and you don't want to move a lot. And you don't need to make a lot of changes. And because of that, it works. It works because they don't have any mountains to hike up, so to speak. And then a lot of times, it doesn't work even then. I always wonder how the hell my dad ended up saddled with two of his kids. I mean, I know there are more. But somehow, my mom and my brother's mom were uninterested enough, or bad enough, that my dad had custody of us. That really is something. I mean, don't get me wrong, he wasn't abusive. Neglectful, maybe. He definitely put us in some situations that weren't any good. But he wasn't cruel. He never has been cruel. But you know, even he clearly thought at some point maybe he would have a family. Or something like it. He couldn't do it. Believing that you can do it isn't enough assurance that you can. I think you only dream of it if it's what you had, and it made you happy. I never had it. It never made me happy."

What she said echoed inside of him. Because it was exactly how he felt. Exactly.

He had never heard anyone say it before.

"Yes," he said. "I grew up in a miserable house. With a miserable woman chained to an asshole of a man. We were miserable kids, who thought . . . We thought we loved our dad. And that he loved us. I could never understand why I felt so bad all the time. He trained us to believe that love and feelings and all that kind of stuff was something different than what it is. It was toxic. I'll fantasize about that. We turned our family into something different. When we gather around the table, it's all of us, with all of our scars, and all that food."

"And you've taken in other people who have been hurt," she said softly.

"Yeah," he said. "We do. We've taken other people who have been hurt because we get it. But I have no desire to re-create this thing that was shitty back when I had it. It was bad then, I can't imagine submitting myself to it now. So that's why I've never had a girlfriend. I never saw the point in building a lie for the sake of not being lonely for a while."

She looked at him, hard. He didn't like it.

"I think there's more to it than that."

"Doesn't matter. I never have to know if there is. Because that's reason enough. Arrangements work just fine for me because an arrangement is all I really need too."

"Do you ever get lonely?"

"Do you?"

She scoffed. "Are you ever going to answer one of these questions without turning it around to me first?"

"No."

He decided to be honest about it. Why should he go baring his soul unless Bix did the same? Hell, she was the reason he was here. Stripped bare and feeling raw.

"Yeah. I'm lonely all the time. But I suppose I don't really know any different. It's being here, being with your family, being with you, that actually showed me how lonely I was. You know when you're cold, so cold that your hands are frozen all stiff, and then they start to warm up. There were numb before, and then they start to hurt. That's what this has been like. I couldn't worry about how bad it hurt, living the way that I did. But I get it now. I feel it now."

His heart felt raw in that moment. He felt more for her right then than he had for anyone or anything in a long damned time.

Maybe it wasn't the best idea to have this conversation naked.

"I'm not lonely. I have my siblings."

"But you and Denver have some issues," she said.

"Show me brothers who don't have issues."

"Well. I guess. I wouldn't know anything about having issues but still being somewhat functional. Because you know . . . everything to do with my brother is a total mess."

"Yeah, I know," he said.

"You said your dad was charming," she said. "And that you thought you loved him."

"Yeah," he said, his voice rough. "That's a hard thing about narcissists. They know how to make you feel special. How to make you feel important. They hold it above your head. This desire to be good in their eyes. To be approved of. My dad was so great in his own estimation, and because of that, I thought he was great too. The way that he saw himself . . . It was larger-than-life, and because of that, I saw him that way too."

It was hard for him to go down this path. Hard for him to revisit it. And he had done it so many times over the last couple of months with Bix. Maybe because it seemed like she understood. And he could tell himself it was because she needed it, the same as he told himself that he couldn't touch her because he was protecting her. But the truth was, something in him wanted assurance from her. Understanding. Because she also had loved a father who had led her down a bad path. Who hadn't taken care of her. He wanted somebody from outside of his family to understand. He didn't know why it was so important.

Only that he burned with it.

And maybe it was like what she'd said. That numb hand. Getting warmed up. Being with her, being around somebody like her, who in many ways was like him, did something to his soul.

He didn't want it. He couldn't turn away from it either.

"I wanted to please him. More than I wanted anything. He knew that. He took advantage of it. I wanted to be like him. I thought he was smarter than everybody else, just the best. And a great dad. I thought my mom was an idiot for leaving him. It's an amazing thing, to carry around that kind of conviction in your spirit, and to realize that every single point of it was wrong. It makes you never want to be that big of a zealot again. Because I knew I was right. Deeply. To the same degree that I know now I was wrong. And that is a special kind of hell. It binds you up. That's another reason I never want to get married. Have a family." He stared at the ceiling. "I don't trust myself to ever have anyone depend on me like that."

Bix said nothing. And then, suddenly, snorted. And laughed.

"I'm sorry," he said. "You find my turmoil funny?"

"What I find funny, Sheriff, is your certainty that a woman would hand all of her agency and decision-making over to you quite that easy. Maybe if you got married, she wouldn't need you to tell her what to think. Maybe she would come with her own opinions."

"That would be enough for you?" They were dangerously close to a subject they had no business talking about.

"I have no idea what would be enough for me. I'm still figuring out . . . everything."

And that was the bottom line of it. Bix was new. In so many ways. This beautiful, sharp, sexy woman who had never even been kissed until tonight was tying him in knots. She was smart and experienced in so many things. And green in so many others. She needed room to grow without any fences around her. And this was not a free-range ranch. Fences were what they did.

And fences were how he kept himself in line.

What he wanted for her, most of all, was to see her run free, and see everything that she could do. Of course, there would be a time when she would run so far, so free, that he would never see her again. She would be nothing but a memory. She snuggled up against him, and he went still. He didn't sleep with women. Not all night. But he couldn't throw Bix out. There was no way.

"I know I have my own room," she said sleepily. "But you're really hot. And I'd rather stay in bed with you. That's my freedom." She cracked one eye open, a wicked little grin on her face.

"Then I guess you should stay," he said.

"Do you know what I want from you, Sheriff?"

"What?" he asked, his chest going unbearably tight.

"I want you to give me all my firsts. So that you can send me on my way. And I won't be naive. Because I'll have done it before."

Yeah. That was it. The best thing he could do.

"Sure thing, Bix."

CHAPTER EIGHTEEN

Bix woke up warm and very, very comfortable. She was in his arms. Naked and pressed against his body. She wiggled her hips, and felt the hard press of his arousal against her bottom. Her face got warm.

Yeah. That had happened. And she was still with him.

She turned over to face him, staring at him intently through the veil of darkness. It must be early in the morning. She didn't have a great sense for the exact time. It didn't really matter. He was here. She was here. She was content in a way she couldn't remember ever being before. It was more than contentment. It was happiness.

He made a gruff, masculine sound and her body responded. Thrilled. She must've laughed out loud, though she hadn't meant to. Because he stirred. He opened one eye, and her heart jumped. "Good morning, Sheriff," she said.

"Bix," he said, his voice sleepy and gruff.

She liked that. Liked that she had woken him up. That her name was the first thing he said. That her face was the first thing he saw.

He had given her a brick.

He had given her more orgasms than she could readily count.

Don't forget. This kind of thing isn't forever. It just isn't. He'll give you your firsts, and then you'll be on your way.

Yes. That was all it was. All it would be.

She knew that. She knew what it was like to live life with one eye always on the potential threat. She knew that you had to live waiting for the other shoe to drop. So why couldn't she just enjoy herself now? She was going to. And that was it. This would be a place that had a natural ending point. There would be a time when it felt right to say goodbye. And when that moment came, she would be ready. She didn't need to be guarded. She didn't need to be in a continual state of reminding herself to be wary all the time. She was in his bed now. She was with him now.

"You want some breakfast?"

"Do you know how to cook?"

She scoffed. "I took care of myself for all that time, and you're not sure if I know how to cook? Please, Sheriff. That's just ridiculous. Now I do need a fire and a small knife."

"What?"

"I'm kidding. I know how to scramble eggs. My van has a stovetop."

Her van. Her van that she had just kind of forgotten. Her van that she didn't need now.

What a strange thing. That for a while it had been everything. The only thing she had. And now it was something she could forget.

It was a quick reminder that while she was going to let herself enjoy this . . . affair, or whatever it was, she was also going to keep wary.

She just needed to keep one eye out. Just the one.

And the other she would keep firmly fixed on him.

She stole his T-shirt and went into the kitchen, getting out eggs and bacon. She could feel him behind her, watching her. She had never had anybody watch her like that before. Like they had nothing better to do than look at her. It made her feel special. Beautiful. She had never felt either of those things before. Not really. She had never felt . . . special. He made her feel like she might be. And she would cook him eggs and bacon for that any day of the week. They were companionable this morning like they had been many mornings, but it was different. There was an intimacy to this that she had never experienced before. One that she enjoyed, that she had never known she wanted before.

He wasn't working off the ranch today, and she took great joy in riding in the truck with him to the construction site.

She gave him an impish look and moved toward him, and then stopped.

"Very good," she said. "You didn't even flinch."

"I don't flinch," he said.

The way his blue eyes stared straight into her made her shiver. And then he wrapped his arm around her neck and brought her in for a hard, quick kiss.

"If anyone has comments to make, they should know I don't have a suggestion box."

She didn't think anyone had noticed that. But even so, she felt dizzy with exhilaration.

She stepped out of the truck and spun in a circle. When she stopped, he was standing right there, looking at her.

"Just happy," she said. "That's all."

It was all. It felt simple. It was maybe the only time in her life happiness had ever felt simple.

He went off to the barn; she went off to brewing.

She was just about done for the day, when Landry's wife, Fia, came into the barn. "Hi, Bix," she said.

"Hi," said Bix. "Are you after some beer?"

"No," she said. "I wanted to invite you to our girls' night."

Bix blinked. "Girls' night?"

"Yeah," she said. "We're going to be doing some baking and watch a movie."

"I . . . Who all goes to girls' night?"

"My sisters. Rue sometimes too. Occasionally Elsie, Evelyn or Violet Garrett. It rotates."

"Oh. Well . . . Yeah. I would like that."

She had never done anything like that before. Not ever. It was wholly foreign. And she wasn't sure if she was a little bit afraid of it or not. But she was Bix Carpenter, and she didn't need to take on any fear.

She had just seen her first naked penis last night, after all.

She was breaking down barriers.

She snickered to herself.

"Yes. I would love to do that."

"Great. Arizona can give you a ride over on her way out from Kings'."

"Sure."

Of course, she hadn't seen Arizona since she had started banging Arizona's brother. But that didn't have to be weird if Bix didn't make it weird. The problem being that Bix was weird, and had a tendency to make everything weird. Oh well. It was part of her charm, maybe?

She would handle it.

She finished up her work, and then went into the barn. She didn't see Daughtry. She gave Denver a wave, and a couple of the other workers.

Denver shot her a keen look. "Are you looking for Daughtry?"

"Yes," she said, grinning sweetly. She could let him wonder.

"He's out back."

She scampered through the barn to the back door, and opened it. He was out back standing in front of a couple of sawhorses with beams placed over them. He had a paintbrush in his hand, and was applying a dark varnish to the wood.

"Howdy, Sheriff," she said.

"Howdy yourself."

She walked over to him, and stretched up on her toes, kissing him, deep and hard. He froze, stopped what he was doing and wrapped his arm around her waist as she kissed him. He returned the kiss, tenfold. Parting her lips and sliding his tongue against hers. She gasped. She could feel him getting hard against her, and she put her hand between them, rubbing her palm over his lengthening arousal.

"I got invited to girls' night," she said, looking up at him. "I won't be home for a few hours. I hope this will save for me."

"You are a little brat," he said.

And yet, there was some sort of pleased light in his eyes, and it made her feel accomplished. And happy.

"Maybe I'll make you something sweet."

"The only sweet thing I need is your ass," he said.

Lightning shot down her spine. "Sheriff," she said. "That's dirty."

"Look what you're doing to me," he said.

She knew that he was just playing along. But it made her feel . . . a little bit guilty almost. Because he was so good. Or he tried to be. And here she was, undoing him.

But he was undoing her all the same. She was the one who had never even had sex with somebody until him.

He was the one who should feel guilty.

She had a feeling he already did. It was kind of his whole thing.

"Arizona is coming to pick me up."

"Well. Have fun," he said.

"You too," she said, looking meaningfully at the bulge in the front of his jeans.

"Rat," he said again.

She wiggled her butt on her way out the door. And a few minutes later, Arizona came driving through the work space. "Are you ready?" she asked.

Arizona was wearing her work clothes too, so Bix didn't feel bad about the fact that she wasn't dressed up for girls' night. She wasn't entirely sure of the protocol of that sort of thing. It was funny, how she had said yes to this. Just jumped right in. When before it had been terrifying to her. Talking to these women. Because she didn't really know how to do the friendship thing. And it had felt so high stakes. She really wanted them to like her.

"Everything going good with the beer?" Arizona asked.

"Yeah," said Bix happily as she got into the truck and buckled her seat belt.

"Everything going good with my brother?"

She turned to Arizona, and she knew her eyes were owlishly wide. "Which one?"

"The one you have a hideous crush on?"

Arizona was giving her far too deep of a look.

And Bix was smart enough to know when you couldn't bullshit a person. "Just fine," she said.

She tried to sound serene. There was no point denying it, though. She did have a crush on Daughtry. More than a crush.

That made her chest feel sore.

They started to pull away from King's Crest and headed to Sullivan's Point.

"He's a good man," said Arizona.

"Oh, I know," said Bix. "He's been nothing but—" she imagined his head between her thighs "—kind to me."

"He's too self-righteous for his own good. But I think it's self-protective."

That was much along the lines of what Bix thought too.

"Yeah. Well. He's not always self-righteous."

She didn't know why she was needling at that. Picking at it. Because it was only going to lead to her admitting that she and Daughtry were sleeping together. But maybe that was what she wanted?

Arizona and the other women were trial grounds for friendship, after all. Friendship bricks. Because she wasn't going to stay here, but she was learning about having a new, functional life here. And if Daughtry was a sex brick, then she supposed . . .

"Yeah," Bix continued. "He isn't always."

"Really?"

"Yeah. He's . . . I mean he's wonderful. Absolutely wonderful. And really sexy."

"He's my brother. I'm not really the audience for that. Happy for you, though."

"Yeah, well, I just . . . You know I'd . . . Sorry. I'm not good at friends. I don't know that I've actually ever had one."

Arizona turned to her, her expression oddly sympathetic. "Yeah, me either. I'm actually kind of just figuring that one out."

"Really?"

"Yeah, I'm what they call prickly," she said. "But I used to be worse. I have a whole thing with Micah. You know, my husband. We . . . Well, I fell in love with him. Back when I was nineteen. And then he went away. I had a horrible car accident and I didn't let anybody know how badly I was injured. How many scars I had left behind. My dad was a real dick about it."

"I've heard your dad was kind of a dick," she said.

"Really?" Arizona huffed. "Well. Daughtry must like you too then."

She felt her face got hot.

"Oh," said Arizona. "Oh. Oh, he's . . . *You're* . . . I didn't realize that."

"It's new," said Bix, fidgeting with her fingernail, hands folded in her lap. "Sorry. I probably shouldn't have . . . It's just that I don't know what else to do. Because I kind of want to talk about it."

"I guess that's what friends do," said Arizona. "I guess. I do wish that it wasn't my brother, though."

"Well. That's fair. I wouldn't want to know anything like this about my brother. But my brother's a horrible human being."

"I'm sorry," said Arizona.

"It's fine. I'm over it. One time he locked me in my room for two days when our dad was out of town. He left me a water bottle. He forgot food, though."

"Bix," said Arizona, "that's awful."

"It's fine. It's just . . . It was sibling stuff."

"That's not sibling stuff," said Arizona.

The way Arizona was looking at her made her uncomfortable. Made her feel pitied.

"I'm not . . . I'm not sad," said Bix.

"Well, some things about your story kind of are," said Arizona.

"Maybe," said Bix, feeling something shift in her chest. "But Daughtry isn't. He's helped me so much and . . ."

"Bix, please don't fall in love with him," said Arizona. "I just think he's . . . Of all my brothers, I know him the least. I can't really figure him out. I don't know what all he's doing and I just . . . I never know with him. He holds himself back. He's impossible to get a read on. And I would say that Justice and Denver are pretty bad bets when it comes to love too, but it's different. They're players. Daughtry isn't a player. But he's broken somehow. Something our dad did."

"Aren't you broken by your dad too?"

"Yeah," said Arizona.

"But you fell in love."

"I did. It's complicated, though. I knew him before that."

"Isn't Landry in love?"

"He is," said Arizona. "But in both of our cases, we fell in love when we were teenagers. And later there was a bunch of stuff, and it was hard, but we fell in love as part of our formative years. Mind you, for both of us, it was part of our trauma. But . . . I'm not saying he can't love. But I am saying, that with everything you've been through . . . I would hate to see you get hurt."

"Don't worry about it," said Bix, that discomfort in her chest only growing more pronounced. "I'm leaving. I mean, once I'm done with all the brewing stuff. I have enough money to get an apartment. I should be able to start online classes. I have goals. And they're not going to be staying here forever. I think I'll move to a city."

"That's great," said Arizona. "I love that you have plans."

What made Bix angry was that her plans didn't feel quite so exciting and present now. School, yes. But the need to leave . . .

Don't let a little bit of sex make you into an idiot. You know better than that.

Just then, they pulled up to the farmhouse. "So is you and Daughtry banging public information?" Arizona asked.

Bix shrugged. "I mean, it's not a state secret."

"Good to know," she said. She turned the engine off, and they got out of the car. The farmhouse was already full, and Bix got reintroduced to the women she was less familiar with. Including Fia's sisters Quinn and Rory, the youngest, Alaina, who she had met the one time, and Elsie Garrett. Arizona and Alaina were both pregnant, about the same gestational age, as far as Bix could tell. Not that she was an expert. And Fia was pregnant too, though not as far along. It was a funny thing, to be surrounded by this sort of energy. She never had been.

It was terrifying and fascinating in turn.

She also didn't really know how to bake, and with Fia's help, she got set up quickly making batches of cookies.

"You'll have cookies to bring home tonight. To Daughtry," said Arizona lightly.

It wasn't her imagination that the head of every woman in the group popped up like a meerkat. "Really?"

"Yes," Bix said serenely. "Because I'm staying with him."

"She's more than staying with him," said Arizona. She looked blandly at Bix. "You did say it wasn't a secret."

"I didn't know that meant you were going to announce it."

"Well, that's fun," said Fia. "Daughtry finally got the stick out of his ass long enough to—"

"He does not have a stick up his ass. I can verify."

That produced a round of chuckles, and Bix felt pleased. Like she was winning a girl talk.

It turned to cheers, and she gladly accepted them. Then they talked about recipes. And due dates, and different ventures at the different branches.

They talked about beer, and movies. And when the cookies were done baking they sat in the living room and watched a rom-com that Bix had never seen before. She was starting to get antsy to get back to Daughtry. Well, she was aroused, was the thing. Just thinking about him.

And the romantic parts of the movie had reminded her that she had a little bit of romance waiting for her at home.

She was sent home with a giant tub of cookies, and Arizona drove her back to Daughtry's house.

"Have fun," said Arizona. "But spare me the details."

Bix laughed, and got out of the truck with her giant cookie tub.

"I hope you'll join us next month," said Arizona.

"I . . . I will," said Bix.

Surely she would still be here then. She wouldn't be done with the brewing project, after all.

And that made her feel happy. To know that she was going to have this time in this community, for just a little bit longer.

Because she really loved it. Treasured it. Above all else.

She walked in through the front door, and was greeted immediately by Daughtry. He grabbed hold of her Tupperware container of cookies, and chucked it onto the couch. "Hey," she said. "That's precious cargo. I baked those."

"Awesome," he said.

"Yeah, it is awesome," she said.

"I wasn't waiting for cookies. I was waiting for you."

A rush of fever need went through her.

That hungry, intense voice doing things to her that she couldn't even fathom. She would never get used to this. Never get used to him.

He pushed her up against the wall and kissed her. Feral. Hungry.

She was shaking when he pulled away, when she put her hands on his belt buckle.

She undid it, then unbuttoned his jeans, lowering the zipper. "I was promised this," she said.

She lowered herself down to her knees, drawing his pants and underwear down his lean hips, bringing herself eye level to his glorious arousal.

She bit her lip, wrapping her fingertips around him, stroking him, her whole body on fire.

She wanted this. More than anything.

She leaned in, touching her tongue to the hot head of him. Then she parted her lips. Taking him in deep, as deep as she could.

She didn't have any experience of this. But she had a deep, dark need rolling through her. It was intense.

She didn't think she had ever fully realized how many emotions she simply hadn't felt for most of her life. Being in survival mode had cut her off from things like this. And now, she felt the glorious brunt of it. The absolute intensity of it all.

He growled, his hands going to her hair. He pulled, leaving stinging sparks behind. And she loved that too. Because being able to enjoy intensity, this discomfort that had no cost, that was a luxury.

All of this was luxurious, and she never wanted to let go of it.

It was pain and glory and power and so was he.

He was everything.

She worked him with her hand, her mouth, the taste of him, the feral noises he made, driving her forward.

Then he hauled her up to her feet and began to strip her clothes away from her body. Right there in the living room.

She had done it. She had driven him over the edge. Driven past the vestiges of his control.

She was responsible for this. She had brought him here.

Not Andrea. Not any other woman. Not for the last year, he'd said.

She was dizzy as he carried her to the center of the living room and removed all of her clothes. Removed all of his. As he kissed every inch of her body and sent her to the heights before taking her there again and again and again.

It was a revelation, and so was he.

He grabbed his jeans, fished his wallet out of his pocket and took out a condom. Of course, he had been planning to ambush her when she got home. So he had come prepared.

Good old Boy Scout that he was. But right now, it was impossible to think of him as anything half so wholesome. He was not wholesome.

Not right now.

He rolled the protection on, and lifted her thigh over his hip as he thrust deep.

She gasped. It was too much. And not enough all at the same time.

He thrust relentlessly into her, this time so much different than their first time. That first time had been about her.

This was about them. About a mutual need that overtook them both. About the glory of it. The absolutely untethered, untamed wonder of it all.

He pushed them both to the brink. Hard and fast and perfect. She gripped his shoulders, wrapping her legs around his waist. She shuddered, shattered, and then he followed her over on a roar.

And she lay there. Feeling undone in the most glorious way. Feeling absolutely, utterly . . . perfect.

"Daughtry," she whispered. "Let's have a shower."

CHAPTER NINETEEN

DAUGHTRY HAD NEVER done that in his life. Lost it and had sex on the floor. Because he couldn't make it to a bedroom. Because he couldn't control himself. He had certainly never thrown a Tupperware full of cookies.

And Bix was looking up at him, bright eyed and happy. Asking for a shower.

"Hell yeah," he said.

Because for now he was just going to pretend that he was a different person. For now, that seemed like a pretty damned reasonable thing to do.

So, naked, he reached out and grabbed the thing of cookies, then lifted Bix up off the ground. He put the cookies in her arms, and carried her in his, down the hall to the bedroom.

Bix chucked the cookies down on the bed. "Will need them later. Sustenance," she said.

She looked up at him and nodded. Gravely.

"You always think about food."

"If you've ever gone without, you think about it a lot."

She made comments like that sometimes. And they just undid him. But then, she did. Altogether. Over much.

He carried her into the bathroom, and opened up the glass shower door. He leaned into the space, and Bix laughed as she turned the water on.

He set her down outside, while they waited for it to warm up.

"I thought you were showering with her. That night when I got home from the bar." She took a deep breath, and his eyes were drawn down to her breasts. So perfect. So pretty.

"Were you jealous?"

"Jealous as hell," she said. "Because I wanted your hands running all over my skin."

She pressed her thighs together, the action making it clear that she was aroused, and that did something to him.

"You're a scamp," he said.

"Obviously," she said.

Steam started to rise from inside the shower, and he wrapped his arm around her waist and pulled her in, beneath the scalding water.

She sighed, and he moved his hands over her skin, got them all soapy and slid them over her curves. Did that until she was panting, until she was arching against him.

"Settle down," he said.

He got some shampoo, washed her hair. Scrubbed his fingers through the silky strands. And when he looked at Bix, he sighed . . .

It almost looked like tears streaming down her cheeks, but of course, that could just be the shower.

It didn't have to be anything else.

Maybe they weren't tears.

She opened her eyes, though, and he could see that they were glassy. "No one has ever taken care of me before."

It was like a punch to the chest.

No one had ever taken care of him before either. And that he was doing an all-right job of it with her . . .

Don't. You don't need to go there.

But it was fine. For now. He just wanted to care for her. He just wanted to give her things. Because she was Bix. And she was special.

He moved his hands over her curves again, then between her thighs, stroked her there until she was sighing.

He felt himself getting hard again, which he would've thought was impossible after that explosion of passion in the living room. But he wanted this. The passion.

It was reckless, he knew, but it was safer than the tenderness that was threatening to cave his whole chest in.

He pushed two fingers inside of her and watched her face as he pleasured her.

Then he backed her up against the shower wall, and positioned himself at the entrance of her body, and thrust inside.

He gritted his teeth. Nearly swearing when he realized what he'd done.

But she felt so good.

He was losing it. Because this wasn't him. He was more controlled than this. He was more responsible than this.

Holding her tightly, still buried inside of her, he opened up the shower door, turned the water off. And stepped out holding her.

She clung to him, and he walked her to the bed, laying her down next to the cookies. "Hey," she murmured when he withdrew from her.

"Condom," he said. "My bad."

But he meant so much more than that. It sounded casual. And he didn't mean it that way. It really was bad. And he really did regret it.

It really was him, as if he had jumped onto a parallel path. One he had decided to get off of years ago.

And now here he was again. He had been careless. And he couldn't be careless with her. He couldn't afford to let feeling, to let need overwhelm him like this. He got a condom out of the bedside drawer and rolled it over his hardened length. Then he went back to Bix, kissing her deep as he thrust into her again.

She looked up at him, her eyes going glassy again as she wrapped her arms around his neck. "Daughtry."

And right then, he would've given her the world. He wanted to slay every dragon that had ever come for her.

The intensity of the feeling that was building inside of him was unlike anything he'd ever experienced before. It wasn't just an impending orgasm. It was more than that. She was more than that.

It was everything. Absolutely everything.

He focused on the pleasure. Focused on the building need within him. On the orgasm that was chasing him down like a hellhound. He focused on that, because it was easier. He focused on that, because it felt good.

And he tried to pretend that it was just sex. And that it wasn't quite so spectacular, and mind-blowing and soul altering because it was Bix. Because she was like a magical creature that had torn a hole through the fabric of his world, stepped inside and cast a spell on him. Affected real change within him. Change he hadn't wanted or asked for.

Bix.

Oh hell.

She chose that moment to open her eyes, to look into his.

And that was what pushed him over the edge.

He clung to her hips as he thrust hard inside of her. "Yes," she whispered. And she began to shudder and shake, coming apart around him.

He thrust deep, giving himself over to his need at the same time she did. And they held each other as they came apart.

Bix rolled over onto her side and he went to the bathroom to discard the condom. When he came back, she was eating cookies.

"Would you like some milk?"

"Yes, please," she said, her mouth full.

He shook his head, went into the kitchen and got two glasses of milk. It struck him how satisfying he found that. Taking care of her like this. Giving to her like this. He came back into the room, and sat on the bed, handing one of the cups of milk to her.

He took a cookie out of the tub and dipped it in the milk. "You really made these?"

She looked proud. "I did. I had help."

He took a bite of the cookie. "Damn, Bix," he said. "This is great."

Right then, it was easy to imagine a future that neither of them actually wanted. One where she baked him cookies. And he made her breakfast. Where they went to bed together every night and got up together every morning. Yeah. That was really easy to imagine right then. But that was only because he was raw, and the sex with her was so mind-blowing it made it difficult to think straight.

"I had a good time with your sister. And everyone else. I kind of understand the friendship thing now. So I told them the story about my brother and they . . . they kind of freaked out. Like what I was saying was crazy."

"What story did you tell them?" All he could think of was the story she told him about her brother leaving her in the woods. It had made him want to kill the guy with his bare hands.

"Oh, and it was just one time my dad left him in charge of me, and he locked me in my bedroom for a couple of days. He gave me some water. I pretended that I was camping. That's funny, because the other time you know when he left me in the woods, I actually was camping."

"Bix," he said. "What the fuck?"

He felt like he wanted to kill someone. Kill something. This rage, this was something he wasn't familiar with. It was a part of himself that he had cut off so long ago it felt foreign.

"I'm *fine*," she insisted. "They looked the same way you did. It's just . . . It was stuff that happened. There's no use getting all traumatized about it."

"But it's fucking traumatizing," he said. "Nobody should've done that to you. Your father should have protected you. Your brother should have protected you. That's what siblings do. My family is dysfunctional, but the siblings all have each other's back."

"Mine didn't," she said. "I just . . . I get it. And I appreciate you being angry for me. The same as I appreciated them being angry for me. But I can't afford to be all upset about the terrible things that have happened. Because . . . because I have to live. I have to live."

"Bix, I . . . It's wrong. What he did to you was wrong."

It was more than that. It made his chest hurt. Made his whole body hurt.

But Bix wasn't . . . It was like she didn't really know. The way they ought to have treated her. What she deserved.

"When you go out into the world, Bix, don't you ever take shit like that from anybody. I can understand not wanting to sit down and be upset about things that happened that you don't have control over, but I need you to be mad enough that you will never accept any of that, ever again. Ever. Do you get it?"

"Yes," she whispered. "It's just . . . I've never been able to afford to be picky about how I was being treated."

"Oh hell, Bix," he said. "I just hate it. I really do. I hate that you were treated that way."

"I hate that you were treated the way you were. So it's mutual, I guess. I promise, I'm not going to accept anything . . . anything bad. Because you've taken such good care of me, I'll expect it from now on."

He felt like a tight band was squeezing his chest. "Well. If I've done anything, I hope . . . Good. Good."

But when they went to sleep, he had the strangest swirl of emotions going through his chest. Contentment, desire, anger.

Because he wanted to throttle her family. The people who had been entrusted with taking care of her, and who hadn't.

He was glad that Bix was so resilient. Angry that she should have had to be.

Mad that she seemed to not understand how extraordinarily awful it was that she had been treated that way.

He really hated that.

He had another day off tomorrow, which was good. He intended to spend it with her.

Because it wasn't permanent. So there was no point holding himself back at all. Because it wasn't permanent, and there would be a natural conclusion one way or another.

And it was supposed to be something he was enjoying. Not something that tore his guts out. But then, nothing was supposed to be able to tear his guts out. Not quite like this. And here he was.

He looked down at Bix. Sleeping soundly. She was so small. She wasn't fragile. And it didn't matter that life had treated her in a particularly harsh fashion; she just seemed to get up and get on with it. She was feisty and resilient in a way that . . .

Well, his response to the things he'd been through had been to shut himself down. But then, Bix wasn't like her dad.

And Daughtry would always have to worry that he was like his.

Because he could remember. He could remember enjoying going and threatening people. Being tougher than them. Smarter than them.

Bix had never gloried in that.

The world had very few people like Bix. That was the truth. People who had been through hell, and who had come out like this. The world had too many people like his father. Like her father. Too many people like him.

And all he could do was hold himself back. While Bix . . .

Bix deserved to be free.

CHAPTER TWENTY

BIX REALIZED THAT she needed to do something with her van. It had been sitting there for too long, and it needed to be started at least. Plus, she had a few things in it that she could probably stand to bring back to the house.

And then she would decide what she wanted to do.

Maybe she would sell it. She could use another vehicle. Something that would be a little bit easier to drive around in.

"Will you give me a jump, Daughtry?" she asked the next day when they were eating lunch together.

"Excuse me?"

"Give me a jump," she said. "*My van*. You absolute pervert." She elbowed him.

They hadn't made any pronouncements about their relationship, but they were not hiding it. And she had a feeling that pretty much everybody knew.

He drove her over to where they had left the van, still concealed in the bushes, and with his help, she got it started. She drove it around to the edge of the back access road to Four Corners, near the farm store, and parked it there in a turnout.

"We can put a for-sale sign up in it," she said.

"You're gonna sell it?"

"Yeah. I don't really want to drive a big orange camper van into my new life, you know? I mean, I also don't want to drive it around town. I'm not driving into my new life immediately." She looked at him, unable to get a gauge on what he was thinking. "That's okay, right?"

"It's more than okay. You know you can stay as long as . . . As long as it's all working."

"Good," she said. "You can tell me, you know," she continued, "if I need to get my own place."

"Why would I want you to get your own place?"

She felt something blooming in her chest. Something like hope.

She knew that this wasn't permanent . . . Except . . .

She was starting to want it to be. Something was shifting inside of her. And she had been so certain that this was going to be temporary, and that she was going to be okay with it. And she felt like maybe . . .

She wasn't an idiot if she felt something for him. She had told herself that she wasn't going to be that person, that she wasn't going to be the idiot virgin, that she wasn't going to be the sad waif who fell for her rescuer. But it was more than that. And what was really funny was that all the people around her seemed invested in her plumbing the depths of her trauma, and she knew she didn't want to do that. But she wouldn't let herself get to the depths of her own happiness. And why was that? People didn't seem to value happiness, herself included. She framed it as being idiotic. While anger and all kinds of other bad emotions seemed to be treated as valid.

She wasn't going to go making any declarations to him right now. She needed to sit with all of this for just a little bit longer.

But . . .

She was starting to think she didn't want to go. That her happiness wasn't out there in some vague, isolated future. That these weren't random bricks. But a foundation. One that she wanted to build off of. Right here. Was that so crazy? Maybe it was. She was starting to care less and less.

She felt incredibly protective of these feelings that were rising up inside of her. Entitled to them. Because yes, all those bad things had happened to her. But so many good things had happened. And she wanted to marinate in those things. To dwell in them and with them. She wanted joy. To claim it. To own it. Identify finding Daughtry and this ranch, this family, as a miracle. It was.

The easy thing would be to walk away. To continue on down the road. To not risk herself. Not invest herself.

But she had been alone for all of her life. For a while it had felt brave. Dreaming about doing school. Dreaming about getting a job at a brewery. Yeah, for a while that had felt really brave.

But it was still walking away. Rather than building on connections. Rather than making more of this, of them. She still wanted to go to school. Maybe she would even get a job away from the ranch. Maybe. She and Daughtry had just talked about how neither of them wanted to get married. Have a family. But she was starting to think that maybe the real bravery was in taking a chance on something that you couldn't actually imagine. Following along in your heart, even if it didn't make any sense. Even if you didn't know the pattern.

To make a whole new path out of something you had never seen before, that was really something.

And if she was so extraordinary, for coming out of the situation that she'd been put in, then she wanted to be the most extraordinary. The most wildly, blindly happy. Because if she had to acknowledge that her past was a tragedy, then she wanted to claim a victory in her future.

They drove away from the van, with a few of her things in a crate. "I don't even think I need these things," she said. "Not really. Some weird kitchen utensils and not much more."

And what she hoped was that his kitchen would just keep on being hers. That she wouldn't need to ever start a kitchen of her own. Which was maybe presumptuous. But she was living in a moment of presumptuousness.

"It seems like a big deal," he said. "Selling the van."

"Yeah," she said. "It does. But . . . it doesn't feel like it's my life anymore."

The most amazing realization was that her new life could be whatever she wanted it to be. Whatever she saw it as. And that the limit on her own happiness didn't exist.

Now, Daughtry . . . She didn't know about him. She was going to have to wait, bide her time. Figure out when the best time was to . . . to say something. Anything.

"You're a big-time beer brewer now, Bix Carpenter."

She frowned. It was funny. That last name. It belonged to her father. Her brother. And consequently, it didn't feel much like it belonged to her. Or like she would even want it to. But the name also spoke of building. And that was kind of interesting.

So maybe she could make the name take on a meaning that was just something for her. Not tied to them.

She had been a carpenter in her own life. She had gotten a brick, and she had started building.

Where she built from here was up to her. And she could confidently say she really felt that for the first time in her life.

Really felt like the control was hers. The agency.

All of it.

She also realized that hope was an ever-expanding resource. The minute you had a little, it grew and grew.

Now she didn't just want to survive. Now she didn't just want to live well and comfortably. She wanted to live surrounded by friends. She wanted to live in this family that she had grown so fond of.

And most of all, she wanted love.

To give love, and have it.

She loved Daughtry. She just did. There was no half-assed way about it. That man was fundamentally lovable.

He didn't think so, she realized. But she wasn't quite sure how to untangle all the threads that had caused that.

It just meant they were going to have to have another honest conversation. Just not today.

She wasn't a coward, after all, but she also wasn't a fool.

They had a good thing going right now, and she didn't want to disrupt it. She wanted to get just a little bit more. Just a little more.

Once they got a for-sale sign put on the van, they went to dinner at Denver's.

Justice and Rue had gone out to Smokey's and Landry and Fia were at home. Which left her, Daughtry, Arizona, Micah and Denver.

She caught her reflection in the glass on a framed photograph. It made her heart stutter. She was glowing. The joy and admiration on her face was so intense it . . . took her breath away. She looked like a woman who cared. And when you cared you had so much to lose.

She knew why it scared her.

Because you're afraid to be happy. Because they're going to hurt if you lose this.

Well. That was the truth. And she was afraid to lose them. All of them.

But him most of all.

She was afraid of losing his touch. Losing her place in his bed.

That was strange. Because with hope did come quite a bit of fear. A sense of scarcity. A desire to defend. It tapped into all of her other emotions. Fear, anger, longing.

It wasn't comfortable.

She had always assumed that people who had a lot of things were completely comfortable. But she was beginning to understand that the more you had, the more you wanted to guard it all jealously.

But this was great. This night. This dinner. She felt so far removed from the girl she had been that first night. That first dinner. And yet she also felt her, right there with her.

Tears welled up in her eyes as she looked at the spread of barbecue that Denver put on the table.

"Hey," said Denver. "Are you okay?"

"I'm fine," she said, wiping at her eyes.

"You look sad."

She shook her head. "I'm not sad."

She did wish that Daughtry would come in and defuse the moment. But everybody else was lagging behind. And it was weird to have her boss catch her in a vulnerable moment.

"I'm just really grateful, to be here. Your family is the best."

Denver got a strange look on his face. "That means a lot, Bix. Given our history, that means a hell of a lot."

She saw his wounds then. The things that he cared about.

He was trying to atone. He might be different than Daughtry but he had a very similar wound.

Finally, everyone else came into the kitchen, and they all sat down at the table, serving big portions all around. And when they were done, they lingered in the living room chatting. It was the single most domestic experience of Bix's life. Then she went back to the house she shared with the man that she loved. They ate cookies. They made love, and they went to sleep.

And the next day, Bix's perfect life shattered.

BIX WAS FEELING pleased by the end of the day, because everything was going well. They were on track to having another successful day of brewing, and she had decided that she was going to go fishing.

She wanted to catch some fish, and surprise Daughtry with the bounty. She could cook him dinner after his long hard day, and then she could strip him naked and do wicked, unspeakable things to his gorgeous body. It honestly seemed like the best idea she'd ever had. So she packed up her fishing pole and went down to the creek, Bear Creek, and when she saw movement on the other side of the water, her instincts went on high alert.

"Who's there?" she asked.

Likely to be a farmhand.

"Oh, there she is."

A chill went down her spine. And out of the bush came her dad and her brother.

"I knew when we saw your van we couldn't be that far from you. Surprise you don't have a still set up in here. But we started brewing a little bit ourselves."

"What the hell are you two doing here?" she asked.

"Now, is that any way to talk to your family, Bix?" her dad asked. He looked as skinny and threadbare as she remembered. His gas station baseball cap was pushed up his forehead, his pants torn and dirty. Her brother didn't look much better. In fact, he looked about the same age as their dad at this point. Hard living would do that to you.

"How do we cross over to the other side?" her dad asked.

"If you're smart, you don't," said Bix. "This is a big working ranch. Believe me when I tell you, you can't brew here."

"We can't?"

"You can't," she said. "I tried. Believe me."

"You look . . . you look different," her dad said, coming to the edge of the riverbank opposite her. "You look like a house pet."

"I work here now. At the ranch."

"You *work* somewhere?"

"Like I said. I got caught. By a cop."

"Well now, how come you didn't get thrown in prison?"

She shifted her weight from foot to foot, suddenly feeling antsy. "Because he didn't arrest me. He lives here."

"Oh, I see how it is. And he *took you in*?"

The really annoying thing, the upsetting and enraging thing, was that she knew her dad was going to assume Daughtry had taken her in as a piece of ass. And she would've loved to have been self-righteous and say that there was nothing going on between them.

But there was. There fucking *was*. And even though it hadn't been like that in the beginning, it was like that now. And she didn't have a self-righteous corner to stand in.

"Yeah, well, he's not gonna do the same for you," she said.

"No," said her dad, "we're not quite so pretty."

"Just get the hell out of here. I don't even know how the two of you got out of prison."

"Commuted sentences," her dad said. "So now we're out. What do you have going here exactly, Bix?"

"I said, I work here. I'm brewing beer."

"You got a spot for your old man?"

The very idea of bringing them into this life, this place, made her want to peel her skin off.

"Why did you even come looking for me?"

"You're family," he said.

"That's never much mattered. What do you want from me?"

"The truth is, Bix," said her dad, "you're the most talented moonshiner of all of us. And we need to get something going again."

"Well, I don't do that anymore. I don't need to. I have a job."

"And a sugar daddy," her brother said.

She crossed her arms and stared Chip down, her rage a flame. "So what if I do? If I got one, you can get one too. Go get one."

"Hell no. You owe us. We're family."

"I don't owe you anything," she said.

Nothing but trauma and pain and hurt. Scars inside and out. She was her own woman because of her own grit. They could go to hell.

"Well now, I'm sure there's some way we could figure out how to make you do it. Something you don't want your sheriff to know about," Chip said, stroking his chin.

They were threatening her. Threatening to blackmail her. And in the past, she would've tried to handle this on her own. She wasn't going to do that now.

Because she wasn't alone. Because she loved Daughtry. Because she had Daughtry. And she was going to go to him.

"If you two aren't gone when I get back, I swear you're going to be sorry."

And she ran. For all that she was worth.

WHEN BIX CAME running up to the house holding her fishing pole, her eyes wide, everything in Daughtry went on high alert.

"Daughtry," she said. "My dad and my brother here. They got out of prison, and they're trying to . . . They think that they can blackmail me into making sure they get a job on the ranch. I don't . . . I don't want them here. I want them to go away."

A monster woke up inside of him. It raised its head, and growled.

"Hang on," he said.

He went into his bedroom and opened up his safe. He got out his badge, and his gun. He strapped the gun to his hip, put the badge in his pocket.

Bix eyed the piece on his hip.

"You don't need that," she said.

"I never assume, Bix."

He got into his truck, and she went around to the passenger side.

"Stay here," he said.

"What?"

"You don't need to come over there."

"The hell I don't. This is my family. This is my responsibility. My drama."

"Get your ass in the house, Bix. I will come home when it's safe, and I'll get you then."

"They're not dangerous."

But all he could think was the stories that she'd told him about her brother. That was a cruel son of a bitch. He knew that much. And he wasn't going to let them near her. Not again. Because he had seen the condition they'd left her in. He'd seen it.

And he fucking hated them.

"Stay," he said. And then he started the truck and drove away. He saw Bix immediately make a beeline toward the river, running like hell itself was on her heels.

Little varmint. She couldn't be told.

He drove down the highway, deciding that he was going to hike in on their side of the creek, the same side he'd gone in on when he had found Bix.

He saw a beater truck, and a bunch of shit lying around. He wasn't surprised.

They were exactly those kind of people. Not just the kind of people who would mooch off of someone else's land, but who would have no respect for it while claiming it was nobody's, too wild to be owned. But they certainly didn't actually mean it. They meant that the world was there *for them*. That any limits prescribed shouldn't apply to *them*. If they could own things, then they would demand everybody else stay away from them.

His anger was at a boiling point. It was beyond.

"Show yourselves," he said. He didn't hear anything. "I'm going to start getting impatient." He put his hand on his gun.

"Easy now," came a voice up ahead. An older man stepped out from behind a tree. "I don't want any trouble."

"Well, mister, the problem is, you're on my land. And I consider that to be trouble."

"Are you Bix's cop?" the old man spit.

"Yes," he said. "I am."

Right now, he was Bix's warrior. Right now, he was everything. Right now, he was going to lay waste to these assholes.

"Daughtry!"

He looked across the river and saw Bix, standing there looking furious.

"I told you to stay home," he said.

"We're family," said her father. "Bix is always going to be here for us."

"That's too bad," Daughtry said. "Because as long as she's here, she won't be. I mean it. I want you off my land, and I never want to see you again."

And that was when her brother appeared. Stepping out from behind a tree adjacent to her father. And Daughtry saw red. He crossed the space without thinking and reached out, grabbing him by the neck. "You sack of shit."

"Hey," her brother said, his voice getting high. Yeah. He wasn't so tough when his opponent wasn't a little girl.

"I know all about you. The way that you treated her. I might just kill you. Nobody's going to dig around here looking for a body. This is my land. And everybody trusts me. I'm the good guy."

"You don't seem like much of a good guy," her dad said.

Maybe that was true. Right now, he didn't care.

He should try to get ahold of himself. Try to find the straight and narrow and get back on it. But dammit, he just couldn't bring himself to do it. These people didn't care.

And he couldn't bring himself to care either. What he wanted was to hurt them. Because they'd hurt the dearest, most amazing person he'd ever known.

He wanted them to hurt too.

"I'll let you in on a little secret," he said. "My dad wasn't just a moonshiner. My dad used to get out there and break the legs of people who didn't pay him back. And I watched. I helped. And now? I've got the law on my side. Nobody would believe you over me. And nobody would ever suspect me of anything. I'm a changed man."

"You're crazy," said her brother.

"Yes. I am. Push me to the edge and see how crazy I can be. Let's see."

"Daughtry," Bix said. "You don't want to do this. You really don't. I know you. I know that this isn't you."

He snarled, "It is me. And this is why I don't let myself get like this. But now it's too late."

"I'm her father," her dad said.

"You didn't do a damned thing for her. You left her to her own devices. She's brilliant and smart and wonderful and it has nothing to do with you. And you," he said, looking directly at her brother. "You are a petty, slimy, abusive coward. And if I squeezed my fist just now and ended you nobody would miss you. Your mother wouldn't even miss you, would she?"

Daughtry really had the guy going now. Terrified. Good. He had terrified his sister. And he deserved no less.

He was shaking now, the adrenaline really going. He saw red. He was at the edge of losing control completely. Even when he'd been his dad's right-hand man he'd never been like this. This was different. Deeper. This felt so gut-wrenching, so personal.

Bix, all skinny and scabbed.

Bix telling him she'd been locked in her room for days. Left in the woods alone.

They'd had her all those years and they hadn't cared for her. He hated them for that.

He hated them.

He heard splashing, and he looked to his right, and saw Bix running across the river.

"Don't," she said. "Do not do this because of me. Please. Daughtry, I care about you too much. I don't want you to do this. It isn't because I care about them. It's because I know you. And I know this isn't what you want. I know it's not. Don't do this. Not for me."

"Who else would I do it for?"

"They're not a danger to me. They're going to leave."

And she stood there, panting, her clothes wet. "Leave," she said to her father and brother. "Because you better believe that he will do what he says. And he didn't even tell you about all the brothers he has, and all the other ranchers on this ranch who will back him up. Who will make sure that he never faces any consequences."

"Go," Daughtry said, letting go of her brother's neck finally. "If I ever see you on my land again, it'll be the last thing you ever do."

He took a step back, and Bix grabbed his arm.

"I never thought I'd see it," her dad said. "A turncoat. Taken up with a cop."

Bix rounded on her dad. "No, Dad. I'm a woman, and I'm making my own life. The choices I'm making are mine. You don't get to decide what I do. What I believe. How far I'll go. I get to decide that. All the decisions I made, I made them because you kept me just hungry enough. Just poor enough. Just scared enough. I'm not scared anymore. I have a bank account. I'm going to college. I'm on a payroll. I'm going to pay taxes. You can't stop me. You don't own me. And I don't owe you anything. I'm proud of myself. And it has nothing to do with either of you."

She looked at her brother and put her hands on her hips. "He's mad about the stuff you did to me. I just laugh at it. You know why? Because you're small. You always have been, you always will be. And you were always threatened by me. Because I'm smarter than you. Because I work harder than you. Because I will always be better. It isn't because I was born that way. It's because it's what I choose. I choose to be better. Than both of you."

That was when her brother lunged at her. Daughtry's rage caught a light and burned bright. He stood between the two of them, cocked his fist back and punched him square in the face. And punched him again. And again.

Bix screamed, her dad ran. And Daughtry hit him, again and again.

"Please," Bix said. Grabbing his arm.

That was enough. Enough to clear the haze, if only for a moment.

She put her hands on his chest, pushed him away. And he realized how far he had gone. And that he didn't feel bad. Not at all. He felt powerful. He felt proud that he had defended her. His woman. His . . .

He was breathing hard, and it was taking time, but suddenly, bits and pieces of reality started to filter in.

He hadn't been like this for so long. Hadn't lost his temper. Hadn't forgotten where he was or what he was doing. Not for a long time. And now he had. Spectacularly.

It wasn't that it wasn't deserved. That wasn't the issue. The issue was realizing how much of that was still him.

He didn't feel a great sense of honor over what he had done. A reluctant call to arms.

No. It had been easy.

"Go," he said. He looked down at her brother. His nose was broken for sure. He had taken a step toward Bix, and Daughtry had been right to defend her. He knew that. He did. But it was all the other stuff, tangled up and messed up inside him.

They hightailed it back to their bigger truck, and started it and drove away.

Bix was holding on to his hand, looking at his knuckles, which were split. She looked up at him. "Let's go back home."

"I'm fine," he said, jerking his hand away from her.

"Oh, stop," she said. She stalked ahead of them to the truck.

"What?"

"You know what!" she said. "You're being sullen and ridiculous."

"I just turned your brother's face into a tenderized steak."

"He shouldn't have tried to hit me."

"You're not happy with me."

"No. I'm not. Because I trusted you. I went to get you, and you didn't listen to me. You took matters into your own hands, and it escalated. But it's fine. It isn't like he's never been punched in the face. And he has deserved it every time. Even if he didn't, it was probably just compensating for times when he deserved to be punched and wasn't. So I don't feel sorry for him. But I feel like you put yourself in a dangerous situation, and that I don't like."

"I'm a cop, Bix. That's going to happen sometimes."

"It's not the same thing and you know it! You know. Just . . . shut up."

They rode back to the house in silence, and when they got back she walked wordlessly inside, and went into the bathroom.

He heard the water running in the bath and went to check on her.

"Take your clothes off, you absolute asshole."

"I just chased those dicks off, I don't even get a thank-you?"

"Thank you. Get naked."

He hadn't expected that. But when Bix wanted him naked, far be it for him to deny her. He took his shirt off, his jeans, everything else.

"Get in the tub, Sheriff."

"What the hell are you doing?" he asked.

"Taking care of you. Now get in the tub."

He gave her a side eye but stepped into the hot water. "You have too many clothes on," he said.

"I'm good." She got soap on her hands and moved to the side of him, running her hands over his shoulders. It felt good. But he didn't deserve it.

He didn't have the strength to stop her.

Some wall had come down inside him and he didn't know how to build it back up. Didn't know if wanted to even if he could.

She moved her hands down over his chest and he grunted. Then she moved to his split knuckles and he growled as she got soap into his wounds.

"Ouch, Bix."

"Well, you should have thought of that before you behaved like an uncivilized grunion."

"A grunion?"

"If the tiny gills fit."

He gripped her wrist and pulled her toward him. "Nothing about me is tiny."

She smiled. "No." Then she kissed his cheek. "Thank you, for defending me. No one has ever done that before. Not like that. Not in any way. It's only ever been you. Always you."

He felt like he was standing on scorched earth, and she was expecting grass to grow around his feet. But he liked it. And he didn't want her to stop.

He wrapped his hand around the back of her head and kissed her, pulling her in hard. She whimpered. He reached down and pulled her shirt up over her head, unhooked her bra with one deft hand. Then he guided her so that she was standing up, so that he could get her jeans off. So that he could lift her down into the tub, fit her right over him.

Everything in him was on fire. His arousal was rampant, his whole body on high alert. Because those walls were knocked down. And there was nothing left. There was no resistance; there was no protection. There was nothing. Nothing but this. Nothing but her.

He wanted her.

For just one moment, he wanted her, without control, without boundaries, without anything. He didn't know what this was. This extreme riot of need that was assaulting him mercilessly. It wasn't anything he'd ever felt before. Wasn't anything he'd ever known. And any other time, at any other moment, he would've pushed it away. But not now. Not now.

His soul felt raw. Everything felt exposed. Every dark, deep part of him. All of the things that he had tried to disguise. All of the things that he had tried to push down.

It was her. It had been, from the moment they'd met. It had been inevitable, this. The ending of all his control. The ending of everything he had tried to construct himself to be.

She hadn't taken the brick and smashed his face, but she might as well have. She had smashed the man that he had fashioned himself into. The idol that he had built of himself. Dead, unfeeling. Not real.

But . . . what was the alternative?

The alternative was the man that had been out there today.

Uncontrolled. Unashamed.

All good when it was directed at protecting somebody, but what if it wasn't?

Because things could get twisted. That was the thing. He had felt conviction on that level when he had been out doing errands with his father.

He had been the one to inflict physical punishment sometime. He could remember that. Punching a man. Over and over again until he agreed to pay. Hurting someone physically and feeling justified because they'd had a deal, and they knew the terms.

And that was the real problem.

Not what he had done today, but it was the path that this kind of behavior led down.

But he couldn't think about it right now. He didn't have the strength to think about it.

Because she was with him, over him, kissing him until neither of them could breathe. Because he could feel her molten, slick center against his arousal, and he wanted nothing more than to sink inside of her.

He wanted her. He moved his hands down her back, down to cup her ass, and brought her hard against his body. She gasped, arching against him, bringing her breasts up to the same level as his mouth. He took one breast between his lips and sucked her hard. Made her cry out with need. Then he did the same to the other one.

Bix.

It would always be her.

And she would always make this thing inside of him come to life.

If he were a different man . . .

If he were a different man, then it would be fine. But he wasn't. It wasn't. And all they had was right now, so he was going to give everything. Everything.

She had said that there was a time limit on this. It was going to have to be sooner. Sooner than he wanted it to be. Sooner than they had imagined.

But this had brought everything out into the open. Every ugly, bad thing.

And he couldn't ignore that. He just couldn't.

He shifted, and that brought the head of his arousal to the entrance of her body.

"Bix," he ground out.

"I'm good," she said. "Cycle wise. It's fine."

He shouldn't. But he was out of control. He shouldn't, but every wall was demolished.

He shouldn't. He shouldn't. He shouldn't. And for the last fifteen years of his life that had been enough. The drumbeat of what he should and shouldn't do, of who he should and shouldn't be, had been enough to keep him from doing things. To make him do the right things. But not now.

Because the bigger drive, the bigger truth, was how much he needed her. And so he brought her down over his length, skin to skin, felt her all glorious and wet and tight around him, and it was like a song inside of his soul.

He lost himself in it. In her.

He had never wanted anything or anyone so much.

He never would again.

Because after this the walls would go back up. After this, everything would be finished. After this, there would be no more.

This was goodbye.

Not just to Bix, but to the man he had become while he was with her.

It had to be that way.

He watched her. With every stroke, as she took each and every bit of pleasure that was afforded to her. He felt like he had been cut open, flayed. He felt like he was being rubbed down with salt. He felt like he had died and gone to heaven. He never wanted it to end.

He held on as long as he could. Until she was shaking. Until she gave up her own release. And then he demanded it again. He put his thumb between them, where their bodies joined and stroked her until she cried out. And then, only then did he let himself go over.

He poured himself into her, and then brought her face down to his, kissed her hard, swallowed her cry of pleasure. His forehead against hers, held her there like that.

She put her hands on his face, and he saw something horribly, indescribably sad in her eyes.

"What?" he asked.

"You break my heart, Daughtry. Because I don't think you know . . . I don't think you know how amazing you are."

"Don't," he said.

"I won't. Not tonight."

He wrapped his arms around her, and held her. They stayed like that until the water was cold. And then he carried her to bed. Because he needed to hang on. To the next few hours, to everything. He needed this. He needed Bix.

And he felt like once the sun rose, everything would change.

CHAPTER TWENTY-ONE

IT DIDN'T TAKE long for rumors of the big dustup to spread around the ranch. When Daughtry passed through in the morning with swollen, busted-up knuckles, there was talk. And well, Bix didn't have it in her to let rumors run rampant.

Not when she could easily clear them up.

"He was defending me," she said.

"That's so romantic," said Rue, softening for a second and looking down at her engagement ring.

"That must put him in an awful temper," said Denver. "You know, he thinks he's better than the rest of us."

"He doesn't," said Bix, feeling irritated that Denver made that assumption. "Have you ever met your own brother? He doesn't think he's as good as anyone. He thinks he sucks. He's wrong."

Denver and Justice exchanged a look.

"It's true," she said. "I don't think you understand just how much he . . . how much he works at being what he thinks is the best that he can be. Not because he thinks he's superior. Because he thinks he isn't."

She ended up sulking for a good part of the day, because she was so damned irritated at how his family had responded.

She knew that they loved him. It was nothing like her family. But still. She understood him. With her whole heart, she understood him. And she was going to have to . . . She was going to have to be brave and tell him. Tell him what she wanted, what she needed. She hadn't been intending on doing it this early. Because there were other things to discuss. But she could sense him pulling away. Freaking out. Last night had been a whole thing. A whole big emotional deal. She could feel him pulling away. She could feel him trying to rebuild the defenses inside of him. She herself was left utterly defenseless against him, so she did not want him getting any barriers up. It wasn't fair.

But then, none of this was about fair.

It was a strange thing. Loving somebody. Loving people. Loving a place. She did. His whole family. Rue. The Sullivan sisters. But Daughtry most of all.

It was like a light had been turned on inside of her. It was the most expansive, altering thing she had ever experienced.

She wanted to be vulnerable for him. She didn't want to get angry. She didn't want to protect herself.

She was ready. Ready to tear strips off of herself. Ready to expose herself.

That had to be worth something. It had to be worth a lot of somethings.

When Daughtry got home from work that evening, her heart lifted.

She ran out of her house and to the truck, and saw that his expression was grim.

"What's going on, Sheriff?"

"Nothing," he said.

"Well," she said. "That's a lie. And I think you know that."

"Don't worry about it, Bix."

"I'm worried. Hey, do you want to go over and make sure they cleared off?"

He looked at her. "Why would I take you if I did that?"

"Because, somebody should be there to stop you from committing a murder if they're there."

"I'm not murderous today."

"That's good. But still. Why don't we go over together? Then maybe we can have some dinner and . . . whatever. Let's just go and make sure that it's handled."

He sighed heavily and got back in his truck. She got into the passenger seat. She didn't think her father and brother were still there. But she wanted him back there. She wanted to be by the cabin when she told him this. She was absolutely jingling with nerves. It was the most intense, extreme experience of her life, that five-minute car ride back over to the cabin.

He parked the truck, and they got out. She stepped slowly into the woods. She looked up, and around.

She was struck by the fact that this place looked the same. But she wasn't the same in it. She had changed. Everything inside of her had changed.

She was different. And she loved Daughtry King. It was maybe the most significant change of all.

Everybody wanted to be loved. Of course they did. Who wouldn't want that? She wanted Daughtry to love her so very much.

But she couldn't ignore the gift of loving him.

When she had soothed his wounds last night—before it had turned sexual—it had just felt wonderful. To have somebody to care for.

It was real. The substance of living.

Surviving was food. Water. Shelter where you wouldn't freeze to death or get eaten by a predator. Living was love.

She knew that now without a doubt.

And there were any number of paths she could go down. Any number of lives that she could live. She had been given the gift of hope. And hope let her see so many options.

But she knew that she really wanted the one thing. More than anything. More than everything.

They walked beneath the trees, until they came to the old outbuilding. She stood there, staring at it. She remembered hiding under the floor when he had first come by. She knew an immense amount of sympathy for poor, scared Bix. She was poor scared Bix now, but she was scared in a different way.

And brave in a different way too. She didn't feel impervious like she had. No. She felt soft. Susceptible to pain. Susceptible to being wounded. But she was almost proud of that. Very nearly.

"Nobody seems to be here," he said. "Of course, they left all their junk."

"We'll clean it."

She looked around the space. "I can't believe it's been just over two months since I was the one squatting here. I . . . It's like a different life, but it's mine.

I know it is. Because I'll never forget it. You saw them. My father, my brother. That's what I come from. That's what built me. It's inescapable. But you . . . This place . . . It changed me. It broke me open. I was protecting myself, all this time. Hiding. Putting up wall after wall of defense to keep myself from being hurt. I had to do that. Because you know how hard it was. You know how cruel my childhood was. If I didn't look out for me nobody would. But when that happens you become small and you become mean. I told you, what I wanted was to be healthy enough, wealthy enough, to be able to help other people. I think I just now realized it was more than that." She let out a long breath. "Love always felt too expensive to me. I never loved anyone or anything. Never even a pet. I never could. I was afraid of it even. But that's the part that keeps you hard. If you can't love anything . . . not even a sunrise, not even where you are . . . then you're just shrunken and cold."

She paced in a circle in front of the cabin. "I caught a fish that day that you saw me. But I couldn't chance cooking it, because you might see the fire smoke. I cried over that fish. Very nearly. That was the kind of thing that got to me. It was all I could allow myself to feel. But never for very long. Because I had to keep going. And here, with you, I've been able to stop and rest. I've been able to find things that I care about. Things that I love."

And right then she turned to him. Then she could see it. The moment his face went flat, cold. The moment the walls started successfully being rebuilt.

"Don't, Sheriff. Please."

"Bix . . ."

"No. I have to tell you this. I have to. Because you need to know. As much as I need to love someone, Daughtry, you need somebody to love you. And I do."

"No," he said. "You don't."

"I do. Don't insult me. Don't insult either of us by pretending you're the kind of man that thinks he can tell a woman what she feels, and I'm the kind of woman that needs to be told. Don't do it."

"I don't want you to," he said. "I made that very clear from the beginning."

"You would've had to make it clear two months ago. I saw you, and I was lost. I just didn't know it. Or maybe . . . maybe I was found. Maybe that's the truth of it. The absolute truth of it. I was found the moment that I first saw you. You reached a hand down to me, and I took it, and it changed everything. And I just want to be able to change even one thing for you. Whether that's cleaning off your bloody knuckles or loving you, just the way that you are, I want to do it."

"You don't get it. That person that you saw yesterday, that's me. Unguarded. Unchanged. Before you, I never had any problems with that guy resurfacing. And I don't want anything to do with somebody that makes me feel that way again. I know that I was justified in trying to help you. But that isn't the point. The point is, I can be that way about anything. I don't trust myself. And you sure as hell shouldn't trust me. Look what I did to your brother. That was overkill."

"It was," she said. "And it was awesome. I liked it. Because nobody's ever cared about me that much."

"I don't have to care about somebody that much to do that," he said. "The truth is, they were on my land. He was about to touch my woman, and that sent me. That's not about finer caring. That's possessiveness. That's the kind of thing my dad felt. If it was his, he was going to claim it, and he could justify anything in the name of that. If he had made a deal with somebody, and they went back on it, then he thought that he got to do anything to them. That lives in me. That is the foundation that built me. And the difference between you and me, Bix, is that I liked it. I liked the power. And I still do. I knew that I could win against your dad and your brother, and I liked it. I like knowing that I'm the one that can end a fight. I have to shut all that down. All of it. All the time. And I cannot be with somebody who . . . who makes me feel these things. I just can't do it."

"It's love, Sheriff. And it makes us all crazy. You just need to deal with it. You just need to accept it."

"It's not love. It's toxic. And it's bad. And I don't want it. I don't want you."

She just stood there, staring, her heart shriveling. He didn't want her. He didn't love her. But what else was new? Nobody did. Nobody had ever loved her; why would Daughtry be different?

He had gotten a look at her family, and he hadn't wanted her. Why would he? Of course he didn't. It was obvious that he wouldn't. Who would? Who would when they had seen all of that?

She felt so ashamed, and so small. It made her want to turn and run and . . .

And that was why he had said it.

It was so easy for her to spiral. For her to believe that he didn't love her. Because of course he would say that.

Of course he would . . . That coward.

He was trying to make her feel awful so that she would leave so that he didn't have to deal with her. So that he didn't have to deal with his feelings. Didn't have to deal with his emotions. Well. Fuck that and fuck him.

"Are you trying to White Fang me?"

"What?" he asked.

"You know. Like the book *White Fang*. You're trying to White Fang me. To tell me that you don't want me and send me out into the wild."

"No. I'm not trying to do that, I am telling you that I don't want you."

"I would at least admit it," she spit. "You fucking dick. You might as well kick a rock at me."

"Bix, I'm not trying to do anything to you. I am just telling you the way that it is."

He was so stubborn. And she was just so angry. She had come here all ready to be vulnerable, and now he was just lying. He wasn't giving her anything in return; he was trying to make her feel bad.

Rage blinded her. She bent down and she picked up a rock, and she threw it at him. It hit him square in the back. He barely flinched, because his muscles were that hard. "Why don't *you* go on and get," she said.

"You're the one that can barely stand it here. You're the one that can barely stand to be around your own family and your own family legacy because you've decided that you're uniquely tainted. Uniquely hurt. Uniquely wounded by everybody and everything. No wonder Denver thinks you're such an ass. You are. I told him earlier today that you don't think you're better than everybody. But maybe you do. And it's so much better to sit up there and be self-righteous than have to get down here in the dirt with the rest of us who feel things."

"That's not it," he growled. "I don't think I'm better than you. I don't deserve you."

"How comforting. A convenient excuse for everything. Must be nice, Daughtry. Walk around with a literal bulletproof vest on, because you're hiding. Protecting yourself, and you tell yourself that you're protecting other people. You just don't want to care. Because the last time you cared that person led you astray. Because the last time you cared, that person didn't actually care about you, did he? You were nothing but muscle to him. And when he couldn't use you the way that he wanted to, he abandoned you. And that's your real problem."

She was furious. And she was . . . Well, she was going to leave without him.

She reached over and grabbed his keys, and then she started to step back toward the truck.

"Where are you going?"

"I'm leaving," she said. "It's what you wanted." She spread her arms wide, the keys jingling. "That's me. White Fang. A lone wolf. So I'm just going to go off and do lone-wolf things. Thanks for the sex and all the money. Sucker. At least I got something out of this. What did you get?" Tears were flowing down her cheeks now. "You didn't get anything. Because I didn't do anything for you. I couldn't give you any work. I couldn't even give you enough love. None of it was enough. None of it was good enough. So I guess this was just one long con after all. Hooray for me."

She got into the truck, and a sob shook her body. She started the engine, and punched the gas. And she left him there, standing behind her. Getting smaller and smaller in the rearview mirror. And she just wanted . . . She just wanted for this to stop. It hurt so bad. And she had said all these things and she didn't even think she meant them. But her chest was this big indistinct radiating ball of pain, so how was she even supposed to know what was true and what wasn't?

The only thing that felt real was all that hurt.

She clutched the steering wheel, trying to find a happy medium between anger and sadness. Instead, she just let it all come. She didn't stop it.

She didn't try to protect herself. And somewhere, in the midst of all of it, she knew that she would be all right. Not in that mean, small way she had survived before.

Even with all this, she was different. She wasn't going to just double down and close off.

This was heartbreak.

It was what happened when you cared enough to get yourself broken.

It was horrible.

Just horrible.

And she knew she couldn't go back to Daughtry's house. So she did the only thing she could think to do.

She drove to Arizona's house.

Because they were friends now. Sort of.

And she needed somebody. She didn't need to be alone. She needed help.

She got out of the truck, and stumbled to the front door. She was just about to knock when Arizona opened it. "Bix? What's wrong?"

"Daughtry . . ."

And then Arizona had her arms around Bix, and Bix could tell that Arizona wasn't much of a hugger. Come to that, neither was Bix. But here they were, trying. "Oh, I'm sorry."

She didn't say she had told her so, even though she had.

"I just really do love him."

"I know," said Arizona. "And he really doesn't deserve it."

Bix hiccupped. "He really doesn't."

"All right, Bix. Let's get you some tea. You can stay here. Until everything gets sorted out."

"I have money," she said. "I can get myself an apartment and I can . . ."

"Let's just give it a minute."

But while Bix wasn't entirely hopeless, she did have one big black spot where hope had been once. And that was the place where her love for Daughtry had once been.

CHAPTER TWENTY-TWO

DAUGHTRY WAITED FOR SERENITY. For something. He waited for control to come back. He couldn't find it. Could feel it. He was bleeding out. He felt like his heart was going to come through his chest. He felt like he wasn't going to be able to keep on breathing. It was a heart attack. Maybe. Or something.

He was standing there in the woods, and he needed to walk back home, but Bix might be at his home. And if she wasn't, it might not be home.

He didn't know what to do. He didn't know where to go. He couldn't recall that ever being the case. Not ever before.

He walked into the cabin, and sat down on the floor.

This was the place Bix had been sleeping when he'd found her.

It made him feel sick to his stomach. All of this did.

He waited. It got cold. It got dark. He still sat there.

He saw a flashlight beam outside, and got tense. If it was her dad and her brother come back for another fight, he was ready to give it to them. Because this was where he was. And it was who he was. And he couldn't seem to find a way to fix it.

The door opened, and he shot up to his feet.

"At ease, soldier," came his brother's voice.

"What are you doing here?" he asked.

"When you didn't come home I hunted around for Bix. Found her. Got the bead that you may still be out here given that she left you. I mean, left you left you. Both here physically, and emotionally."

"Because I told her to," he said.

"Yeah, I got that. Something about you trying to White Fang her."

"I don't even know what the hell that means."

"I think you do. And I also think it's accurate. Sounds like you said a bunch of hurtful things to drive her away."

"Excuse me, you have the emotional literacy of a cabbage—what are you doing here lecturing me?"

"Oh, did it sound like a lecture? I didn't mean it to. I was just repeating the things that you did back to you. If it bothers you, then you have a problem with yourself, not with me."

"You judge me."

"Yeah. I do. Because Bix is a cool woman. And you're never going to find anybody else like her. So I don't actually know what you're doing. But then, you've always been a mystery to me. I don't know what you want, Daughtry. Do you?"

"Yes. I want to do the right thing. I want to be better than our father. I want to be better than he raised us to be."

"Join the club," said Denver.

"We don't go about it the same ways."

"No kidding. That could be why we fight so much."

"We don't fight that much," said Daughtry.

"Why don't you just work at the ranch?"

"Because," he said. "Because everything to do with the ranch is tied up in all the old stuff, and anything that is tied up in the old stuff is just . . . It's too hard. All of it. I can't stand it. Okay? Is that what you want to hear? I don't know what I'm doing. I just know that I don't want to feel. I don't want to feel the way that I did. Because back then, I could feel all these things, and it was just . . . It would explode. And Dad used that. He used me. And the thing that I felt deepest, the thing that I felt most proud of, was our family. Was being Dad's son. How can you be that wrong and not know it? Don't you ever wonder that? How you can be that wrong, and have no idea?"

"I don't worry about it," Denver said. "Because I can't. I have shit to do. Right or wrong, good or bad, I do what needs doing. As long as taking care of you, taking care of the people in the community Dad messed with, takes up my time I won't get off the path. I would've thought that you would have a similar feeling. You joined law enforcement. Doesn't that tell you everything you need to know?"

"No. Because suddenly, there's Bix. And all of my feelings are too big to handle again. And I don't know how I'll know when I'm doing the right thing, and when I'm doing the wrong thing. When I'm angry because it's justified, and when I'm just on a power trip."

"You know, I don't believe you. I bet she didn't either. I think you believe that. I think you're the only one that does. I think you were the only one that believes that you might actually go off half-cocked one day. It's a pretty neat story that you're telling yourself. And I get it. I do. Bottom line, though, I was older, and I saw more of Dad than you or Justice or Landry. I think he did a particular kind of hit job on you three. Because you all loved him. Very much. And you got involved in his world, and I did too. But it was different. I . . . I was trying to protect you. I wasn't very good at it. And I'm still not. Because if I was, then you and I wouldn't be at odds all the time, and you wouldn't have rejected the one woman who was dumb enough to fall in love with you."

"You don't owe me anything," said Daughtry.

"No. I don't. I get that. I've actually done a lot. I still don't feel redeemed, or whatever it is you're waiting to feel. Just so you know. It's complicated. I get that. I tried. I'll never get over what happen. I'll always wish that I had done more. Done better. Done different. But I didn't. So I guess my question is . . . are you really afraid of yourself, or are you just afraid of loving somebody again? And being blindsided. Because from my point of view, that's the cruelest thing that ever happened to you. The way you loved Dad, only to have to realize, to fully realize, that the version of love you'd been sold all your life was a total lie. You might lose it again, right?"

"Denver . . ."

He didn't like his brother's words, because they scraped against something inside of him. Because they felt too damned true.

Because yeah. It didn't feel real that Bix loved him. And it didn't feel like she should.

They were wrong, though. He did feel bad. Afraid

of the feelings inside of him. Because they were just so big. They were so big, and if he loved her and then she didn't really love him, it . . .

Well, hell.

It was all that. All of it. And he wanted to reject her before she could reject him. Because he had loved a narcissist, and his dad had played him. And that was how he had recognized love for all these years, and it made him afraid of it now.

Afraid of himself. And the capacity he had to love the wrong person in the wrong way.

But Bix wasn't a narcissist. She wasn't wrong. Bix was the best person he knew. She was principled. And she was good. She was feisty. Kind of a liar, but kind of in an obvious way, which was cute.

She was cute.

And she cared about him. Cared for him. And he had . . . he had tried to hurt her. Tried to hurt her so that she would leave him when he was expecting it. And not when he wasn't. So that he could be in control.

And what hit him then was that it was closer to being his father than he would've ever wanted to be. By trying to not be like him, by trying to avoid pain and attachment, he was somehow bringing himself closer to the old man than he would have ever believed.

"It isn't that I don't care about the ranch," he said. "I care too much. And anything that I care too much about, I try only to do about half of."

"I hope you didn't only do half with Bix. She deserves better than that."

He shot his brother a flat glare. "I wanted to figure

out a way to fix the way the town saw our family. Because that was actually still more distant than digging in and fixing the family itself. The distance is my fault. I'd . . . I'm just so . . . Listen, I'm not afraid of having a gun pointed at me. I'm not afraid of a high-speed chase. I'm not afraid to get into a fistfight. But I am really afraid of some of the things that I feel."

"I get that," Denver said, his face shrouded in shadow. "Believe me. I get that. And I know all about bids for atonement. But you have an opportunity here that's pretty amazing. And I would hate for you to miss out on it because of Dad. Mostly because I just don't think he should have any more of us than he already does. And if you can't love her out of spite, which is frankly what I would do, then just love her for you. Because wouldn't it be better than just being sad?"

"I don't know," Daughtry said. "Living with her, day in and day out and always feeling all these things."

"I think they call it being happy. Having not experienced it firsthand, I wouldn't know. But you've been happy, Daughtry. The happiest I've seen you. Anything that makes you feel like that is something worth hanging on to."

He sat there, in the dark, looking around the cabin. This cabin that felt so emblematic of Bix's bravery. Of how far she had been willing to go.

He had taken care of her physically. But emotionally . . . she had given him everything.

It was more than a brick.

It was more than a handful of stardust.

It was all the stars in the sky.

Bix, who'd had so little to give, had opened her heart to him generously, and what had he done? He'd been a coward.

He had deserved everything she had shouted at him.

"So are you going to come back or what?"

He nodded slowly. "Yeah. I think I will."

"Are you going to patch things up with Bix?"

He stood there, in the darkness. And the most crushing, horrifying, terrifying joy he'd experienced began to filter through his body. "I could, couldn't I?"

"Yeah," said Denver. "You could."

"I could be happy."

"Yes, Daughtry," Denver said slowly. "You could be."

He could be happy. He could be with Bix. He could be in love.

And he realized then that it wasn't about banishing all of the hard feelings. It wasn't about not being afraid. It was just about knowing that loving her was worth it. Whatever the risk, the reward would be greater.

He loved her.

And that was all there was to it. There was no going back, no protecting himself from it. No changing it.

Bix Carpenter had changed him. His whole world. His whole soul.

And he needed to tell her.

BIX WAS DOWN at the river throwing stones. Because what else could you do when your whole world had broken apart, and your heart felt like it was full of jagged glass, and you still needed to work the next day, and make plans for your whole future? She was proud of herself. Sort of. Because she was standing. So there was that.

She closed her eyes and let the wind ruffle through her hair.

She knew who she was. She was Bix. She had more now than she had before. She had more now because she loved Daughtry, even if he was too scared to admit he loved her too.

He did.

She had to believe he did.

She wasn't in despair.

She would rather be with him than not. But she would be okay. She would be.

"I thought I might find you here."

She turned around, and saw Daughtry standing there.

"What are you doing?"

"Looking for you. Finding you. I stayed at the cabin until after dark. Then I went home and didn't sleep much. I knew that I needed to talk to you."

"Did you have more mean things to say?"

"No. I need to take back all the mean things. I'm sorry. I *was* trying to do that thing you said."

"White Fanging."

"Yeah. I was."

Her heart went to a standstill. "Go on."

"I was trying to do that because I was totally freaked out. And you were right. It's not because I'm really afraid I'm going to do something awful. I've lived too much and learned too much. I do know what's right and wrong. That's an excuse that I've been telling myself for a long time because keeping myself on a leash means keeping myself from feeling too much. Keeping myself from being hurt. I've made so many little choices in my life that amount to trying to keep myself at a distance with things and people that I care about, that I didn't even realize I was doing it anymore. It all got buried underneath this story that I told myself about needing to be in control. Because of the things in my past. And it's legitimate. I did some bad things. But I've done a lot of good things. And somehow, I never let them be enough. It isn't about protecting other people. It's about protecting myself. You are absolutely right about that."

"Oh," she breathed.

She felt afraid to hope. But she didn't want to be. Because hope was one of the greatest gifts of her time here. Other than Daughtry.

So she opened up her heart, and she let it flow through her.

"I hope that you're here to say what I want you to, Sheriff."

"I want stardust, Bix. All that magic. That's us. The whole sky full of stars. I want you. I want to love you. And I want you to love me."

She set down her rock, and ran toward him. She wrapped her arms around his neck, and held him tight. "You want to love me, or do you love me?"

"I love you," he said, fierce and glorious. "And I want to love you for the rest of forever."

"I want that too," she whispered.

"If that means you need to go away first for a while,

that's okay. If you need to go to school, if you need to have other experiences, I'll be here when you get back."

She shook her head. "No. I've already decided that any opportunity I want is going to fit around our life together. Because love really is the most amazing thing. Love is the thing I didn't have even a little bit of before. And now I have so much of it I'm full to the brim. Now I understand. I understand the romance novels. And the songs. And the self-help books, oddly. Somehow it kind of helped with those two."

He laughed. "Good. Me too. I was . . . I was living half a life. And I thought it was all I was going to be able to have. And I'm terrified. I'm terrified of messing things up with you. I'm terrified of not being good enough. I'm terrified that you'll leave me. But I'm even more terrified of what it looks like if we don't try."

"One thing you should know about me, Sheriff," she said, "is that I am good at a few things. I'm good at surviving, and I'm good at making moonshine. I am damned good at loving my man. Forever and ever."

"Well, I am not good at making moonshine. But I can promise you that I'll love you. With all of me. You know that I'm stubborn. So once I decide to do something, I never stop."

"Now, that I believe," she said.

"I want to marry you," he said. "I want you to have my name, have my babies. I didn't want that before. I couldn't imagine it. But now that it's you I can. Now

I'm not imagining the house I grew up in. Now I'm imagining you and me."

"I want that too. I really do. Because, you know . . . I was thinking, why have my dad's last name when he doesn't mean anything to me? When I don't feel part of that family. I decided the name itself could mean something. But I would much rather take your name. That's more than a brick. That's a whole ranch. A whole family."

"Yes, it is."

She looked across the river at that little house where he found her. Everything was different now.

She had thought she needed a new starter for her van. But that wasn't it.

What she had needed had been here all along.

What she had needed was love.

* * * * *

Read on for an excerpt from
The Rogue by Maisey Yates.

CHAPTER ONE

RUBY MATTHEWS HAD her life together. She had a perfect little house, with a perfect little yard. And she had a very perfect little dog. She had the perfect engagement ring and the perfect fiancé, deployed at the moment, and a perfect wedding dress in her closet waiting for her very perfect day.

It was important to Rue that she had those things, because her life growing up had been very, very far from perfect. Things being the way they were now felt right, after the chaos of her upbringing.

Everything had a place. A perfect, neat place where it belonged.

All of her yarn organized by weight and fiber in little baskets in her extra bedroom.

Her dresses belonged in rainbow-colored order in her closet.

Her beloved grandmother's ashes belonged beneath a cherry tree at King's Crest, the place she loved most in the world.

Asher belonged by her side as her husband, and their wedding was in one month, which meant it was almost time for that to happen.

And Justice? He belonged right up at the front of the church when she and Asher had their wedding.

Because he was her best friend in the whole wide world, and he was her man of honor. It was his place.

Oh, Justice.

It was impossible to oversell the impact of Justice King. When he walked into a room, he created a ripple; you couldn't *not* notice. He was tall, halfway over six foot, with broad shoulders and sandy brown hair. His eyes were a deep green that seemed almost otherworldy. His jaw was square, his nose straight, his lips…

She had heard a woman say once that his lips were made for sin.

Rue wasn't sure what that meant but it had stuck with her.

He was her best friend. The greatest guy she knew.

Except he was late for his suit fitting because he was a careening, disastrous mess who washed his face only when she reminded him to. Or when he was going out to pick up women, which he did a lot.

It could be argued that Justice's place was actually in the dog pound, because the man was nothing but a hound. But she was way too fond of him to argue that point.

She was getting anxious because she had been waiting with the seamstress in her front room for ten minutes, and Justice hadn't answered his text and he was eight whole minutes late. The seamstress had been early.

Rue herself was always early, and Justice was always late.

It made her want to…

But just then his truck pulled into the driveway and her heart lifted. She was so, so glad to see him. Because time was wasting and she hated wasted time.

He parked his truck and walked through her front door without knocking. Which made her feel a strange note of wistfulness, because when she moved in with Asher, Justice wouldn't be able to just do that. They would be being newlyweds and having…sex and things.

It would change Justice's position in her life.

She frowned.

"You're late," she said.

"Sorry, Rue," he said, his voice sounding scratchy and unrepentant. "I'll do better next time."

He always said that. And Rue could only assume that his version of best worked for her on some level or she wouldn't have made him such an integral part of her existence.

"When, at the next tux fitting or my next wedding?" she asked.

He grinned. "Yep."

"The only way I'll be having two weddings is if the first one is ruined because the man of honor is late." She gave him the evil eye and Sue Quackenbush, the seamstress, gave him a swift once-over.

"Come on over here," she said.

She began to measure him without preamble, and Rue watched the proceedings closely. Justice gave her a smile, and a wink as Sue measured down his inseam.

"Careful," he said.

"I know what I'm doing," she responded, brusquely.

Rue liked it when a woman wasn't flustered by Justice. It was far too easy for him to get a reaction out of women. They shouldn't reward his bad behavior.

"Where were you?" Rue asked, because suddenly she was suspicious.

"In bed."

She couldn't help herself; she let out an exasperated sigh. "You're a cowboy, Justice. How do you end up sleeping past noon?"

"Easy. I party till the cows come home. Then I feed the cows. Then I go to bed."

"Lord." She scrubbed her hand over her forehead.

"Okay," said Sue. "Go in the next room and put these on." She pulled some pants, a vest, a shirt and a jacket off her rolling clothes rack. "They'll be close. Then I'll put some pins in and make the alterations."

Justice went into her bedroom without checking with her first. It was clean, thankfully. She knew that.

He emerged a few minutes later and she was stunned speechless. Motionless. Thoughtless.

She knew Justice better than she knew anyone. She knew him after a hard day's work. She knew him as a third-grade boy who wouldn't read and who'd had to take lessons from her, a girl who was a whole grade younger than him. She knew him as a protector, a terrible poker player, a first-rate playboy.

But she'd never known him in a tux.

Good. Lord.

He was going to be unstoppable. She was going to have to warn her female family members, and Asher's, who came from out of town to be safe and vigilant where he was concerned because…

In a tux he was lethal.

All the broad, muscular lines of his body were so sharp in that suit. The black bow tie made him look like Cowboy James Bond.

She'd seen him cleaned up, but this was another level.

Justice had actually rendered her speechless.

"Well…well, that's fantastic," she said.

"Yes," Sue agreed. "Just a few alterations to make."

She was speedy with her pins, and far too quickly, Justice was back and changing out of the tux. "You're going to make a great decoration at the wedding," Rue said.

She was only half kidding. Having him on stage looking like that was a boon. She could save on flowers. Who needed them when you had all that cowboy to look at?

"Thanks, Rue, I always wanted to settle down and live a quiet life as something more aesthetic than useful. I'd be a great paperweight."

In spite of herself, Sue, who was really quite stoic, blushed. Justice was a whole thing and he couldn't be stopped.

"I'll have the altered suit back by the end of the week," Sue said.

"Great," Rue responded. "I'll talk to you then."

Sue hung everything on her rolling rack and collected her supplies, before leaving Justice and Rue alone in the house.

"I bet I could pull her if I wanted to," he said.

"She has been married for thirty years and has nine children."

"Your point?"

"Lord above, Justice, not everyone is an idiot over…that sort of thing." She gestured wildly at him.

"If they aren't then they aren't doing it right."

She cleared her throat. "So where were you really?"

"In bed. Really. I had a late night."

Oh. That was code for hooking up. She knew Justice well. Good for him, really. It was fine that her sex life was sporadic. She wasn't jealous. It was a hazard of an eight-year engagement to a man who'd been deployed for the majority of that time.

She wasn't…that sexual anyway. She liked it. She liked being close to Asher. But it wasn't a huge factor in her life. What she liked best was the stability. The promise that he would be there for her always.

The certainty she felt with him.

He was her high school sweetheart. Her one and only. And their wedding was finally on the horizon.

So, Justice could wham-bam-thank-you-ma'am whoever he wanted to. That was empty. She had *love*. So there.

So very there.

"Well, at least you showed up without the scent of the workday clinging to you." If she smelled too deeply there might be a hint of perfume, though.

She wouldn't smell deeply.

"You coming for dinner tonight?" he asked.

She spent most nights with the King family. After her grandmother's death last year she'd felt so alone.

Her grandma had been the most constant figure in her life. She might not have raised her, but going to her house every day after she'd done school at the little one-room schoolhouse at Four Corners Ranch had been her salvation.

Her parents' house had always been a mess of angry words and beer bottles. Rue hated the disorganization. Her own room had always been spotless.

And her grandmother's house had been a haven of sunlight and cookies. She and Justice had both spent days there, often. Her death had been tough for him too, not that he'd actually said that. Justice wasn't a big one for emotional sincerity.

Though, after the funeral he'd seen her crying behind the church and he'd taken her in his arms, hard and tight.

He'd smelled like the earth, the sun and Justice. So familiar, and so necessary in that moment when the church had been full of all the family she didn't know that well, while they said goodbye to the one person she had.

She cried into his jacket and left tear stains behind.

It had helped her hold it together later so she hadn't had to cry on Asher.

But ever since then she'd eaten dinner at the main house at King's Crest more often than not. King's Crest was Justice's family ranch, part of the broader ranching collective of Four Corners Ranch, the largest ranching spread in the state of Oregon.

Sullivan's Point was home to produce, baked goods and a farm store. McCloud's Landing was an equine therapy center. Garrett's Watch was a cattle ranch, and King's had been too up until recently. They still did their cattle, but they were expanding. They had a new wedding venue they were almost finished with. It was going to be gorgeous but she couldn't wait for it to get done to be married there.

Also, as much as she loved King's Crest, she really did think she needed a church wedding. It felt more grounded and traditional. But the reception would be at King's. They'd offered her the barn and outdoor area they used for town hall meetings—the big all-ranch gatherings they had once a month to discuss their business and make new proposals, dance, eat and have a good time.

Asher had been a little bit *meh* about it, but the truth was, he was always a little *meh* about the ranch.

He didn't *get* it; that was the thing. How could he?

Four Corners had always been a family. Even if, much like her own, it was dysfunctional in some ways. The school had been small, and they'd all known each other—even if she and Justice had been closer to each other than to anyone else.

Justice was popular; he always had been. He played kickball, baseball and backyard football with the rowdier kids. She had taught some of the other kids who preferred to sit to crochet, then eventually knit and the ones who were interested would sit with her in relative silence while sports occurred.

They'd had different kinds of home lives; she had never really talked about her situation with anyone but Justice.

The dirt, the trees, the view of the mountains, that would always be a profound part of her. Asher seemed to find it inconvenient that she liked to spend time there.

But it was fine. Asher would get it eventually, she was sure. Because no, she wasn't going to keep eating dinner six nights a week at King's when they were married, but they would definitely go over sometimes. That was just how it was.

Justice and his family were part of her life.

"Yes," she said. "I'd love to come to dinner. I might bring some bouquet pictures too. Maybe Penny and Bix can give some input."

"You think Bix is going to tell you what flowers to get?"

Bix was Justice's brother Daughtry's fiancée. She was unorthodox to say the least. Rue had an interesting time with her. Not that Penny was much better. A headstrong, feral woman who had been taken in by the Kings when she was a teenager, after her dad had died.

"Maybe I'll hold back unless Fia's there." His sister-in-law. There was no point showing flowers to his sister, Arizona, either.

It was sometimes a little sad not to have a passel of close female friends, though she did like the women of King's Crest. But Justice was the one whose opinion would always matter most. He would always be the one who mattered most.

"Probably a good plan."

"I only have a month, Justice. Thirty days. And then Asher and I are finally going to be married and…"

"And what flowers you carried won't really matter."

She looked up at him, shocked by his uncharacteristic show of…sentimentality. It was deeply unlike him. "That's really sweet, Justice."

"Is it? You didn't ask me why the flowers won't matter."

"Oh. Dear. Why won't they matter?"

"Because men don't give a shit about flowers. All he'll care about is what you're wearing, or not, under the wedding dress."

She scoffed and tried to hold back the color she could feel bleeding into her cheeks. He was outrageous sometimes and it was embarrassing, even though she should be used to it. "That isn't true."

"It is," he said. "Trust me, I'm a man."

"But you aren't a man in love," she said.

"What…difference would that make? I'm still never going to care more about a bouquet than a bra."

"But the whole thing matters when you're in love. All of it. It's not about sex. It's about caring, and saying vows and…"

"The sex should matter," he said.

"But it isn't the point."

He squinted. "It's not?"

"No. And that's why you're stuck in bar-hookup Groundhog Day, where you wake up at the same time every morning with a different woman in your bed, doomed to repeat it again the next day."

"First of all, is that supposed to sound bad?"

"Yes!"

"Second, I don't wake up in the morning with anyone but me. I don't spend the night with women I don't know. It's dangerous. You could get robbed. I practice safe sex."

He smiled then, and she couldn't be annoyed at him. Because that was how he was.

"Okay, get out of my house," she said, pushing at his shoulder. "I have to go take inventory at the yarn store."

Her grandmother's yarn store was forty minutes away, in Mapleton, and it had been part of her inheritance. It was an established shop with a full staff, but Rue worked there full-time and she loved it. She was a serious yarn addict. Her stash was the only thing in her house that was overflowing.

It was organized, though.

By fiber, weight and color.

"Okay then, see you at dinner."

He left then, and got in his truck. As she watched him drive away, she couldn't help but sigh in a contented sort of way.

Everything was perfect.

Everything was in its rightful place.

CHAPTER TWO

JUSTICE STACKED ROCKS until his muscles ached. Until the tyranny of the night before released his hold on his head, and his muscles. The only way to survive partying this hard was to work harder.

The older he got, the more that was true.

At thirty-three it wasn't like he was an old man, but the hard living was definitely beginning to catch up with him. So he was doing the best he could to outrun it any which way he could. Because the alternative was to grow the fuck up. And he wasn't planning on doing that anytime soon.

He wondered, not for the first time, what his life would be like when he was less tethered to Rue. Sometimes it felt like she was the only thing holding him to basic human decency.

She was definitely the only and best part of his valor.

It wasn't like she was moving away or doing anything drastic. Rue never did anything drastic. She was a constant. The eternal port in the storm that he had grown up in. His best friend in the entire world. His better half, some might say.

She deserved the world.

He was happy as hell that she had found a man that made her happy. That she was moving on and having the kind of normal life that they hadn't been able to imagine when they were kids.

Watching her win at this made him feel… He was proud of her. She deserved this. She deserved everything and more.

"You're up early."

He turned and saw his brother Denver standing there, staring at him. His tone was dry. Because it was 4:30 p.m., he was not up early. He had gotten up early to go to Rue's. But this was a normal time for him to be up and about.

"Fuck you," he said.

"Good morning," his brother returned.

"I've already run errands today. Don't be so high and mighty."

"Oh yeah? What were you up to?"

"I had to go to a tux fitting. The wedding is in just a couple of weeks."

"Oh that's right. The wedding. I can't believe it."

"Yeah. Me neither."

"Do you ever feel weird about that? Like everybody getting married and moving on. Even Penny."

They both shook their heads. Even Penny was off and married. Landry was, Daughtry was. And honestly, he felt much the same about them that he did about Rue. It was good for them. It was good if you could run from the shit in your past and get some more better.

"Yeah, I guess it's a little bit strange. But…I don't want to change anything. I'm happy."

"Are you?" Denver asked.

"Yeah. I mean, I got laid last night."

"Thank you for sharing, Justice, I really value knowing about your sex life."

"I like to keep an open line of communication with us, bro. I feel like it is really good for the soul."

"You're bragging."

"You could get laid if you felt like it."

"Some of us work. I mean, we really work, we don't stroll into the barn at our leisure."

"Your thoughts on my life aside," Justice said, "I've done what I set out to do. I never wanted to fuck anybody up the way that Dad did us. The way that he did Mom. And here I am. I'm a decent brother, I like to think. I do help you on the ranch, whatever you say, and I have a lifelong friend. And I have managed to maintain that friendship since I was eight years old. Given our upbringing, I feel like that is winning. Great for other people if they want something that looks a little bit more traditional. I don't."

"Can't say that I do either," said Denver.

"Yeah. I mean, that's kind of a big hell no."

"And that's fine," said Denver.

He couldn't remember the last time he ever thought his big brother questioned much of anything, but he could see that he was.

"What's got your panties in a twist?" Justice asked.

"We're the last two," he said.

"The last to what?"

"Everyone else on this whole fucking ranch is gone and gotten themselves married. The Garretts, the Mc-Clouds and the Sullivans. All married."

"Honestly, all I hear is that everybody went and stepped in a bear trap, and you're musing about whether or not we should want to step in a bear trap."

Denver laughed. "I dunno. I guess my concern more is that there is something eternally wrong with us."

"Who cares if there is? We haven't dragged anybody into our shit."

"Good point."

"Go out and get laid, Denver," Justice said. "That will deal with all of your emotional turmoil. You'll remember that there are ways to connect with people that don't require you upending your entire life."

"Yeah. I know."

In all seriousness, his brother was a good dude. But he was hard. And harder to know. They were all like that, he supposed. They had a bit of a reputation around town for being…unsociable. Daughtry had made it his mission to improve the King family name in town, after their dad had done a good job of running it through the mud. The rest of them… Their younger sister, Arizona, had always been known to be prickly and mean. Landry was legendary if only for the explosion that had occurred between him and Fia Sullivan when they were in high school. Denver was well-known for being a hard-ass of epic proportions.

And Justice? Well. He was known for having fun. He was a good time, not a long time, and everyone knew it.

He couldn't say that it had earned him any respect around town, but it had certainly allowed the townspeople to see that the Kings could be harmless. Or if not harmless, something a little closer to fun than deathly serious assholes. Or scumbags.

So there was that.

Of course, Daughtry had gone and hitched up to a former convict, Landry and Fia had gotten together— but only after they had revealed they'd secretly had a child together back when they were teenagers, who they were now raising together—and Arizona had reunited with the love of her life, which had sorted her personality quirks right out. The Kings were on the straight and narrow, except for Daughtry. Who had been kicked off of it a little bit. But honestly, it looked good on him. Happiness looked good on all of his brothers.

He had been happy for a long time, personally. Because he had figured out the secret to that. He had a full life. A good family. Good friend. And he had manageable expectations for himself. And that was the best a man could do in his situation, he figured.

The alternative was marinating in trauma and other bullshit and he wasn't interested in that, thanks. Thinking too much didn't lead anywhere good.

"You coming out to dinner tonight?"

"Yeah, I figured."

"Let's head that way."

He hopped in his brother's truck and let him drive him across the property. King's Crest was, in his opinion, the jewel of Four Corners Ranch. He knew that the other families would fight for that distinction. But Justice had never shied away from a good fistfight. So, it didn't worry him any. His brothers' trucks were sitting in front of the farmhouse when they arrived. The stately old place had been in the family for generations.

Just like the ranch itself.

A collective run by the McClouds, the Kings, the Garretts and the Sullivans since the 1880s. It was the largest ranching operation in the state of Oregon. They weren't factory. They worked the land by hand; they had over a hundred employees. The employees often lived on the ranch, worked on the ranch. Their kids went to school on the ranch. They were an ecosystem in and of themselves. And it was only growing. The Sullivans had made a store on the property where they could sell their items directly. And the Kings were in the process of working at diversifying their cattle operation.

They were building a venue so that people could have conferences, weddings, birthday parties. Guest cabins for people to stay in. Justice was happy to go along for the ride. His favorite thing that they had started up was headed by his sister-in-law Bix, who had an affinity for brewing, and had started a beer label for the place. They had all gotten together and come up with their own distinct variety of beer, and it was about to go into stores, which was definitely a boon.

Bix had been a moonshiner prior to her marriage to Daughtry, and she was the cutest, scrappiest little thing. He really did think his brother had won the lottery with that one.

Bix and Daughtry were about in the farmhouse when they arrived, and so were Arizona and her husband, Micah.

"Hey kids," Justice said when he came in.

"Well," Arizona said. "As I live and breathe. Justice King. Without a hangover."

"Oh, I had one. I just worked it out."

"Good for you," she said. "Is Rue coming?"

"I expect so. Unless she has wedding stuff."

Asher wasn't back in town yet, so she was still spending most nights out at King's Crest. But that was normal. She and Asher had been together for eight years, and he had been deployed on and off for many of those years. He hadn't been a Four Corners Ranch kid. Meaning he hadn't gone to school on the property, even though he was from the area. He had been bussed to school an hour away in Mapleton, and so she hadn't met him until she had started working at her grand-mother's store in town. She had fallen for him pretty quickly. At least, that was how Justice had felt. She was cautious and sweet, was Rue. And she had never been big into the dating scene. He couldn't blame her.

Her parents had been a hot mess and a half. Certainly not the kind to give you aspirations of great romance.

So she'd been extremely choosy when it came to dates and all of that. He had actually been a little bit disturbed when she'd gotten real serious about Asher. When they'd started…apparently sleeping together. It wasn't like she had gone and announced it; there was just a point where it was clear that was happening, and Justice's initial take on that had been pretty dim. Be-cause she was like a sister to him, and it had felt like another thing he wanted to protect her from. He just wanted her to not get hurt.

But she hadn't gotten hurt. They'd stayed together. It was definitely hard on her when Asher was gone. But one thing he admired so much about Rue was that she was levelheaded even when she was falling in love. He had always heard that women got a bit loopy over that kind of thing. Hell, he'd seen men do it too. Love, he knew, was one of the single most dangerous things on earth. It gave people an extraordinary amount of power over another person. And it could create a hell of a lot of damage.

The way that Rue had managed to get into a relationship, and stay in that relationship, while maintaining her home, her career and their friendship, had actually shown him something. But then, Rue had always been a window into some foreign, fascinating thing. She had always been different. Different than what they had been raised in. Different than what they had been surrounded by. A source of peace.

He had never been able to quiet himself long enough to learn anything in school. But when Rue taught him, he was able to sit and listen. She broke it down for him in such a way that she made it all feel possible. He wouldn't even know how to read if it wasn't for her. Forget algebra. So, if anybody could do love and marriage and make it all work, keep their sanity and all of that, he really wasn't surprised that it was Ruby Matthews.

His phone vibrated, and he looked down. Right on time he had a text from Rue saying that she would be there fairly directly. He smiled. He didn't respond. She knew he saw it.

And she wouldn't expect for him to respond directly either. It just wasn't how they did things.

They began to get dinner on the table—barbecue and all the trimmings, which was a staple of the King family diet. They did beef. And they did it well. And anything the Kings did well, they did hard. From work to sex.

He liked that about them. They were definitely a better iteration of the family name than their father had been. And to that he could raise a glass.

Rue appeared a bit later with a craft bag hanging off of her arm, and a folder under her other.

"Hey," he said, moving to the door and taking everything from her, unburdening her immediately.

"Hi," she said, smiling.

"Tell me," Arizona said, sticking her head out of the kitchen, a mischievous grin on her face. "You are really going to get my brother to wear a tux?"

"Yes," said Rue. "Because I'm getting married in a church like a civilized person, and he has to dress like a civilized person."

"The trouble is," Micah said, "I've never had the impression that he was a civilized person."

"I'm not," said Justice.

Denver chose that moment to join the conversation. "Oh, he sure as hell isn't. But he will move heaven and earth to make sure that Rue has the wedding that she wants. He's not civilized. He's a damned good friend."

"That's the truth," said Rue.

Rue, for her part, gave him a level of loyalty that he knew few people ever saw. He often wasn't quite sure what he had done to merit it. Yeah, he'd been there for her. He was protective of her. He cared for her. But in comparison, he was an absolute disaster area. Walking caution tape. And she was…perfect.

"I will show up and do whatever I'm told to do," he said. "This is her wedding, and the bride gets whatever she wants."

"You're a good man, Justice King," Arizona said.

"Oh I'm positively great when I'm on loan. But I wouldn't be any good long-term."

Rue laughed. "I don't know. We are pretty long-term."

"You know what I mean."

"Yeah," she said, wrinkling her nose. And that hurt a little bit, but it was fair. Rue was realistic about him. There was nothing wrong with that. She knew him. She knew him well.

They served up dinner, and sat around the table. And he watched as Rue smiled and interacted with his siblings. Family, maybe. That was maybe what he offered. Because for all that they had been broken and damaged during their upbringing, the Kings had done a good job of rallying around each other, and holding each other tight. They had been through hell, in some regards. Their father had been a pretty high level narcissist who had done a lot of damage in the community. And had twisted up his kids all kinds of ways. It was what had given Justice a healthy distrust for love. Because he had watched their father manipulate how much they had loved him. How much they had wanted to please him. That was when Justice had exited people-pleasing stage left. It had been clear to him that there was nothing but danger in that. And that was when he decided the life of a hellion was the one for him.

It was safer. For all involved.

"He looks great in his tux," Rue said. That knocked him out of his reverie a bit.

"Do I?"

"You know you do," she said. "You know you always look good."

"It is a tragedy," Arizona said, shaking her head. "No matter how many times I warned the female populace about him, his powers are too strong."

He rolled his eyes. "Listen. We all have to play to our strengths." The truth was, he knew that he was shaped the kind of way women like. He was good-looking, he supposed. But more than that, he was fucking fantastic in bed. Because part of being raised by a sociopath was making a decision about whether or not you were ever going to use people the way that he did. And living the life of a man-whore meant engaging in behavior that could come across as using somebody. That was why he went out of his way to be the best partner possible. A woman got a lot out of the night with him. He was not a selfish lover. If she didn't get off more than once, there was no point as far as he was concerned. He made it his mission to rock worlds. It was his version of being a better man.

He might not be able to offer forever, but he compensated for what he couldn't offer.

They finished dinner, and he walked Rue out to her truck. "I didn't get a chance to show you all the stuff in the folders. I'm trying to choose flowers."

"Oh. Did you want to come back to my place for a bit?"

"No," she said. "It's okay. I... Asher ended up getting delayed back at the base. So he isn't going to be here for a couple more days. Would you help out?"

"Whatever you need."

"Well, I need help choosing some things for the bouquet. Not the flowers—I had to have those grown over a year ago, but she thought that it was a good idea for me to hold off on ribbons and things until closer to the time, so now I have an array of things to look at. Just fine details. And then, I need to do my final dress fitting with Sue. I was kind of hoping you would come."

"You want me at your dress fitting?"

"The final one. To make sure everything's good to go. In case I lost weight or gained it, or whatever. Obviously most of this was done a year ago."

"Obviously," he said.

There was nothing obvious about that to him. But then, that was Rue. Always prepared. And he couldn't imagine that she actually needed his input on anything. But, she did like to double-check a box, and so he knew it was important to her to make sure that everything was thoroughly managed.

"What time do you need to meet?"

"I need to go to the florist at nine."

He grimaced.

"Is that okay?" she asked.

"Yeah," he said. "I just won't go out tonight."

Because the truth was, he would do anything for Rue. She was on the path to her perfect life, and he wasn't going to let anything mess that up.